How would *you* like to have a disc set in the middle of your forehead which glowed pink whenever you felt sexually aroused? This is the basis of Brian Aldiss's amazingly funny and original novel, set in a near-future Britain where the discs are to be made compulsory – but not before a lot of hilarious and even frightening events occur, suggesting that perhaps it's not quite such a good idea to wear one's – er – 'heart' on one's forehead . . .

Also by Brian Aldiss in Panther Books

Greybeard
The Moment of Eclipse
The Male Response

Brian Aldiss

The Primal Urge

Panther

Granada Publishing Limited
Published in 1976 by Panther Books Ltd
Frogmore, St Albans, Herts AL2 2NF

First published by Ballantine Books Inc
Copyright © 1961 by Brian Aldiss
Made and printed in Great Britain by
Hazell Watson & Viney Ltd
Aylesbury, Bucks
Set in Linotype Times

*This absurd attempt to popularize various sorts of
morality is dedicated to EDDIE COONEY and OSCAR
MELLOR because they were the first to hear about it in
'The Gloucester Arms' – and for better reasons.*

CONTENTS

AUTHOR'S NOTE

Just as it would be difficult—and fatuous—to write a history of twentieth century art without mentioning Picasso, I have found it impossible to draw this contemporary picture without mentioning a number of the pillars of our society, from Mr. Jack Solomons to Air Chief Marshal Dowding; I have presumed enough to impute to some of these public figures opinions on the hypothetical matters contained in my novel. One particular victim is Mr. Aldous Huxley, who has most kindly permitted me to take this liberty with him. May I beg the other sufferers to be similarly indulgent, reminding them that such is the price of fame and *semel insanivimus omnes*? Of course I realise that their actual opinions could hardly fail to differ from those I have ascribed to them. But their presence here, even if involuntary, has lent me moral support in rough waters.

The same seeking for life-lines has caused me to use a number of branded goods in my pages. I would, accordingly, like to thank the manufacturers of Kosset Carpets, Odo-ro-no, Cooper's Oxford Marmalade and several automobiles for the sense of security their products have afforded me.

Likewise with institutions. The Harlequins, the British Government and the National Book League are real, and I for one am glad it is so. But the representatives of the British Government who appear in these pages are *not* real; my Minister of Health, for instance, is no relation to any past, present or forthcoming Minister of Health; for this also one may be grateful.

These qualifications accepted, all characters in this book are fictitious and are certainly not intended to represent anyone living or dead; the institutions in it are purely make believe; such actions and opinions as are ascribed to these characters or institutions are imaginary; even the weather is too good to be true. Readers are asked, nevertheless, to bear in mind the lines of George Santayana:

Even such a dream I dream, and know full well
My walking passeth like a midnight spell.
But know not if my dreaming breaketh through
Into the deeps of heaven and hell.
I know but this of all I would I knew:
Truth is a dream, unless my dream is true.

B. W. A.

PART ONE

A PUTATIVE UTOPIA

"We burn." (Title of poem by Dr. Marie Stopes)

I. A Fox with a Tail

For London it was one of those hot July evenings in which the human mind is engulfed in a preoccupation with the moist palm, the damp brow, the armpit.

Sweating continently, James Solent emerged into the motionless heat of Charlton Square. With a folded newspaper raised to his forehead in an odd defensive gesture, he came down the steps of the grey trailer onto the grass and paused. The door of Number 17, where he lived, beckoned him; but competing with the wish to go and hide himself was a desire to overhear what three men nearby were saying.

"Such a gross imposition could only be swung onto a politically indifferent electorate," one said.

The second, lacking words to express what he thought of this sentiment, guffawed immoderately.

"Rubbish! " the third exclaimed. "You heard what the Minister of Health said the other day: this is just what's needed to give Britain back her old sense of direction."

It was the turn of the first man to burst into mocking laughter. Seeing Jimmy standing nearby, they turned to stare curiously at his forehead.

"What's it feel like, mate?" one of them called.

"You really don't feel a thing," Jimmy said, and hastened across the square with his newspaper still half-heartedly raised. He let himself into Number 17. From the hall he could hear Mrs. Pidney, the landlady, drowsily humming like a drowned top in the kitchen. The rest was silence. Reassured, Jimmy discarded his paper, revealing the disc on his forehead, and went up to the flat he shared with his brother. Fortunately Aubrey Solent was out, working late at the BIL; that undoubtedly saved Jimmy an awkward scene. Aubrey had grown uncommonly touchy of recent weeks.

The flat contained the usual facilities, a kitchen, a living room (with dinerette), Aubrey's large bedroom and

Jimmy's smaller bedroom. Everything was so tidy that the one glossy-jacketted LP lying in the middle of the carpet looked to be posing. Skirting it, Jimmy hurried into his room and closed the door.

Just for a moment he played a tune on the panelling with his finger tips. Then he crossed to the looking glass and surveyed himself. The suit Harrods had made him before he began his new job in January was daily growing to look better on him, more like him; for the rest he was twenty-five, his brown hair not objectionably curly, his face round but not ugly, his chin neither aggressive nor recessive.

All, in fact, he told himself, sighing, alarmingly ordinary. "Oh, ye of the average everything," he addressed himself, improvising, as he frequently did, a rhymed oration, "Oh, ye of the average height, overtaken by taller folk, under-taken by smaller folk . . . an average fate one might certainly call a joke."

One feature only was definitely not, as yet at all events, ordinary; the shining circle, three and a half centimetres in diameter, permanently fixed in the centre of his forehead. Made of a metal resembling stainless steel, its surface was slightly convex, so that it gave a vague and distorted image of the world before it.

It looked by no means ill. It looked, indeed, rather noble, like a blaze on a horse's brow. It lent a touch of distinction to a plain face.

Jimmy Solent stood for some minutes before the ward-robe mirror, looking at himself and, through himself, into the future. It was a time for wonder: he had taken the plunge at a period when to plunge or not to plunge was the consuming question. He was one of the first to plunge, and the seal of his precipitance was upon him. His preoccupa-tion was gradually banished by the barking of the loud-speaker in the square outside. Slipping off his jacket, Jimmy went over to the window. His outlook here was generally less interesting, being more respectable, than that from his brother Aubrey's bedroom windows. *They* looked out on to backs of houses, where people were unbuttoned and being themselves; Jimmy's window, in the front of the house, stared perpetually out at façades, where people put on closed little public faces.

Now, however, there was life in the square. This week, a big grey trailer, so reassuringly similar to the Mass Radi-ography units, stood on the seedy grass beneath the plane trees. A queue of men and women, most of them in summer dresses or shirt sleeves, stood patiently waiting their turn to enter the trailer. At five minute intervals, they emerged singly from the other side of it, generally holding a newspaper, a handkerchief, or a hat, to their foreheads, disappearing without looking to left or right. A few spectators idled about, watching the queue; at the beginning of the week there had been cameramen. From the bedroom window—from safety!—it all appeared rather comical: at once unreal and typically English. Jimmy found it hard to realise he had come through that same mill only twenty minutes ago; just as the government had promised, his forehead did not ache at all. Though he prodded it experimentally, his disc neither moved nor ached. The marvels of modern science were indeed marvellous.

The man in charge of the loudspeaker, being hot and bored, was not talking into his microphone properly. Only occasional phrases were intelligible. One bit sounded like "We are free to sit here in a fine old state"; he must have been saying something equally preposterous, like "freer citizens of a finer state."

". . . government's assurance . . . many eminent doctors agree . . . nothing but healthful . . . far from being an affront to national modesty . . . greatest assets . . . no expense . . . only a minor operation . . ."

The voice mumbled like a cloud of bees, and the minor operation was a major operation taking place all over the country: for the grey trailers were parked by now in the centre of every town and village from Penzance to John o'Groats. The whole population was potential queue-fodder. Jimmy came away from the window.

Somebody was moving about in the living room. Jimmy straightened his tie. It was unlikely to be Aubrey, but Jimmy called out, "Is that you, Aubrey?" and went to see.

It was not Aubrey. It was Aubrey's girl, Alyson Youngfield, if the noun "girl" may be used here ambiguously. She had discarded her summer gloves and was fanning herself with the discarded LP sleeve. Jimmy's face lit at the sight of her.

"He'll be late this evening, Alyson," he told this charming creature settling herself on the divan with the elegance of a puma. Her fairness took on a special quality with the July weather; under the neat blonde hair, her skin seemed to ripen like wheat.

"Not to worry," she said. "I didn't really expect to find Aubrey at home, but it's cooler here than in my bed-sitter. It gets like an oven just under the roof. Let's have a little hi-fi to combat the heat, shall we?"

In that instant Jimmy saw she was looking at his forehead. It caused him none of the embarrassment anyone else's regard would have done; with pleasure, he wondered whether an acquired tactfulness or natural kindness caused her, when she saw his glance, to say matter of factly, "Oh, you've got yours. I must get mine tomorrow."

With gratitude, to draw her into a conspiracy, Jimmy answered incautiously, "Are you really? Aubrey won't like that."

He knew at once he had said the wrong thing.

"Aubrey will eventually be wearing one himself; you'll see. It'll come to us all in time," Alyson said. But she said it stiffly, turning her fair head with its most immaculate locks to gaze at the window. As always, Jimmy found himself reflecting how hard it was to gauge the precise relationship between her and Aubrey. A serious quality in Alyson and an evasive one in Aubrey made them both not entirely easy people to estimate.

"I'm going to a party this evening," he told her, to change the subject. "At the BIL, Aubrey's HQ; I'm sorry you're not coming. I shall have to be getting ready soon."

"I don't envy you," Alyson said. Nevertheless she watched him keenly as he walked into the kitchen. He there assembled a carraway roll (Jimmy did not so much enjoy carraway rolls as endure them under the impression they were fashionable), a slice of camembert cheese, a spoonful of cream cheese, a wedge of butter and pickings from the garlic-flavoured salad which reposed in the refrigerator. Hesitating a moment, he poured himself a glass of dry Montrachet; it was not quite the thing with the cheese, he realised, but he liked it.

"Come over here, Jimmy," Alyson said, when he appeared in the living room with his tray.

He went over at once to where she was sitting on the divan. She was wearing the green suit with the citron lining that Aubrey had bought her at Dickens and Jones. Underneath it, she wore a citron blouse, and underneath that could have been very little; all the same, Alyson looked warm. And, ah, undeniably, warming.

Changing her mind about whatever she was going to say,

14

Alyson remarked, "You are too obedient, Jimmy. You must not come when just anyone calls you."

"You're not just anyone, Alyson," he said, but missed the required lightness of tone such an obvious remark demanded. He took his tray sadly into the dinerette, from where he could still see her ankles and calves, curved like a symbol against the plum background of the divan. They looked, indeed, very beautiful; as if he were having his first glimpse of the Himalayas, Jimmy felt humbled by them. Then a hint of colour made him hold one hand up before his face; a pink radiance covered it. The disc on his forehead was doing its stuff.

Feeling both shattered and pleased, Jimmy lingered over his meal. The Montrachet was very good. He sipped it, listening to the music from the record-player. A band featuring an overharsh trumpet flipped through the current trifle called "You Make Me Glow"; that tune had been lucky; the show in which it was sung had been running for some weeks before the Prime Minister made his sensational announcement. Yet it might almost have been written for the occasion and brought unexpected fortune for the songwriter, who found himself over-night the author of a hit and able to afford the enemies he had always dreamed of.

"Fate decreed
Your effect upon me should be so:
You not only make me knock-kneed,
You make me glow.
Presently,
Or when all other lights are down low,
Your touch will kindle me, you see
You make me glow."

Alyson switched it off.

"What I was going to say, Jimmy," she exclaimed, speaking with an effort, "is that I feel rather appallingly glum just now. It's the sight of all those people queueing out there—and all over London—I suppose. They're so *patient*! Nobody seems quite to have grasped how epoch-breaking these ER's, these Norman Lights as they call them, really are; not even people who are against them, like this politician, what's his name, Bourgoyne."

"Let's not get onto politics," Jimmy said. "You know how we always argue. Stay as sweet as you are."

15

Although he expected her to take him up on that, she said nothing, moving her legs restlessly. She began to hum, "You Make Me Glow," but broke off as if realising the idiocy of the tune.

"I sometimes think the opposite of amusement is not boredom but peace," she said. She was deliberately misquoting a current poster, and Jimmy laughed.

"I'm not sure sometimes that boredom and peace aren't the same thing," he said and, having said it, thought it silly. Alyson evidently did not.

"A lot of people feel like that," she replied. "Perhaps otherwise they would never have consented to have their foreheads tampered with; they're eager for anything that makes a change. It's understandable enough." She sighed luxuriously and added, deliberately guying the pathos of what she said, "We're the generation what missed the war, lovie. Remember?"

Jimmy liked her saying that. It put them on an equal footing, for although Alyson happened to be his brother's mistress, she was Jimmy's age to within a month; Aubrey, six years older than Jimmy, had been born in 1930, thereby missing the war too, but he had been excluded from Alyson's remark. Alyson was perceptive; she seemed to know exactly how and when Jimmy felt uncomfortable.

"Don't be glum any more," he advised. "It makes you look so huggable that no one could be expected to have any sympathy for you."

Alyson gave no answer. Contentedly, Jimmy finished his meal and went to take a shower.

Thirty seconds under the hard, cold spray was enough. He towelled himself, applied Odo-ro-no, sucked an Amplex tablet to remove any anti-social traces of garlic, and dressed for the party. As he did so, he looked out of his window again. The queue outside the grey trailer was no shorter; the shadows in the square were longer.

These ER Installation Centres, to give the trailers their proper name, had dispersed themselves over a bewildered Britain on the previous Monday morning. It was now only Thursday evening, and already some 750,000 people up and down the country, had the Register painlessly—and perpetually—embedded in their brows.

The great conversion, in fact, had begun with many of the omens of success. Although much of this was due to the careful government campaigning which had preceded the

16

conversion drive, the personal appearance of the Prime Minister on TV, wearing his ER, on the evening before the grey trailers opened their doors, had undoubtedly won over thousands of doubters to the cause he favoured. Even the Opposition conceded his speech had been powerful.

His disc gleaming interestingly but unobtrusively below his shock of silver hair, Herbert Gascadder had said to the watching millions: "I beg each one of you to realise that only a superficial view can hold that the ER is a menace to society. If you think more deeply, you will see the ER as I do, as a badge of liberty. We have, as a nation, always been diffident about expressing ourselves; that, perhaps, is why some sociologists have called loneliness one of the great curses of our age. The ER is going to break down that barrier, as well as many others.

"The ER is the first invention ever to bring man closer to his fellow men. Even television, that great institution by whose medium I am able to speak to you in your homes to-night, has proved a not unmixed blessing—in fact, often a disruption—to family life. Over the ages, since we ceased to huddle together in caves, we have inevitably drawn further apart from one another. Now, I sincerely believe, we shall find ourselves drawn nearer again, united by those common impulses which the ER makes apparent.

"Yet I would not have you think of the ER as something fantastic or crack-brained, a mere aberration of science. It will, in fact, have the same effect as any other invention, once we are accustomed to it; that is, to make a slight but inevitable modification to man's daily life. We can only continue to exist by a policy of change in this highly competitive world. Let us thank God that the ER is a *British* invention. More, let us show our thankfulness by getting our ER's installed as soon as we can, so that by simplifying our private lives we can all pull together and make this nation, once more, a land of opportunity."

"How Gascadder would love me now," Jimmy thought, glancing again at his brow in the mirror while he adjusted his tie. His ER was still there, slightly larger than a penny, a symbol of patriotism and of hope.

"Be a good boy and don't drink too much," Alyson advised, as he finally appeared, ready to leave the flat.

"Don't be so motherly!" Jimmy said. "We are meant to be Unlovable Young People."

"Good God!" she exclaimed. "That! It's hard enough being People!"

For a moment he shuffled by the door, looking at her. The rest of the room was nothing; she, sitting there in her Dickens and Jones suit, had an extra dimension, a special reality, a future in the balance. "Good-bye, Alyson," he said, and went out to the most momentous party of his life.

Jimmy was usually unassuming; yet the feeling had grown on him lately that there was some sort of help he could give Alyson. What help, he did not know; Alyson made no deliberate appeals and, aware of their potentially awkward position in Aubrey's flat, they both confined their conversations to light chit-chat. Yet the something which remained unsaid had been growing stronger ever since Jimmy arrived at the flat. One day soon it would emerge from its hidden room into the light.

What convinced Jimmy that this was no illusion of his romantic imagination was the contrast between Alyson's and Aubrey's natures and their relationship with each other. Alyson was both intelligent and tolerant—but her comings and goings at the flat had a casual quality which implied little passion for Aubrey. Aubrey was a withdrawn young man; the streak which in his brother appeared as diffidence had been transmuted in him into aloofness. He was "correct," in manner, dress and choice of church, food, and book. He was a conformist with a career. In short, he was hardly the type to take a mistress; Alyson was hardly the type to become his mistress. They ought to be either husband and wife or strangers, and that was the crux of the matter.

A smell of sausages coiled juicily about the landing. As he descended the stairs, Jimmy could hear them frying.

The kitchen door, as usual, was open. Hilda Pidney spotted Jimmy as he reached the hall and came out, as she always did unless one was moving very rapidly, to exchange a few words. She was stocky and fifty, with the face, as Alyson once remarked, of one crying in a wilderness of hair. Despite her miserable expression, she was a cheerful soul; her first words now struck exactly the right note with Jimmy.

"Why it suits you a treat, Mr. Solent!"

"I'm so glad you think so, Mrs. Pidney," he said, putting his hand up self-consciously. "I see you've got yours."

18

He had, in truth, the merest glimpse of it through her mop of hair.

"Yes, I went straightaway at nine o'clock this morning," she told him. "I got there just before the trailers opened. I was second in the queue, I was. And it didn't hurt a bit, did it, just like what they said?"

"Not a bit, no."

"And I mean it is *free*, isn't it! " She laughed. "Henry's been trying to make it work already. I ask you, at my age, Mr. Solent. I can see I'm in for something now! "

He laughed with her without reservations.

"I think these Emotion Registers are going to give a lot of people a new lease on life," he said.

"You know what people are calling them," she said, grinning. "Nun Chasers or Normal Lights. Funny how these nicknames get round, isn't it? I'd better get back to me sausages, quickish-like. Cheerio."

As Jimmy let himself out of the front door, he thought: "She wasn't coy. She has accepted it in the proper spirit. Three cheers for Mrs. Pidney and the millions like her. They are the backbone, the backbone of England; such vertebrae, one dirty day, will rise and slay the pervertebrae."

He strolled gently towards Park Lane, where he intended to capture a taxi, making himself enjoy the heat by contrasting it favourably with the cold, rain-bearing wind which had been blowing only a few days before. Everyone behaved much as usual in the streets. Considering that the grey trailers had been hard at work everywhere for four days, surprisingly few people had additions to their foreheads, but those few were attracting no interest. The man and woman in the bright red Austin-Healey, the cadaverous commissionaire, the two squaddies sunning themselves on the corner of South Audley Street, all wore their Emotion Registers as to the manner born. The cabby who answered Jimmy's raised hand also bore the new token. Into every class, the ER's were finding their way.

The party to which Jimmy was going, Sir Richard Clunes' party, was being held in one of the formidable blocks, Kensington way, which had been built at the end of the last decade. It was—with a few exceptions like Jimmy himself—a British Industrial Liasons party for BIL personnel, and therefore more in Aubrey Solent's line than Jimmy's, for Aubrey was a BIL man; Jimmy was entangled in literature. But Sir Richard, while promising to lend Jimmy a portrait for an exhibition he was organising, had genially invited him to the party at the same time, on the principle that younger brothers of promising executive material were worth suborning in this way, particularly as party material was always scarce at this season of year.

It was a small party: Jimmy could see that as soon as he arrived—much smarter than the literary parties to which he was more accustomed, which were generally toned down by provincial novelists with no style or reviewers with no figure. These were London people; more, BIL people! — BIL people living useful days and efficient nights. "They're already at their primes, I'm sure they read *The Times* at breakfast," Jimmy told himself, glancing round as he shook hands with a beaming Sir Richard and Lady Clunes. Sir Richard had mobile eyebrows and a chin the shape of a goatee. His manner flowed with milk and honey, and he engaged Jimmy in pleasant talk for two minutes precisely.

"Now let me see who you'll know here, Solent," Sir Richard said, as that halcyon period drew to its scheduled close. "Ah, there's Guy Leighton, one of our most promising young men. You'll know him, of course—he has been working on the K. R. Shalu business with your brother. Guy! Can you spare us a moment, my dear boy?"

A dark young man who balanced perpetually on the balls of his feet was expertly prised from a nearby group and made to confront Jimmy. They bowed sadly to each other over their champagne glasses, with the polite dislike one partygoer so often feels for another. Guy and Jimmy were no more than acquaintances; their orbits only intersected when their invitation cards coincided.

"Shall we dance?" Jimmy said, and then, very seriously to counteract this facetiousness, "This looks a worthy gathering, Guy."

"Worthy of or for what, Solent?" the dark young man parried. He could have been no more than four years older than Jimmy, but his habit of using surnames seemed to give him a good decade's start. "The usual set of time-servers one finds at these bun-fights: no more worthy than the next man, surely?"

"*Looking* more worthy," Jimmy insisted. It was not a point he cared to labour, but he could think of nothing else to talk about. Gratefully, he accepted more champagne in his glass.

"You, if I may say so," Guy said, cocking a sardonic eyebrow at Jimmy's forehead, "look positively futuristic."

"Oh. . . . the ER. Everyone'll be wearing them in time, Laddie, yew mark moi words," Jimmy said, with that abrupt descent into dialect with which some of us cover our inadequacies.

"Possibly," Guy said darkly. "Some of us have other ideas; some of us, I don't mind telling you confidentially, are waiting to see which way the cat will jump. You realise, don't you, you are the only person here wearing one of the ghastly things."

He could not, announcing Armageddon, have shattered Jimmy more thoroughly.

"You're all living in the past, you scientific fellows. These are the nineteen sixties, the Era of the ER," he replied, but he was already looking round the large room to check on Guy's statement. Every brow, high or low—some of them were the really interestingly low brows of genius— was unimproved by science. The wish to conform hit Jimmy so hard that he scarcely heard Guy's remark about oppressed minorities.

"The Solent pioneering spirit . . ." he said.

"And another thing I ought to tell you," Guy said. "I'm sure you will not mind my mentioning it. People in the swim refer to these discs as Norman Lights; after the firm of Norman which invented them, you know. I rather think it's only the lesser breeds without the law who refer to them as ER's—or nun chasers, which being pure music hall might just possibly catch on. Of course it's too early for any convention to have crystallised yet, but take it from me that's the way the wind's blowing at the BIL."

"I'll be terribly careful about it," Jimmy said earnestly. He concealed his earnestness by a parody of earnestness; Guy, the born Insider, had just the sort of information one listened to if one hoped to get Inside oneself.

And then the group of men and women from which Guy had been separated flowed about the two young men, and a welter of introductions followed. Everybody looked well, cheerful and in good humour; that they were also interested in Jimmy lessened his interest in them. As if they had been waiting for a signal, they began talking about the registers; they were *the* topic of conversation at present. After a long burst of animation, a pause set in, during

21

which all eyes turned on Jimmy, awaiting, as it were, a sign from the fountainhead.

"As the only fox with a tail," he said, "I feel I ought not to give away any secrets."

"Has it lit up yet, that's what I want to know?" a commanding man in heavy glasses said, amid laughter.

"Only once, so far," Jimmy said, "but I haven't had it more than three hours."

More laughter, during which someone made a crushing remark about fancy dress parties, and a sandy woman said, "It really is appalling to think that everyone will know what we're thinking when we have ours installed."

A man, evidently her husband by the laboured courtesy with which he addressed her, took her up instantly on this remark. "My dear Bridget, will you not remember that these Norman Lights go *deeper* than the thought centres. They register purely on the sensation level. They represent, in fact, the spontaneous as against the calculated. Therein lies the whole beauty of them."

"I absolutely couldn't agree more," the heavy glasses said. "The whole notion of submitting ourselves to this process would be intolerable were it not that it gives us back a precious spontaneity, a *freedom*, lost for generations. It is analogous to the inconvenience of contraceptives: submit to a minor irk and you inherit a major liberty."

"But don't you see, Merrick," Guy said, perching himself on tiptoe to address the heavy glasses, "—goodness knows how often I've pointed this out to people—the Norman Lights don't *solve* anything. Such an infringement of personal dignity is only justifiable if it *solves* something."

"Personal dignity is an antique imperialist slogan, Leighton," a smart grey woman said, giving Guy some of his own medicine.

"And what do you expect them to solve?" Merrick of the heavy glasses asked, addressing the whole group.

"Abolishing the death penalty entirely last year didn't solve the problem of crime, any more than contraceptives have done away with bastards, but at least we are taking another step in the right direction. You must realise there are no *solutions* in life—life is not a Euclidean problem—only *arrangements*."

The smart grey woman laughed briefly. "Come, Merrick," she said, "We can't let you get away with that; there

22

are no 'directions' in the socio-ethical meaning you attribute to right."

"Oh, yes, there are, Susan," Merrick contradicted imperturbably. "Don't reactivate that old nihilist mousetrap. There are evolutionary directions, and in relation to them the Normal Lights are an advance. Why are they an advance? Because they enable the id for the first time to communicate direct, without the intervention of the ego. The human ego for generations has been growing swollen at the expense of the id, from which all true drives spring; *now*—"

"Then surely these Norman Lights are causing a reversion," Bridget interrupted. "A return to the primitive—"

"Not primitive: primal. You see, you've got to differentiate between two entirely separate but quite similar—"

"I can't help thinking Merrick's right off the beam. However it comes wrapped, an increased subservience to the machine is something to reject out of hand. I mean, in the future—"

"No, wait a moment, though, Norman Lights aren't machines; that is to say, they aren't instruments for the conversion of motion, but for the conversion of *emotion*. They're merely registers—like a raised eyebrow."

"Well, I'm still capable of raising my own eyebrows."

"And other people's, I hope."

"Anyhow, that's not the point. The point is—"

"Surely a return to the primitive—"

"The point is, to wear them voluntarily is one thing; to have this law passed by our so-called government is quite—"

"And who elected this government, Susan? You, Susan."

"Don't let's go into all that again! "

"After all, why drag evolution into this? How can a mere mechanical—"

"My dear man, mechanisation is a natural step—natural, mark you—in man's evolution. Really, some people's world pictures are so *antiquated*. Darwin might as well never have sailed in the *Beagle* at all! "

"I cannot honestly see how anyone could expect anybody—"

"All I'm trying to say is—"

"—in the nation's best interests. Everyone bogged down by inhibition, and then like a clean slash of a scalpel—"

"If you've ever observed an operation in progress, Merrick, you will know surgeons do not slash."

23

"—comes this glorious invention to set us free from all the accumulation of five thousand years of petty convention. Here at last is hope handed to us on a plate, and you worry—"

"Last week *he* was attacking and *I* was defending."

It was at this point in the argument spluttering round him that Jimmy, listening in interested silence, found that a man he had heard addressed as Bertie was tipping rum into his—Jimmy's—champagne from a pocket flask.

"Give it a bit of body," Bertie said, winking conspiratorially and gripping Jimmy's arm.

"Thanks. No more," Jimmy said.

"Pleasure," Bertie said. "All intellectuals here. I'm a cyberneticist myself. What are you?"

"I sort of give exhibitions."

"You do? Before invited audiences? You'd better count me in on that. I tell you, when I get my red light, it's going to wink in some funny places." He laughed joyously.

"I'm afraid these are only book exhibitions," Jimmy said, adding, for safety, "Clean books."

"Who's talking about books? They're full of antique imperialist slogans," Guy said, butting in and making a face at Susan. "Don't change the subject, Jimmy. There's only one subject in England at the moment—it's even ousted the weather. You, presumably, are more pro NL's than anyone else here. Why are you pro?"

"For practical reasons," Jimmy said airily. The champagne was already making him feel a little detached from the group; they were only talkers—he was a pioneer. "You see, entirely through my own stupidity, Penny Tanner-Smith, my fiancée, broke off our engagement last week. I hoped that if she could see how steadily my ER glowed for her, she would agree to begin again."

There was much sympathetic laughter at this. Susan said, "What a horribly trite reason!" But Merrick said "Bloody good. Excellent. That's what I mean—cuts through formality and misunderstanding. Our friend here has inherited a major liberty: the ability to *prove* to his fiancée exactly how he feels about her; try and estimate what that is worth in terms of mental security. I'm going to get my Norman Light stuck on tomorrow."

"Then you disappoint me, Merrick," Guy Leighton said.

"I cannot wait on fashion, Guy; I have an aim in life

24

as well as a role in society," Merrick said amiably. It sounded as if he knew Guy fairly closely.

Gazing beyond them, Jimmy could see Sir Richard still welcoming an occasional late arrival, his eyebrows astir with hospitality. A tall, silver man had just come in escorting a tall girl with a hatchet face who, in her survey of the company, seemed to "unsee the traffic with mid-ocean eye," to borrow a phrase from a contemporary poet Jimmy disliked. The man smiled and smiled; the girl seemed barely to raise a grin. She wore the silver disc on her brow.

"There's someone—," Jimmy said, and then stopped, foreseeing an awkward situation. But Guy had also noticed the newcomer; he became tense and his manner underwent a change.

"Oh, *she's* here, is she!" he muttered, turning his back on that quarter of the room and shuddering as if he had witnessed a breach of etiquette. "I say, Solent, here's a chance for us all to try out your gadget."

"Include me out," Jimmy said hastily. "I don't like public demonstrations. Besides, I can tell from here that she would have no attraction for me; she doesn't look as if she could make a firefly glow."

"You haven't met her yet," Guy said, with surprising fierceness.

"You never know what's in your id," Bertie said, appearing again with his pocket flask. "Or in hers, Freud save us." He crossed himself and nudged Merrick, who did not smile.

The inevitable, as it inevitably does, happened. Guy, with unexpected delicacy, did not go over to the newcomers. Instead, Sir Richard and Lady Clunes ushered them over to Jimmy's group in a frothy tide of introductions, among which two waiters sported like dolphins, dispensing drink.

"Martini for me this time," Jimmy said and, turning, was introduced to Felix Garside and his niece, the hatchet-faced girl, Rose English.

Seen close to, she was no longer hatchet-faced, though her countenance was long and her features sharply moulded; indeed she could be considered attractive, if we remembered that attraction is also a challenge. As Rose English glanced round the company, she was making no attempt, as most of the others present would have done upon introduction, to conceal the engagement of her mind and feelings in her surroundings. In consequence the unconventional face, less a mask than an instrument, drew to itself the regard of all men and most of the women. Her countenance was at once intelligent and naked; invulnerable perhaps, but highly impressionable.

Her clothes, although good, seemed to fit her badly, for the jacket of her suit, in the new over-elaborate style, did her disservice, making her look to some extent top heavy. She was tall; "rangy" was the word which occurred to Jimmy. She might have been thirty-five, perhaps ten years his senior. Under her cheekbones faint and by no means unattractive hollows showed, ironing themselves out by her mouth, which, together with her eyes, belied the hint of melancholy determination in her attitude.

Her eyes rested momentarily on Jimmy's brow. She smiled, and the smile was good.

"Et tu, Brute," she said and then turned with a suspicion of haste to talk to Guy, who showed little inclination to talk back; though he remained on the balls of his feet, his poise had deserted him. This at once disappointed and relieved Jimmy, for he discovered he was flushing slightly; Merrick and several of the others were watching his Norman Light with eagerness.

"It is just turning faintly pink, I think," the sandy woman said. "It's rather difficult to tell in this lighting."

"The maximum intensity is a burning cerise," a clerical-looking man informed them all.

"Then cerise will be the fashionable colour next season," Lady Clunes said. "I'm so glad. I'm so tired of black, so really tired of it."

"I should have thought it ought to have registered a little more than that," Merrick said, with a hint of irritation, staring at Jimmy's forehead. "Between any normal man and woman, there's a certain sexual flux."

"That's what it'll be so interesting to find out," Lady Clunes said. "I am just longing for everyone to get theirs."

"Oh yes, it'll be O.K. for those who're exempt: a damn good sideshow, I'd say," Bertie remarked, precipitating a frosty little silence. The new ER bill just passed through Parliament, which specified that everyone should have a Norman Light fitted by September 1, exempted those under fourteen or over sixty; it was generally agreed that this upper age limit would preserve the status quo for Maude Clunes. Her friends were waiting, hawk-like, to see if she would have a disc installed.

Guy, to fill the gap in the conversation, brought Rose

back into it with a general remark. Seizing his chance, Merrick bunched heavy eyebrows over his heavy spectacles and said, "Miss English, your having your Norman Light installed so promptly shows you to be a forward-looking young lady. Would you cooperate in a little experiment, a scientific experiment, for the benefit of those of us who have still to, er, see the light?"

"What do you wish me to do?" she asked.

He was as direct as she.

"We would like to observe the amount of sexual attraction between you and Mr. Solent," he told her.

"Certainly," she said. She looked around at each one of them, then added, "This is a particular moment in time when our—my—responses may seem to some of you improper, or immoral, or 'not the thing', or whatever phrase you use to cover something you faintly fear. In a few months, I sincerely hope, such moments will be gone for ever. Everyone will register spontaneously an attraction for everyone of the opposite sex and similar age; that I predict, for the ER's function at gene level. And then the dingy mockery which our forebears, and we, have made of sex will vanish like dew. It will be revealed as something more radical and less of a cynosure than we have held it to be. And our lives will be much more honest on every level in consequence."

She spoke very simply, very intensely, and then turned to look into Jimmy's eyes. Listening to her, watching her moving mouth, seeing her tongue once briefly touch her lips, taking in that face a sculptor would have wept at, Jimmy knew his Norman Light was no longer an ambiguous silver. He caught a faint pink reflection from it on the end of his nose. When the rangy girl surveyed him, he saw her disc redden and his own increase output in sympathy. She was so without embarrassment that Jimmy, too, remained at ease, interested in the experiment. Everyone else maintained the surprised, respectful silence her words had created.

"A rosy light!" exclaimed the sandy woman and the momentary tension relaxed.

"Not by Eastern casements only. . . .!" Jimmy murmured. It surprised him that, although he still glowed brightly, he consciously felt little or no attraction for Rose. That is to say, his fiancée, Penny Tanner-Smith (not

27

to mention Alyson Youngfield), was still clear in his mind, and he felt no insane desire to go to bed with this strange, self-possessed woman.

"The attraction is there and the ER's detect it," Rose said. "There lies their great and only virtue: they will force a nation of prudes to recognise an incontrovertible natural law. But, as I say, they work at gene—or what will no doubt be popularly termed 'subconscious'—level. This force lies like a chemical bond between Mr. Solent and me; but I feel not the slightest desire to go to bed with him."

Jimmy was amazed at how unpalatable he found this truth, this echo of what he had just been thinking; it was one thing silently to reject her; quite another for her openly to reject him. This absorbed him so completely he hardly listened to the discussion which flowed around him.

Merrick was shaking Rose's long hand; she was admitting to being a "sort of brain specialist." The wife of the clerical-looking man was squeaking something about "like a public erection. . . ." and urging her husband to take her home. Everyone was talking. Sir Richard and Felix Garside were laughing at a private joke. Bertie was signalling to a young waiter. Drink and olives circulated.

When Sir Richard excused himself to greet someone else, Jimmy also slipped away to another part of the room. He was disturbed and needed time for thought. From where he stood now, he could see Rose's back, a rangy figure with a handbag swinging from her crooked arm. Then a heated discussion on the effects of colour TV on children rose on his left and broke like a wave over him. Jimmy joined in vigorously, talking automatically. He emerged some while later to find the subject held no interest for him, though he had been as partisan as anybody; muttering a word of excuse, snatching another drink, he went into the corridor to stand by an open window.

Here it was distinctly cooler and quieter. Jimmy leant out, looking down four stories to the untidy bottom of the building's well. He lapsed into one of the untidy reveries which often overcame him when he was alone. His thoughts went back to Rose English, the woman with the unlikely name, and then faded from her again. Euphoria flooded over him. A waiter brought him a drink. He groaned at his own contentment. The world was in a hell of a state: the political tension in the Middle East was high, with war threatening; the United States was facing a worse reces-

28

sion than in 1958; the British political parties were bickering over a proposal to build a tunnel under the Severn; gold reserves were down; the whole unstable economic edifice of the country, if one believed the newspapers—but who did?—tottered on the brink of collapse; and of course the ER's would deliver a rabbit punch to the good old status quo of society.

But it was summer. It was summer in England, hot and sweet and sticky. Everyone was stripping off to mow a lawn or hold a picnic or dive into the nearest dirty stretch of river. Nobody gave a sod. Euphoria had its high tide willy-nilly, come death, come danger. The unexpected heat made morons of us all, quite as effectively as did the interminable wretchedness of winter.

He sighed and breathed the warm air, full of discontent and indifference, those hallmarks of the true-born Englishman. As Jimmy withdrew his head from the window, Rose English was approaching, coming self-assuredly down the corridor.

"Hello," she said, without noticeably smiling. "I wanted some cool air too. People should not give parties on nights like this."

"No," Jimmy replied, rather glumly. Yes, she had something about her.

"I didn't mean to embarrass you in there, Mr. Solent."

"Jimmy, please. I've got such a wet surname." He had trained himself not to wait for laughter after making that modest joke. "You didn't embarrass me; as you say, everyone'll soon be in the same boat."

"No, I didn't mean that. I mean, I hope I said nothing to hurt you."

"Of course not." His Norman Light was glowing; without looking directly, he could see hers was too. To change the subject, he said, "I could do with a swim now."

"Same here." He thought it was a schoolgirlish phrase for somebody of her seriousness to use and wondered if she was in some way trying to play down to him.

"I know a fellow—he was at Oxford with me—who's got a private swimming pool. Would you care to come for a bathe with me?"

"Thank you. I should really prefer dinner," she said. He knew by her tone she thought he had tried to trap her into that; how could she believe him so subtle? He took one of her hands, thinking at the same time he must be a little

29

tight to dare to do so. A lunatic notion blossomed in his brain, swelling like a blown balloon.

"I've just thought of the idea!" he said. "Quite spontaneous—there's no catch. An evening like this is wasted in a place like this; it'll probably pour with rain tomorrow! We could go out and have a swim with them—Hurn, their name is—and then we'll still have time for a meal afterwards. Honestly! I mean how about it? It's a genuine offer. It would be great fun."

"Perhaps it really would be great fun," she said pensively. A waiter, watching them interestedly, gave them gin-and-its. And all the while a drowning Jimmy-inside was telling him, "She's not your kind, kid. You don't like the cool and stately type. She's nearly as big as you are. She's too experienced: she could blow you into bubbles. She's too old for you—she must be thirty-five if she's a day. I warn you, Solent, you'll make the biggest gaffe of your life if you persist in this bit of foolishness."

"You can ditch Uncle Felix, can't you?" he implored her, grinning ingratiatingly, and swallowing the gin-and-it.

"Uncle's no obstacle," she said. "He's staying afterwards to talk to thingme—Clunes."

"Come on, Rangey!" He said, taking her hand again. "Nothing's stopping us. Nobody'll miss us. Down that drink and let's go while the going's good."

Jimmy-inside noted with disgust the lapse into basic American and the abuse of adverbial "down" as a verb. He also noticed that this large, handsome girl was about to surrender herself to Jimmy's care. "She's a wonderful creature! Just be careful, that's all I can say," Jimmy-inside sighed, and went off for the night.

They put their glasses on the window sill: superstitiously Jimmy slid his over till it touched Rose's. Then he took her arm and hurried her down the carpeted stairs. The unending roar of the BIL party died behind them.

"You're telling the truth about this swimming pool, Jimmy?" she asked.

"Wait till you see it, Rangey!"

From then on she seemed to banish entirely any qualms she might have had. It was almost as if the idea had been hers rather than Jimmy's.

II. A Towel in Common

The innocence, simplicity and diffidence which formed a good proportion of Jimmy Solent's character were often ousted by male cunning; now mixed drink had precipitated their expulsion. Anyone who drinks at all knows there are a hundred degrees of sweet and subtle gradation between sobriety and the doddering old age of intoxication; Jimmy was a mere thirty or forty notches down the slide, and still firing on most cylinders. Only his old aunt Indecision had been shut away.

He conjured up a taxi directly Rose and he got outside and urged it to Charlton Square as fast as possible. Knowing something of the oddness of women, he had realised the cardinal fact that once they had bathing costumes and the question of nude bathing was thus disposed of, the whole stunt would seem, by comparison, respectable. He wanted to borrow Aubrey's car: taxis to and from Walton-on-Thames would be expensive. He had yet to tell Rose exactly where the pool was, for fear that she would object that it was too far away.

Jimmy found when he reached the flat that Aubrey had evidently come in and gone out again with Alyson. That was bad; perhaps he had taken the damned MG. Moving like a clumsy wind, while Rose sat downstairs in the ticking taxi, Jimmy seized his own swimsuit and Alyson's from the airing cupboard—it would have to fit Rose, or else. Sweeping into the kitchen, he pulled two bottles of Chianti from the broom closet which served as wine cellar. Then he was downstairs again, shouting goodnight to a surprised Mrs. Pidney, and back in the taxi with his arm round Rose.

At the garage they were in luck. The MG was there. Aubrey and Alyson would be walking; it was a nice evening for walking, if you did not have to get to Walton. Jimmy paid off the taxi and bustled Rose into the coupé.

"They're looking at us as if you're trying to kidnap me," Rose said, waving a hand in indication at a couple of mechanics.

Jimmy laughed.

"No, it's because we're both bright pink," he said.

Laughing, they backed out of the garage. Jimmy drove with savage concentration, fighting to keep the whiskers of drink away from his vision. They could crash on the way back and welcome, but he was not going to spoil the evening now. He was full of exaltation. He had won a prize!

"Had an old car when I was up at Oxford," he shouted to her. He should not have said it; he reminded himself of Penny, who had ridden in that car. Dear little, dull little, Penny! Penny had not the sheer presence of this great luscious lascivious lump. . . .

"What happened to it?" she asked.

. . . nor that *look* in her eye.

"Sold it to Gabby Borrows of Corpus for £20."

You still owe me £4 on that deal, Gabby, you sod.

"He got a bargain, didn't he?"

What, off me, Ikey Solent! ?

"You should have seen 'Tin Lizzie'! She was about tenth hand when I got her. And what am I sitting here talking to you about automobiles for, Rangey, my sweet pet?"

He drew into the side of the road without signalling, braked, and took a long, deep kiss from her. She shaped up round him immediately like a young wrestler. Together, they plunged. The next thing he recalled afterwards was cursing loudly because he could not unhook her brassière. It popped most satisfactorily, and he slid his hands over her breasts, cupping them, kissing them. They excited and bemused him; he hardly realised what he was doing.

"Let's have a swim first, sweet," she said, gasping.

Jimmy struggled up and looked at her. They were bathing each other in pink light. It was like a warm liquid over them. The long face had undergone a change. Her brow was wide and tolerant; every line of her face had relaxed, so that she seemed plumper, less mature, even less sure of herself. Here, now, she was beautiful. He took a long look at her, trying to remember it all.

" 'And threw warm gules on Madelaine's fair breast,' " he quoted, half-shyly. "Have some Chianti?" Just how much had she drunk before the party, he wondered, that she should ever want him?

They drank gravely, companionably, out of the one glass Aubrey kept stowed in his locker, then drove on. Jimmy covered the road more slowly now. For one thing, he had caught the savour of the evening; it was something peaceful, relaxedly relentless—a kind of homecoming. He was going to be a proper man and take the correct tempo; Rangey would appreciate that. She knew and seemed to tell him exactly how these things should go. For another thing, he was having misgivings about the Hurns and their pool.

Rupert Hurn had been at Merton with Jimmy. Their friendship had not been close, but twice Rupert had taken Jimmy and another friend to his home. They had met Rupert's younger sister (what *was* that plump child's name?), and his docile mother, and his pugnacious little stockbroker father; and they had swum in his pool. But the last visit had been two years ago. Rupert might not be at home; the family probably would not remember him. They might even have moved. Jimmy's idea began to look less bright with every mile they made.

He mentioned no word of his misgivings to Rose. If the evening was going to spoil, it should do so without any help from him.

The sun was setting as the MG passed Walton station. To Jimmy's relief, he remembered the way clearly and picked up Ryden's Road with confidence. He could recall the look of the house now; it crouched between two Lutyenesque chimneys; the porch rested on absurdly fat pillars and a laburnum grew too close to the windows. Jimmy had passed the place before he realised it; they had had the sense to chop the tree down.

He backed into the drive and climbed out. Rose climbed out and smoothed herself down. She took his arm, looking at him quizzically; her irises were a perturbing medley of green and brown. Jimmy wondered how on first impression she had seemed unattractive.

"Er . . . come on," he said. Their Norman Lights had ceased to burn. He stepped between the fat pillars and rang the bell; in reply, a mechanism in the hall said "Ding Dong Ding Dong". There was no other sound.

"Perhaps they're out," Rose said. "There are no lights anywhere. Surely they won't have gone to bed yet?"

"You're beautiful," Jimmy said. "Forgive me for not mentioning it earlier. You're beautiful, wonderful, unique."

The door opened, and a very young man thrust his head out. After a searching glance at them, he stepped onto the porch, pulling the door to behind him. He wore a soft black suit with a mauve bow tie and big suède shoes; he had a (violently) contemporary fringe-cut to his hair, while on his brow an ER disc glinted metallically. His little, enquiring face was at once sweaty and fox-like.

"Who are you? You aren't Fred," he said, surveying them anew.

"Touché," Jimmy said, with an attempt at what he called his society laugh. "What can we do to redeem ourselves?"

"What do you want?" the young man asked, refusing to be deflected into a smile.

"We are friends of the Hurns," Jimmy told him. "We beg entry in the name of hospitality—or don't they live here any more? Tell me the worst."

"Which Hurn do you want? They're nearly all out."

"For heaven's sake," Rose said, making a determined entrance into this asinine conversation, "Who are you, a bailiff?"

The young man shot her the look of dumb endurance one sees on the faces of wet dachsunds. He was about to speak when a girl appeared in the open doorway, wearing a severe blouse and slacks, the austerity of which was relieved by a hundredweight of charm bracelet clanking on her left wrist. In the dim light, she looked very young, very lovely. She also wore an ER, though her hair was swept forward so as partly to conceal it.

"Jill!" Jimmy exclaimed. The name of Rupert's sister had returned to him suddenly, just when vitally needed. Jill!—That podgy creature who had swooned over Rock Hudson and played Jokari from a sitting position had transformed herself into this moderately svelte little armful. He wished two years had done as much for him.

"My giddy aunt, you're—aren't you Jimmy Solvent, or someone?" the girl said.

"Solent. Wish I was solvent. Fancy your remembering my name!"

They clasped each other's hands.

"My *dear*, I had a perfectly silly crush on you once. You used to look so sweet on the back of a motor bike!"

"Cross my heart, I still do," Jimmy said, sliding in the nicest possible way round the fringe-cut, who stood there nonplussed by this turn of events. "This, forgive me, is Rose English; Rose English, this English rose is Jill Hurn."

"And this," Jill said, swinging up the charm bracelet in the direction of the scowling youth, "is my boy friend, Teddy Peters. You'd better come in. Were you looking for Rupert, because he's not here. He's in Holland."

34

"Each to his destiny," Jimmy said easily, forging into the hall. "Actually Rose and I came to ask you if we could have a swim. It seemed a shame for a couple like us to waste a bath like yours on a night like this."

With Jill leading and Teddy following, they had reached a living room at the back of the house. A teleset radiated dance music softly from somewhere upstairs. Jill switched on a light on a corner table; in the illumination flowing over her face, Jimmy saw she was too heavily made up and a trifle spotty. All the same, it was a good attempt for—what?—sixteen, she would be no older. She headed for an expensive cocktail cabinet, moving with a copy book grace.

"You must have a drink," she said. "Daddy and Mummy are out." That was a slip, although it told Jimmy nothing he had not already guessed. To readjust the role she was playing (and that little lout Teddy wouldn't have noticed the slip, Jimmy thought), Jill sloshed whisky into three glasses, squirted soda at them and doled them out like Maundy money. She reserved something else for herself; perhaps a Pepsi-cola.

Jimmy took his glass, looking askance at Rose, wondering just how she was feeling. She took a sip and said, "What a lovely room you've got here"—which greatly cheered Jimmy; even half stewed, he could see it was a ghastly, ostentatious room.

"It's beautiful," he lied. "Your chandelier must have been particularly expensive. And your Jacobean radio—gramophone."

"Let's get back upstairs, honey," Teddy said, speaking for the first time since his setback on the porch. Turning to Rose, he added, with a sort of rudimentary parody of Cagney courtesy, "We were dancing."

"How heavenly," Rose said gravely. "I love dancing."

Jill, tilting her tightly covered rump like a snub-nose, was edging Jimmy into a corner. He was content to be edged until the vital question was answered; this now popped impolitely out of him again: "Can we have a swim?"

She did not answer at once, being busy breathing somewhat industriously.

Her eyes were ludicrously wide. Her perfume was as painful as a trodden corn, and then she smiled. The performance would be better in a year; in eighteen months you would not be able to tell it from the real thing. Perhaps, indeed, there wasn't a real thing: only a series of undetectable fakes. It might be one of those shams which Rose said that Norman Lights would abolish. Apropos of which, Jill's, old boy, was turning pink on you. Keep your ruddy genes to yourself, you in the ruddy jeans. It's useless getting sanguine over me. Title for a song....

"Of course you can swim, Jimmy," Jill was saying. She had made her voice husky for extra appeal; perhaps, Jimmy thought, she did it by holding Pepsi-cola at the back of her throat; and he watched her mouth eagerly to see if she dribbled any. "Only you see, Jimmy," she continued, "Daddy isn't very broad-minded about couples swimming after dark—we had a lot of trouble in the spring with Rupert and an awful girl called Sonia MacKenzie—you ought to hear about *that* some time—but of course *I'm* broad-minded, so I don't care, but you'd better be out before Daddy gets back. Teddy and I would come with you, but Teddy can't swim."

"Pity about that," Jimmy murmured.

"Here's the key to the changing hut," Jill said, handing over a large label tied to a tiny key. Her hand touched his and stayed there. He stroked her chin with his free hand.

"You're an absolute darling," Jimmy said. "I love you, and I'll remember you in my will."

"I never think that's a very practical suggestion," she said frowning. The remark amused Jimmy considerably; he choked over his whisky.

"As you can see," he said, "owing to present commitments, I am unable to offer you anything more practical!"

Still laughing, he turned to find Rose dancing a slow quickstep with Teddy. Both of them still clutched their drinks. Both scowled in concentration. Both were showing faint pink on their ER's.

"Hey, you're meant to be swimming!" Jimmy said, forgetting his manners. Catching hold of Rose round the waist, he dragged her away, turning to wave at the other two as he pushed her through the door. Shoving her down the hall, he got her into the open and shut the front door behind them.

"That was very rude!" Rose said admiringly. Under the stars she drained the last of her glass, let it drop onto the gravel, and slid forward into his arms. They kissed, rapturous with reunion. In the house they had been apart: it was another world. Now they were together again, the evening once more on their shoulders like a tame raven.

36

Jimmy grabbed the Chianti and the swimsuits out of the car. "I just don't give a damn," he thought wonderingly; "not a damn!"

"Hang on here a moment, pet," he whispered. "I'm going to take the car just down the road a bit, in case the old man comes home early and spots it."

"What old man?" she asked curiously.

"Any old man, Rangey, my love, my bright shiner."

He seemed to be away an age, finding an unobtrusive place for the car and relieving himself heartily into a hedge, but when he returned Rose still stood in the centre of the drive and asked him again, with the same puzzlement in her voice, "What old man, darling?"

"Jill's old man. Old man Hurn. Come on; let's go see the puddle."

The swimming pool was at the rear of the house. By daylight it looked small and impoverished; the concrete was a maze of cracks, the diving boards both drooped. Now, camouflaged by night, Aphrodite could have risen from it without putting it out of character. On the other hand, the changing hut (the Hurns showed a surprising modesty in not labelling it 'the pavilion') was even smaller, darker and stuffier now than by daylight. Inside the door with the frosted glass window was one room with a partition down the middle, opposite sexes who changed there together being trusted not to look round it—a simple-minded but ideal arrangement, Jimmy thought.

"Can you see to undress?" he asked Rose.

"Yes, by the light of your ER," she said.

"Sorry," he muttered, turning tactfully away.

"How's the costume?" he asked, when they emerged into the night air a minute later.

"A bit tight."

"So'm I. Feel O.K.?" She looked like a lusty goddess.

"Hungry," she said, wrapping her arms round her middle.

"We'll eat later, that I swear: Jimmy'll never let you starve. The night's young!"

Suddenly he knew indeed that the night was young and he was young. The excitement of the dark purred through his body. In one grand flash, he recalled all the events of the day, getting up, his work, having his ER fitted, the party, Rose. It was all unreal, bygone, prehistoric. A new era had begun; the ER's were going to change everything. In Merrick's words, he had inherited a major liberty.

He raced round and round the lawn, puppy-like.

"The world's begun again, Rangey my love," he shouted. "You and I are the only ones to guess it yet, but the jolly old millennium began today? Hurray! Life's the greatest invention yet! "

"Not so *loud*, Jimmy," she said. "You're crazy! "

"Nuts to you, you great big lovely ploughable adult of a woman," he called. Charging at the pool, he bounded in and disappeared with a resounding splash. Rose followed more gracefully, diving off the side of the bath.

"Distinctly frappé," she said in a small voice, as they swam together. She shook her head vigorously in distress.

"Where have they kept this pool all day?" he asked. "Feels like liquid oxygen. Death to the loins."

"Oh Jimmy, I do feel funny. I think I'd better get out."

He put an arm round her shoulders. Her flesh was as heavy and cold as refrigerated meat.

"Come on then, pet," he said. "I'll give you a hand out. You'd better go indoors and have a warm-up. A sip more whisky's what you need."

"No, wait a tick. . . . Ug, better now, I think. It was just one of those momentary things. Sorry. I seem to be functioning properly again now."

Rose trod water, and then they began swimming slowly round the tank like a goldfish in a bowl. The water had evidently had a cooling effect on their genes, for their Norman Lights no longer glowed, spoiling what might have been rather an unusual effect.

"Are you sure you're all right, Rangey?"

"I told you I was."

"The water's quite hot when you get used to it."

"What I was thinking."

He floated on his back, gazing into the clear night sky with its complement of stars. Somewhere way up there was a super-civilisation which had solved all its troubles and wore new suits every day; it was not having half the time he was.

"I think I'm ready to get out," he said. "How about you, Rangey?"

"I could stay here till dawn now I'm properly in. One becomes acclimatised, you know."

He drifted over to her. Her face and the reflections of her face seemed to palpitate before him like butterflies in a cupboard. Reaching out, he caught and kissed her; they climbed together up rickety wooden steps, trotting over short grass and gravel to the changing hut.

There, Jimmy thoughtfully locked the door on the inside, and proceeded with the next stage of his master plan. Waiting a moment, he called softly in mock-consternation. "Rangey, what a fool I am! I forgot to bring any towels."

"You are lying to me, Jimmy, and I hate lies," she said from her side of the partition.

"I'm not lying!" he said angrily. "I did not bring any towels. I was in such a hurry I forgot."

In the faint light, he noticed as he spoke a towel hanging on a hook, on the rear wall of the hut. Rose presumably had found one too and believed Jimmy had provided it. Snatching it off the peg, he bundled it up and thrust it under the seat. Then he bounded round the partition.

"If you've found a towel, you'll have to let me share it, pet," he said. He saw at once that she had one.

"Go away, Jimmy," she said quickly, clutching the towel round her body as he bathed her in his ruby light. "I haven't got any lipstick on yet."

He was too intent to laugh.

"It's a lovely warm towel!" He exclaimed, grabbing a corner of it. "Don't be greedy! It's big enough to cover two of us! How about saving me from the foggy, foggy dew? I'm shivering."

The odd thing was, that when they were pressed together under the towel, Jimmy did begin to shiver. Excitement made him shiver as he felt her wet limbs wet upon his. He ran his hand down the great hyperbola of Rose's back, sliding it over her buttocks and gripping them, then working it round her thigh.

"Oh, Jimmy, you know I'm hungry!" she wailed.

"For God's sake, give me time," he said.

She did. He fed upon the riches of the wide world on that cramped wooden floor. Sometimes he wondered, with only the mildest concern, whether she would not suffocate him, sometimes whether she would not crack his ribs; sometimes whether he had not bitten off more than he could chew, but always he rose triumphantly to face a fresh attack, always they were matched. She had spoken at the party against making a mockery of sex; of that she was not guilty; the core of earnestness Jimmy sensed in her was there even in her gladdest abandonment; she swam with him up the mountainside of love like a salmon leaping up a waterfall. In the end, he was flooded with a delighted and transcendent surprise, cast on a shore beyond Ultima Thule. Exhausted, thrilled, jubilant, panting like a dog.

"Oh, darling . . ." Rose sighed at last, "what a rough brute you are!"

"Me! You're the brute!—you're the beauty *and* the beast. Rangey, you're all things. Rangey, how old are you?"

"Don't ask petty questions," she said, giving him a final hug, tugging his hair gently, kissing his neck.

"But I know so little about you!"

"That's just as well for you," she said, getting onto her knees. He tried to pull her on top of him again but she wisely would not come, so he got up and fetched the Chianti bottle. She was dressing as fast as she could and would take no wine.

"We must be filthy from this beastly floor!" she said. "It's all gritty and beastly. Don't they ever sweep the damned place?"

"Wonderful, heavenly floor!" Jimmy said. "We'll come and visit it and lay an offering to Venus on it every anniversary of this date, won't we?"

When she did not reply, he knew he was being hearty. More, he knew they would never come here again. He was about to say something else when she seized his arm. Footsteps sounded outside on the concrete path. A pause while the grass muffled them. Then the handle of the changing hut door was turned. Jimmy clapped his hand up to his forehead to cover his ER in case it should be visible through the frosted glass, but it had ceased to glow. They listened while the footsteps receded.

"We could always have said we were waiting for a bus," Jimmy said.

"Jill's old man keeps late hours," Rose said tugging on her skirt. "It's past midnight."

"And a good time was had by all. Oh, Rangey, I love you so! This has been such a wonderful evening for me. I can't really believe your name is English Rose."

"Does it sound so very unlikely?" she asked, with a strange seriousness in her voice.

"Very," he said. It astonished him that he should be feeling suddenly irritable with her, and hid it as best he could; we resent those who please us, for they can guess our weakness. "I'm going to get you a meal now, woman."

"Really?" She relaxed at once. She was nearly dressed.

40

He regretted it was too dark to see anything of her under-clothes; such things were a mystery to him. Pulling himself together, he blundered round the partition to put his own clothes on.

"Where, Jimmy?"

"Where what, pet?"

"Where are we going to eat?"

"Your uncle Jimmy knows a dirty little Chinese restaurant off Shaftesbury Avenue which stays open till two in the morning."

She came and stood on his side of the partition then, to show him she was proud of him. When they were finally ready, they crept out of the hut, leaving the key on the outside of the lock, and walked quietly round the pool. Its surface was as still and black as oil. Keeping on the grass as far as possible, to avoid the scrunch of gravel, they skirted the house, where no lights burned.

A voice softly called "Goodnight!" from above them. They looked up to see Jill Hurn leaning out of her bedroom window, shadowy under the eaves. She must have been there a long while, watching for them. Jimmy raised a hand in silent salute to all good things and led Rose back to the car.

They ate their chow mein, sweet and sour pork and crispy noodles in quiet mood; when, after the meal, Rose insisted on catching a taxi and going off alone, Jimmy protested without vehemence and yielded without delay.

They were tired and had nothing more to offer each other.

It was a quarter to two when he let himself into 17 Charlton Square, and after three before he fell asleep. When he awoke next morning, it was to find his sheets full of earth, dead grass and dirt, picked up from his session on the changing hut floor; appearances suggested he had had an aborigine in bed with him.

III. At the IBA

The Home of the International Book Association, where Jimmy worked, was a tall, undistinguished building just off Bedford Square. Unlike its rival and elder sister, the

National Book League, the IBA claimed no Regency graces. There was American capital behind it: it was modern and proud of it.

As you went through plate glass doors into a foyer ambushed with cactus, a sign in sanserif announced, "Only books stand between us and the cave. Clyde H. Nitkin." The IBA ran mainly on dollar lubrication supplied by the Clyde H. Nitkin Foundation, and the words of the great man, at once original and obvious, were in evidence throughout the building. In the cafeteria downstairs, among the Mojave Desert décor, was "To read is to strike a blow for culture. Clyde H. Nitkin." In the Main Exhibition room on the ground floor was "Speech is silver: silence is golden: print is dynamite. Clyde H. Nitkin." Up in the library, appropriately enough, was "Only by libraries can man survive. Clyde H. Nitkin." And, most touching heart cry of all, reserved for the board room up by the roof, was "Dear God, I would rather be an author than Clyde H. Nitkin."

This morning, Jimmy came in rather late. He stood for a moment in the rear of the foyer, exuding general goodwill. It was only six months since he had come to live in London and take this, his first job. Pleasure still filled him at the thought of it; he surveyed everything with a contentment at once filial and avuncular. Posters and book jackets jostled convivially here under busts of Shakespeare, Sophocles and Edna St. Vincent Millay. Mr. J. B. Priestley would speak on the 18th next on "What the Canadian Theatre Means." Angus Wilson's new play "Regular Churchgoers" in its fifth week at the Criterion. Thyroid Annerson's new play at the Stumer. The new Francis Bacon exhibition—the one with the laughing dogs—at the Hanover Galleries. Kingsley Amis to speak, mysteriously, about "The New Distaste" on the 25th. The posters at least were quietly, staunchly English.

The book jackets struck a more exotic note. Peter Green's name appeared on the serpent-haunted jacket of his large new novel "Patinotoxa's Donkey." Monkeys chased themselves round the latest Mittelholzer title from Secker's. A formal jungle surrounded the word "Popocatepetl" on Edmund Wilson's new collection of travel essays. Orange prisms crashed across "Berg and the Instability of Our Times." It was all, Jimmy told himself, at once homely and exciting. "The hoi polloi are rather coy at facing the printed word, but mad dogs and publishers care nought for the midday herd," he intoned to himself.

He nodded amiably to Mrs. Charteris, the receptionist (somehow he could never think of anything to say to that woman) and went to his room. This room, lying beyond the Main Exhibition chamber, was isolated from everyone else in the building; nevertheless, it was nice to have a room at all, and Jimmy, who was second-in-command of exhibitions while Dirk Hanahan was away being ill in Boston, relished its privacy—especially this morning.

He was in a golden daze. He wanted only to sit quietly and think of the raptures of last night, with Rose alive in his arms. His room was almost bare; even the inevitable bookcase contained little more than Webster's Dictionary and a pile of IBA pamphlets on people like Svevo. A Ben Nicholson relief on one wall only added to the austerity. That suited Jimmy well; the fewer external distractions the better.

The intercom on his desk buzzed.

"And now a word from our sponsor," Jimmy groaned.

He depressed one of the ivory keys and said "Solent" in a suitably crisp tone.

"Scryban here, Jimmy. We're having an informal discussion on next month's activities, just pooling a few ideas. You'd better be in on it from the exhibition angle, I think. Would you kindly come up, please?"

"Certainly." That was a blind. Jimmy felt perfectly fit, except for a dry mouth, but he just did not want to face people this morning. However, Scryban was Scryban and business was business. . . . In Jimmy's drawer lay a manila folder labelled "Haiti Exhibition"; he debated taking it up with him to Scryban's room but, as that exhibition would not be held until September, decided it would look irrelevant or self-important or something equally horrid. Instead, he took the lift up to Scryban's room.

"Literature is a jealous god: serve it in deeds and words," adjured Clyde H. Nitkin from eye level.

Four people were already closeted with Scryban. Donald Hortense, the IBA librarian, a science-fiction magazine tucked in his pocket, winked at Jimmy. He was the only one here Jimmy could really say he knew. Mrs. Wolf, a little, lipsticked woman with a big, difficult husband, smiled at him: Jimmy smiled back, for Mrs. Wolf was always very sweet to him. Paul de Perkin, whose office door bore

43

the enticing word "Social," acted up to his label, indicating a chair for Jimmy and offering him a cigarette. The only person to ignore Jimmy's entrance was standing looking out of the window; this was Martin "Bloody" Trefisick, who called himself a Cornishman, though his detractors claimed he came from Devon. He was the declared enemy of Mrs. Wolf, and his office door bore the oblique message "House Organ".

Sitting sideways behind his desk, his neat knees crossed, was Conrad Scryban, the Managing Director of IBA. Jimmy had quietly admired this man from their first meeting; so effectively and unassumingly was he the English literary man, that Jimmy felt sure there must be fraud in the fellow somewhere. It made him roughly ten times as interesting as any of the other solid but transparent characters in the room.

Apart from Scryban and Trefisick, everyone in the room already bore a Norman Light on his forehead. It lent an air of strangeness and newness, like a paperback found among Roman relics.

"Splendid," Scryban said vaguely, as Jimmy sat down between de Perkin and Mrs. Wolf. Scryban's baldness, like a tonsure, gave him a monastic look which his clothes quietly refuted. "We were saying before you joined us, Jimmy, that next month, being August, is rather a dog month generally. Anyone who is anyone will be no nearer Bedford Square than Teneriffe. Nevertheless, we are duty bound to offer some sort of diversion to such of the general public as wander through our doors. . . . Have you, I wonder, any suggestions? I hasten to add that none of the rest of us have."

"Actually, I believe the centenary of the publication of 'The Cloister and the Hearth' falls some time next month," Mrs. Wolf said cautiously.

A hush settled over them. "I ought to suggest something," Jimmy told himself, as gradually the dread of being laughed at by Trefisick was dwarfed by the dread of being considered unimaginative by Scryban. He cleared his throat.

"How about some sort of tie-in with politics?" he asked the company generally, following up with a brilliant improvisation: "I've been thinking about the Nitkin pearl that every poem is a pincer movement. Couldn't we drag out some contemporary examples of that?"

"I can see the implications," said Scryban, appearing

44

actually to view them in a far corner, "but how exactly do you visualize . . . I mean, what I don't see . . ."

He was too gentle to name what he did not see, but Jimmy suspected it must be the same thing he himself did not see: just what the deuce he was suggesting. He tried a counter-move.

"Well, how do you feel about the present political situation?" he asked.

Scryban did not immediately answer. Instead Paul de Perkin leant forward, his face gleaming with interest, and said, "I think you have something promising there, old boy. Do you mean the international situation?"

"Heavens, is he really fool enough to think I've got something?" Jimmy asked himself drearily, and then decided that de Perkin, also unsure of himself, was also trying to appear bright.

"Yes, the international situation," he said at random.

"Ah now, let me see," said Scryban, conscientiously. "We have the Western bloc on one side and the Soviet bloc on the other, have we not? And the Middle East shuttling tediously about in between. That is how matters have been, internationally, for some years, I believe, and I confess I find it an uninspiring situation: an unfruitful situation."

"We are all in a perpetual state of non-combatancy," Mrs. Wolf said. Jimmy liked the remark and laughed; she smiled at him and laughed herself.

"All very trying for everyone," Scryban agreed. "One may, in fact, quote the words Donne employed in a somewhat different context: 'The foe oft-times having the foe in sight, Is tired of standing though he never fight.' "

"We shall see a change now," Trefisick said, wrestling to fit his broad shoulders into the window frame. "These ER's completely topple the status quo at home; they are bound to have repercussions abroad. Without being in any way a prophet, I'd say that chaos will come again. Britain is already the laughing stock of Europe."

"That just isn't so! *The Guardian* says Scandinavia is green with envy," Jimmy said hotly, venturing for the first time to contradict Trefisick.

"Really? In those very words?" asked Scryban, interested at last.

"I see the *New Statesman* is less outspoken about Tory intrigues than it was last week," de Perkin observed. "And certainly the Commonwealth seems to commend us. . . . Especially Australia; I always think Australia's very forward looking. . . ."

"There was a paragraph in the *Telegraph*," Mrs. Wolf said, looking round as she whipped out her paper. They had all brightened considerably under the new topic of conversation. "Here we are. It points out that we have inaugurated a social invention whose power potential is far greater than that of the hydrogen bomb."

"And we go and use it on ourselves!" Trefisick exclaimed bitterly. "My God, but I never saw such bloody folly. You'll never catch me wearing one of the beastly things, I can assure you of that!"

"Life has grown too complicated, Martin," said Scryban gently. "We have said that so often in past years that it has become a platitude. Now that something has come along which, it is claimed, will simplify things for us, surely we are morally obliged not to look our gift horse in the mouth—especially when they are free on the National Health Scheme?"

"But *will* these damned gadgets simplify life, that's what I want to know?" Trefisick said pugnaciously, squaring his shoulders by inserting his thumbs in the top of his trousers. "Have they simplified *your* sex life, Solent? What about yours, de Perkin? Find things easier for having a tin medal over your nose?"

"I've only had mine a day," Jimmy said, simultaneously feeling his cheeks redden and cursing himself for not standing up to this man.

"You'd better ask all my mistresses about that, Trefisick," de Perkin laughed feebly, and Jimmy cursed him for being another time server.

Mrs. Wolf rolled up her *Telegraph* pugnaciously. She was at least forty-nine, and every wrinkle showed; but for a second defiance gave her back her youth. "This damned gadget as you call it, Martin, has certainly not simplified my life," she said without heat, her sharp teeth gleaming as she faced Trefisick. "On the contrary, it has complicated it. My husband and I are in the situation which comes to many couples: we are out of love with one another. Whereas for years we have manoeuvred unceasingly to hide this state of affairs from each other—and from ourselves—*and* from other people—we can no longer conceal it. The Norman Lights confront us with the truth."

"I'm sorry to hear that," Trefisick said, rubbing his neck, abashed; he added, despite himself, "All the same, Veronica, you've proved my point about their being a menace."

"Not at all," she said. "For the first time my husband and I are free to be perfectly honest with each other. I have only hope for the future; forced to acknowledge the facts at last, we may reach something better than a dead compromise." She paused. "I'm sorry. I shouldn't have . . ."

"Dear Mrs. Wolf," Scryban said, lifting his hands from his knees and replacing them there, "I refuse to allow you to apologise. What you say only makes us respect and admire you the more; our vegetable love for you grows marvellously quicker than empires. You do show—"

"I'm just trying to show you," she interrupted a little breathlessly, "that these Norman Lights really should have our utmost faith: they are the first scientific invention ever to make us face ourselves."

They had been embarrassed by revelations about Mrs. Wolf's marriage before. Silence burst over them like an exploding muffin.

"Well, thank you all very much for coming up and giving me your ideas. We'll think along the political line, shall we?" Scryban said, with more haste than usual. "Now I'm sure I'm keeping you all from your coffee. I would just like to say, if I might, that though I disapprove of ER's personally, I find it difficult to understand why all the criticism of them from the culture camp, from people like Betjeman and Clark and Ayrton, has confined itself to aesthetic principles. I find those of you here who have your Registers installed"—this was said with a deprecatory smile—"of an enhanced appearance."

As they left Scryban's room, Donald Hortense materialised at Jimmy's left elbow. He was one of Jimmy's closest friends, which made him rather less than more endearing at present, Jimmy's lover's soul feeling far from chummy.

"I don't believe you said one word in there," he accused Donald.

"That takes bags of courage, especially when one has nothing to say. Did you get that portrait for your exhibition off Sir Richard Clunes?"

"I got the promise of it when we're ready for it, which is all I wanted," Jimmy said. "And I went to a cocktail party he gave last night. A business do."

47

"Oh? And what do the Corridors of Power boys think about nunchasers?" This was Donald's method of referring to anyone in bureaucratic or scientific circles, however lowly.

They seem on the whole to take to the *idea* of them a deal more enthusiastically than do we Corridors of Eng. Lit. boys."

"Not surprising; we're a backward-looking lot. Our glories lie behind us, *pace* Nitkin," Donald said, without much interest. "Come on down to the café for a chat. There isn't a blessed thing to do this morning in the library."

Jimmy agreed, catching a glimpse in his mind's eye of a pair of faultless breasts thrusting towards him on the road to Walton. The IBA seemed curiously insubstantial this morning.

"What did you think of the she-wolf washing *and* ironing her dirty linen in public?" Donald asked.

"I thought it was jolly brave of her to speak out to Bloody Trefisick the way she did. I admired her for it."

"You're hopeless, Jimmy. That wasn't bravery, you ass, it was masochism, if ever I saw it. She's a masochist and her hubby must be a mash-assistant."

"You don't believe a word you say, Donald," Jimmy reproved, but he felt slightly tired of the other's habit of jokingly imputing perverted values to every conceivable relationship; it was, of course, the result of Donald's being what he was, and of the law's attitude to what he was. "When allowances are made, it's what I've always said, It's only 'uman nature after all," Jimmy rhymed to himself. All the same, he would not dream of mentioning Rose to Donald, much as he longed to rhapsodise about her to someone.

In the cafeteria they sat at a corner table, just out of striking distance of a giant American aloe cactus. Donald sat genially with his elbows on the table. Despite too beautiful tailoring which enveloped him, he looked like a rugger forward just off the field, his hair spikey, his nose slightly flat. He had a healthy look about him; Jimmy already accepted the fact that Donald's light glowed intermittently in his presence.

"Had a poem accepted this morning, me boy," Donald said. "*Mandragora* took it—the one about the turds, that Tambimuttu turned down."

"I remember. Good! Congratulations. It should appear

in about three years." Jimmy enjoyed none of Donald Hortense's poems, but he found them oddly memorable—partly because, as a member of the Scribist movement, Donald only composed poems which were seven brief lines long.

"Of course, I'm going to have to change my entire method of writing poetry," Donald said thoughtfully. "What a lot of people have not realised is that Norman Lights are going to put a new aspect on everything," Donald said. "For literature, it'll be a far more sweeping change than any of the multitude of changes it's already undergone this century. It'll mean writers having to learn a new language even more difficult than Shaw's forty letter alphabet would have been: the language of changed mores and responses in the external world. Willy nilly, poetry and the novel are dunked back into a realm of exploration."

"I suppose so," Jimmy agreed. "A writer writes most richly of his childhood. Facing the new set-up will be a tax on him. Any novelist not tackling the immediate present will be classed as an historical novelist."

"Not only that. The NL's will bring a state of flux which is going to last for years, as all the ramifications seep through every level of society. A synthesis, an analysis, will be a more demanding task than ever—*and* its value more questionable. Because no sooner do you get the novel or what-have-you written than your specimen is out of date. Have you seen *Vogue*?"

Jimmy shook his head. He had never seen *Vogue*; Donald always had. Women's fashion magazines were irresistible to the librarian; through them he caught glimpses of a vast, busy world with which he had not the slightest connection.

"There's an interesting article in it by Grigson," Donald said: "Versatile type, Grigson; I admire him for it. He's attempting to predict the effect NL's will have on such womanly wiles as make-up and hats—and hence on the whole conception of female beauty. He thinks that at first hats will be designed to *conceal* NL's and then, later, to *reveal* them. As a long range prediction, he emphasises that we have supplied our bodies with a new sexual focus, which he thinks may supplant some of the others in superficial importance. So that by about the mid-seventies bare breasts may be quite the thing; they just won't seem anything to be excited about any more."

"It's something to look forward to, anyhow."

"Infantile traumas springing up right, left and centre," Donald exclaimed, gulping down his coffee in disgust. "Well, I must be awa'."

When Jimmy returned to his little room, he pulled the Haiti folder out of the desk and opened it. On the first sheet of paper, he had written boldly, "Books in Haiti since 1804." It was going to be a good and unusual exhibition: *his* exhibition. He ought to write straight away to the faculty of Pisa for photographs of Queen Marie-Louise's grave; sufficiently enlarged, they would fill the awkward alcove at the far end of the Main Exhibition hall. He began a rough sketch to indicate the sort of camera angle he required.

In no time, his pencil stopped. Blankly, gently, he gazed into space. The soft and nutritious thought of Rose slid over him. As if silent upon a peak in Darien, he seemed to have discovered a new ocean of truth. He perceived that most of the books in the building, and nearly all the books he had ever read, had lied; that his friends and acquaintances had deceived him; that his parents and teachers had misled him; that few, in fact, except a smattering of sages mislabelled voluptuaries, had ever staggered on his mighty discovery. Physical love was good!

Jimmy recalled St. Augustine's nauseating comments on women; he recalled the diatribes of Puritans and Victorians; he recalled the dirty jokes he had heard and told; and he seethed with anger. It was all a pack of contemptible rubbish, foul, unhealthy lies and illusion! There was no beauty like the indulgence of the flesh, no cleanliness like a woman's intimate cleanliness.

Yes, though women like men might be bags of offal and intestines and secretions, what sweet chemistry could be brewed between them.

He recalled all the modern novels he had consumed in which passion was shown as a dark destroyer or, at best, as a parched desert. How crudely those authors had misread. Truth lay buried in the body and could only be reached as Jimmy had reached it last night. The plunge was what absolutely must be taken. And though one had wings, the dive into the burning lake was necessary for life.

Jimmy Solent, as may perhaps be gathered from this summary of his feelings, was practically a stranger to the wilder alchemies of the human system. A diffident creature

50

his experience hitherto had been limited to: one foray undertaken in a more or less scientific spirit eight years ago, with a girl at the seaside; the tide had come in before they could reach any definite conclusions; one diversion at an Oxford party with a girl called Diana who was reading mediaeval law, a diversion which had been interrupted at an extremely crucial moment by Penny (this was the reason for Penny's breaking off her engagement with Jimmy); and several trial runs with Penny herself which, while not unsatisfactory enough to rank as failures, had hardly—as Jimmy now realised—been stylish enough to qualify as successes.

Rose had style. What had been a mere tussle with Penny became a gallant conspiracy with her. The strange temples that they had built last night had been as disciplined as Salisbury Cathedral and yet as riotous as Gaudi's Barcelona; with Penny, to continue the architectural metaphor, only a sort of stodgy Broadcasting House was possible.

This was due to far more than the contrast in Rose and Penny between experience and innocence, between thirty-five and twenty-two. It was due to a difference in attitude which would express itself, not only in all the outlets of love but in every facet of their involvement with the outside world. That was why Rose seemed to have brought the millennium to Jimmy: he was sure he had seen through a spy-hole into a complete—and infinitely desirable—existence.

The more Jimmy explored all the agreeable sensations which filled him, the more uneasy he grew. The contradiction puzzled him, until its source suddenly became clear. He had to have more of that wonderful world, and he had not got Rose's address. He had not had the elementary intelligence to get her address, and she had not suggested another meeting.

He was at lunch in the IBA cafeteria when this oafish bit of stupidity occurred to him. He set down his cup with such force that his friends jumped in alarm.

"I've just remembered—I've got to make a phone call," Jimmy told Donald Hortense and Sylvia Redfern, the IBA sub-librarian.

"Crikey, man, it'll wait till you've finished your coffee, won't it?" Donald said. "You haven't forgotten it's a bob a cup here, have you?"

51

"This is going to be a private call," Sylvia said, "You can tell by the look on his face."

Bitterness was detectable in her tone: she had hoped to make Jimmy's ER light, and had failed.

As soon as he could decently get back to the privacy of his office, Jimmy did so. There were two possible ways of procuring Rose's address, through Sir Richard Clunes or through Guy Leighton; Guy was the obvious choice, although Jimmy bore him little love and Aubrey had to be phoned first to obtain Guy's number. Finally, however, there was that competent voice of Guy's in Jimmy's ear; odd how even a voice can sound as if it is balanced on the balls of its feet.

"Hello, Solent. This is so sudden. What can we do for you?"

Without finesse, Jimmy asked for Rose's phone number. There was a distinct pause on the line.

"Had you met Miss English before the cocktail party last night?" Guy finally asked.

"No; I thought you knew I hadn't. Why do you ask?"

"Look, Solent, it runs quite contrary to my principles to ladle out free advice, and I say this purely by way of friendship, but really if I were you I should steer quite clear of the Iral fraternity at present. Do you understand?"

"No, I'm sorry, Guy, I don't understand. I didn't mention Iral; I just asked if you knew where I could find Rose."

The voice at the other end assumed the slightly constricted tones of martyrdom as it said, "As perhaps you may have heard, the Norman Laboratories, which invented the Norman Light or Emotional Register, are controlled by Iral Chemicals. They rival Monsanto in size, and this new product is giving even ICI a twinge of regret; you may have noted, if you keep abreast of such things, how Iral shares have jumped recently. Felix Garside is a director of Iral. Rose English is his niece. I am not at liberty to say too much, but if this NL deal with the government fails to come off, Rose and everyone else are—er, going to be in trouble."

"I don't follow you," Jimmy said, feeling disquieted by this information. "Surely this NL deal *has* come off? Everyone has to have one fitted by the first of September, by law."

Guy laughed dryly.

"You submerge yourself in books too deeply, Solent," he

said, "or you would have observed considerable opposition to Norman Lights—opposition which grows as public opinion becomes more enlightened. It is more than likely that the government will have fallen by September the first."

When he had absorbed this, Jimmy heard himself say weakly, "It may be as you say, Guy, but I don't honestly see how all this should affect my seeing Rose."

"I'm trying to explain in your own best interests, why I think you're plunging in out of your depth, Solent."

"Good heavens, I'm not asking you to worry if I drown. All I want to know is how I can get in touch with Rose."

"Then I'm sorry but I do not know. To my knowledge, which is limited, she is rarely in London. Goodbye, Solent. You must have a drink with me sometime."

Jimmy put the phone down and sat being quietly angry. An additional item in his fury was an inability to see just how much of Guy's rudeness was deliberate. When he had really come to the boil, he marched out into the foyer to Mrs. Charteris, the receptionist. For once he could think of something to say to her. He asked her for the London telephone directory and looked up Iral.

IV. "You Don't Feel a Thing"

That afternoon, when the IBA had closed most of its doors (only the library, cafeteria and lecture rooms were still open) Jimmy walked gently in the hot sun, paying more attention than usual to his surroundings. Two IBA typists, bottoms jolting, passed him hurriedly and were whistled at by two lowly members of the Army, that blue-jowled mother-surrogate. The soldiers wore ER's, which did not glow at the girls; their whistles had been purely automatic, a signal to each other rather than to the typists. A small percentage of the crowd bore the metal discs on their foreheads.

An array of posters met Jimmy's eye at the end of the street. Beside "The toast is—Melloaf!" the toucans drinking Guinness, Jack Hawkins in "First the Beachheads," and the now familiar U.N. poster saying "The opposite of Peace is not War but Death," was the new government poster on which a pretty but suitably reticent-looking girl wearing her ER announced "I'm respectable now; nobody will pester me when they can *see* I'm not interested." Under this unlikely statement was the legend "YOUR life will be Simpler," but as Jimmy passed the half acre of paper he saw somebody had scrawled on it "We don't want sex in our home."

He bought a *Standard* from the newsboy at the corner. Only a third of the front page was given over to the Test Match against Ceylon. The rest bore a heading " 'Big' Bill Bourgoyne says: Lights Bring Darkness." Under the headline, a report said: "Amid Opposition cheers, 'Big' Bill Bourgoyne, Socialist member for Sludge (East), claimed that ER's, brilliant new inventions of Norman Laboratories, would bring about a New Dark Age. 'Don't listen to Government claims that they are going to make life better,' he shouted during a stormy scene. 'They are only going to make the Police State stronger.' The Commons were meeting to discuss the new Double Daylight bill.

"Will Bourgoyne, forty-six-year-old M.P. and TV star, famous for his outbursts when the ER bill was passed early this year, is leader of the Bourgoyne Group holding a protest meeting in Trafalgar Square this evening. The ranks of his 'Hands Off Sex' campaign, as one of his critics has pointed out, are made up of ageing ladies who appear never to have had their hands on. Tonight's meeting should be lively, notwithstanding.

"When Bourgoyne claimed that ER's were camouflaged mind readers, Mr. Peter Thornton, from the government benches, shouted 'That is dangerous and unscientific nonsense! Emotion Registers are man's greatest contribution to social living—you are a Victorian prude.' There were cries of 'What have you got to hide, Bourgoyne?' The Speaker brought the house back to the subject in hand, which was—later closing in public parks. It had been suggested that glowing ER's might help park attendants to locate late visitors."

Jimmy smiled and headed for the tube. He could see little hint in the activities of Bourgoyne that the government was threatened; Guy Leighton did not know what he was talking about; the fellow was obviously too eager to impress. If trouble had been coming, it would have come before the bill was made law. But the party in office had laid its plans with care and those who spoke out against the motion were easily made to seem opponents of progress and oppressors of the mixed-up young, if not downright dirty old men. "Every man is not a proper champion for truth," said Sir Thomas Browne, "nor fit to take up the gauntlet in the cause of verity," and the case against the ER was quickly brought to disrepute by the obvious crankiness of many of its detractors.

Even so, the installations of an ER on every forehead in the kingdom would have remained forever a dream but for one factor: the very revolutionariness of that invention. As *Time* commented, "Pixilated by novelty, Britain decides to put love-light above eyes." The whole thing was launched like a surprise attack. There were contributing factors also which won over, if not public support, public acquiescence for the Government ER campaign. The Prime Minister, Herbert Gascadder, and his very able Minister of Health, Dr. Warwick Bunnian, were careful never to alarm anyone by employing the word "sex"; they merely mooted a design for common sense living with clarified emotional standards in which ER's would do for the blood what traffic signals did for the highways. It was left to the opponents of the design to use that terrifying three letter word, with the foreseeable consequence that they thereby stirred up prejudice against themselves. The true aspects of the debate, as so often happens, were lost, and Sense v. Sex was presented as the issue at stake.

Humbler and saner levels of the great British public might still have repelled the new notion from behind a barricade of prudery. But under the first concerted frontal attack it had ever faced, that prudery collapsed; it had been a poor, frail thing, a middle class myth of hardly more than a century's standing. The heritage of the past, Chaucer's, Shakespeare's, Wycherley's, Boswell's, revived overnight, and the majority of people found themselves eager to discover which of their acquaintances actually felt how strongly about them; it was worth revealing one's own feelings to find out. *And* the ER's were free on the National Health Scheme. That simple economic fact tipped the scale —despite the equally simple fact that the next Budget would have to find the needed millions.

While the bill was before the Commons, the *News Chronicle* Gallup Poll asked the country two questions and got their revealing answers:

'Will you feel conspicuous in your ER (Norman Light, sex detector, etc.) when everyone else is also wearing theirs?"

Yes	No	Don't know.
31%	24%	45%

"Shall you be interested in seeing other people's reactions to you and to each other?"

Yes	No	Don't know.
93%	2%	5%

Ask the nation any question—did you wake up this morning?—and at least five per cent will always not know; no doubt it is always the *same* five per cent. The fact remained: the country's traditional love of privacy was overturned by its traditional love of "having a go." The ER bill went through and became law. Four months later, the grey trailers were attracting queues throughout the country.

The trailer in Charlton Square looked to be doing a brisk business as Jimmy went past it that fine evening. It cost him an effort to realise he had been wearing his own Norman Light for only twenty-four hours, so busy had that time been. Yesterday he had met Rose for the first time: tonight he was, he hoped, going to meet her again—for he had phoned through to Iral and had finally been connected with a secretary who had grudgingly, and only in exchange for Jimmy's name and address, informed him that Miss English stayed at the Debroy Dalmar when in London. Jimmy was going to that lustrous hotel as soon as possible; he needed a shower and a snack and then he was going.

"When lovely woman stoops to folly, he who helped to egg her on should see she stoops again before the in-clin-a-ti-on is gone," he muttered, adding to himself, "Don't try to be hard and bright about her, laddie: I can tell you're soft as butter underneath."

He showered and walked about the flat in a gaudy silk dressing gown, assembling a rapid meal. He dressed and was out of the house before his brother arrived, and strolled, in the very best of moods, towards the Debroy Dalmar, wondering dreamily how comfortable the beds would be there. It took him a quarter of an hour and he enjoyed every step. His shoes, bought a month ago, had just learnt to fit his feet properly. The air was so warm and still that the boundary between his flesh and the external world for once became unapparent, making the whole evening an extension of his content.

The Debroy had its awning out, and pretended, in a dignified way, to gaze over the mediterranean. The foyer was pugnaciously unostentatious and overwhelmingly discreet; an Indian woman in a gold, silver and blue sari moved through it like a spirit, giving Jimmy one breath of chypre. He sought another, but the perfume had gone. Smiling rather vacantly to himself, he stood where he was, looking about him, enjoying the eight-guineas-a-day atmosphere, neither blasé enough to ignore it nor naïve enough to feel guilty about it—just, in fact, smiling vacantly. Then he jumped into action and went over to Reception, where a beautiful young man stood behind a curving palisade of beech and elm. "Here's why the Debroy needed a charge that so exceeded Claridge's: to keep this lamb Charles-of-the-Ritzed and Austin-Reeded." Jimmy intoned to himself.

In answer to Jimmy's enquiry, this lamb, his manner suggesting he had been born and bred in the Quay d'Orsai, regretted that Miss English had driven off about forty-six minutes ago and was not expected back until after the week-end. Jimmy admired the "about forty-six minutes" and hated all the rest. Limply, he wandered out again into the malicious evening. It was too hot and his feet were tired.

For an illusory moment, he seemed to see Rose clearly, sprouting mirage-like from the pavement. She wore her tight skirt and the bulky jacket which made her look top heavy; her long, rather rugged, face was smiling. Jimmy knew why he loved her. It was because she was *adult*. Other women with whom he had associated at all closely, perhaps through a principle of unconscious selection, had been timid creatures, mere girls, afraid to follow definite lines of action (such as sleeping with you). Rose lived as she wished: again he pictured the masterly detail of her life. She could decide and abide by her decisions. She stayed at places like the Debroy Delmar and drove off for week-ends God-knows-where—and with God-knows who. Her mystery and temptation deepened. Meanwhile, it was only Friday. Three dreary days had to pass before she was again accessible; Quai d'Orsai had regretted he had no other address for Miss English. Jimmy's loins positively ached with physical desire. For him, this sensation was new; and it was worse than hot feet.

In the nearest pub he could find, Jimmy sat moodily over a tepid lager. He wanted no distractions; he wanted merely to soak in melancholy; a queasy wriggling coupled with horrifying irregular breathing told him that the fat man alone at the next table was bursting to converse with him. Stubbornly, Jimmy refused to look, fixing his gaze instead on the bar-side TV, in which two comedians told a joke about ER's ". . . and so *he* said, 'Well, how should I have known?—I'm colour blind!'" Wild applause, whistling, stamping.

Jimmy thought that mysterious curve under Rose's cheek-bones was exactly echoed by a curve along the inside of her thighs, but he needed to check to make sure. Following the comedians were three acrobats performing, on one-wheel bicycles, the ballet "Swan Lake." The lager was nearly gone; should he go or have another?

Glancing gloomily up at the TV screen, he saw that the cameras were sweeping over Trafalgar Square, where people clustered like pigeons round the Landseer lions. The Bourgoyne Group had started its meeting; everything was as orderly as a congregation of Lord's Day Observance Society officials. Under banners bearing the words "Suppress Science!" "Hands off sex!" and "Beware Second Norman Conquest!" a meagre man addressed the crowd in an academic tone. He spoke from notes, without gestures.

". . . . since the Industrial Revolution. England's green and pleasant land has been eradicated, my friends—by science. Yes, by science. Look around you and see what it has done! But it is only getting into its stride. The new despotism has only just begun. Oh yes! This new invention, this so-called Emotional Register, strikes a deadly blow where we shall feel it most: in our thoughts. Yes, your thoughts and feelings are no longer sacred. They are to be harnessed to the machine. It is no longer legal to keep your reactions to yourself. We shall become a nation of robots unless you give us your support and your pennies now."

An influx of customers to the bar obscured Jimmy's view of the screen. He got up and leaned against the bar to see better.

"And that was Percy Warren, Chairman of the Suppression of Science Society, which has just publicly associated itself with the Bourgoyne Group," announced the hushed voice of the announcer. He was talking through an open mike; faint in the background were the strains of a brass band playing "Oh, Peaceful England!" "And as I stand here, I can see the Friday evening crowds coming slowly down Whitehall, and the tops of the historic buildings about me are still gilded, still beautifully gilded, with the rays of the setting sun. And even the starlings seem to be hushed. And now everyone is waiting for the next speaker, William Bourgoyne himself. I can see his car, his Armstrong Siddeley Sapphire, waiting for him near the National Gallery. And now he is going to speak."

Bourgoyne in action looked very like the Labour leader, John Burns, who had once spoken from between these same indifferent lions. He had what is termed a good presence which, coupled with an ample beard and a resonant speaking voice, generally compelled respect from his audiences.

"You've heard of Herbert Gascadder," he began, without preliminaries. "He is our Prime Minister; he and his Cabinet have brought disgrace upon us. They've brought us disgrace *internationally*. Can you imagine our allies the French having any nonsense with these Norman Lights? Of course you can't! They've always managed without them—so have we. And we can go on managing without them. We have been disgraced *nationally*. When these badges of the devil are installed, what son is going to care to face his mother, what sister is going to face her brother?" (Someone in the crowd shouted, "We don't all feel that way about our sisters!") I warn you, family life will be shattered at one blow. But most of all, we have been disgraced *personally*. Whether or not these registers function as they are supposed to do is immaterial; the fact remains, it is an insult to expect a man or a woman to have a tin badge welded to his or her forehead. It's shameful! It is a descent into savagery. Soon we shall be issued with rings to go through our noses!"

He was working himself up now, but Jimmy in the bar felt only an increasing restlessness, perhaps because the TV cameras were also growing restless, and fidgeting about the crowds, or even taking a peep at Nelson up on his column, when they should have been concentrating on that hypnotic beard. Or perhaps, Jimmy reflected, he suffered from that typical failing of the British mentality: he could not grasp that when a problem graduated into the realm of politics it did not thereby lose its reality.

This Bourgoyne business, as far as he was concerned,

59

although more absorbing than, say, the Test Match, was about as relevant to everyday life. Wearing an NL was a personal decision—and in his case he had had no doubts—against which all that Europe or a continent of mothers thought was immaterial; perhaps he would have felt differently had his parents been alive.

"But we can resist!" Bourgoyne was shouting. "If you will give me your support, we can resist. Britons never, never shall be slaves of the Lamp. We must take a leaf out of Ghandi's book. Passive resistance means effective resistance. If *none* of us submit to these metal brands, the whole country cannot go to jail, can it? Men, be Men! Women, be Women! Resist this disgrace! Keep Gascadder out of your private life!"

"Of course, he's right, you know," a woman sitting over a gin said to the company round the bar. "It is a bit of a cheek, when you come to think of it, *making* us wear the things."

"At least it'll stop men marrying us for our money, Nancy, love," the barmaid said, winking all round.

"Is that so much worse than marrying for sex?" an angular man in a pin-stripe inquired severely. There was a tiny silence; the word was tolerable in print, the meaning welcome in innuendo, but spoken, when everyone was drinking together all nice and friendly-like in a nice respectable pub . . . Well, of course, they'd have to get used to it. It was a sign of the times.

"Look at old Freddie over there," the barmaid said, pouring a bitter. "You wait till he gets his fitted. This place'll be bathed in pink all the time, like the Folly Bare-Jair."

In the laughter that followed, the fat man was heard to say, "Still, they say you don't feel a thing."

"Don't you believe it," the pin-stripe who had made the unpopular remark said. "My daughter Else, who's a trained nurse, says there are two little wires behind that plate which go right through into your brain." This remark also produced a silence.

"Ah, you're all wet," someone said.

"I don't know what they want to come interfering with me and my old missus for," the fat man said miserably into his Crippenson's, "We were perfectly content as we was."

V. Breakfast with Paper and White Nylon

The fact that most surprises most people in most revolutions is their unrevolutionary quality. Life goes on, whether the barricades go down or stay up. This is particularly so when the issue is ill-defined and the national drama is largely enacted in individual bosoms. Blood is a great heightener of tension, and there was no blood.

Or very little. The Day after Bourgoyne's speech was the first Saturday on which the grey trailers, known officially as ER Installation Centres, were operating. More people are more restless on Saturdays than on any other day of the week. In Glasgow, a party of demonstrating undergraduates emerged from Sauchiehall Street and overturned a grey trailer standing in Kelvingrove Park. In Pontypool, a postman assaulted a housewife whose Norman Light, he claimed, had glowed at him; later, it was established that her light had merely been reflecting the colour of his mail van. In Frinton, and one felt it was somehow typical, a seaside guest tried to remove the ER he had had installed that morning, and was taken to a hospital. In Bickington, North Devon, an old lady of seventy-five put her head in the gas oven rather than submit to such newfangled devices; as she was safely over the statutory installation age limit of sixty, the gesture was largely fruitless. On Orkney, a determined brigade of islanders led by Eric Linklater repulsed the seaborne medical unit which tried to dock with a cargo of ER's. On the West Cliff at Bournemouth, a young lady was charged with causing an obstruction; for a modest half-crown a head, a queue of enthusiastic young men were attempting, by kissing her, to make her Norman Light glow and thus win ten cigarettes.

But these incidents were as nothing beside the march of world events. Despair on Wall Street, despots in Jordan, despond over the City. Earthquakes in Greece, revolt in Roumania, sackings in the Egyptian Army. Two-man space ship being planned at Woomera, report of sea monster off Belgian coast, yeti tracks sighted by First International Himalayan Expedition. Terrible fire in Georgetown, British Guiana, sensational mass murders in Milan, dope ring exposures in Marseilles. And, of course, film star marrying, Royalty on tour, darling baby panda at the zoo, three drowned at seaside resort. Oh, and the Test Match.

Between these large scale worries and the usual personal preoccupations with money, food, love, sport, prestige, tax evasion, work, and class, the problem of the ER never really received due attention, although its cruder aspects were on everyone's lips. People tended either to go and get theirs fixed on and be done with it, or to wait until their friends got theirs. Abstract thought as a national trait is something even the ubiquitous TV quiz shows have been unable to foster.

In this respect, as in so many others, Jimmy Solent was the average citizen. He went about that Saturday with hardly a constructive thought in his head. Cupid, that grim reaper, had got him.

In the evening, his brother Aubrey took him in a fit of exasperation to see the new Thyroid Annerson play, "No Anchorage But Ithaca," at the Stumer Theatre. Then for a little while the spectre of the Rose was banished from Jimmy's mind. Before a black backcloth, under execrable lighting, the mackintoshed figures of Odysseus and his crew confronted the bespectacled figure of Circe. She came forward and offered him a bunch of flowers.

ODYSSEUS. What are these?

CIRCE.   Flowers: the purple violet that grows in the timid shades of the island.

ODYSSEUS. What are they for?

CIRCE.   What are flowers for? If I ransacked the learned places of the world I could not find a sillier question. Do you not possibly think these flowers ... lovely?

ODYSSEUS. Why, they are poor little things, a mere mouthful of grass. I asked you what you brought them for.

CIRCE.   The stupidity of my hope! I hoped you might like them. I hoped they might appeal to you. Their simple beauty, I thought, might

62

ODYSSEUS. touch one chord of concord, one string of humanity in you.

ODYSSEUS. Humanity and flowers are stranger bedfellows than sun and chastity. Keep these frail posies for gardeners and snickering country lovers. Odysseus needs them not.

CIRCE. I have known many great men capable of responding to the violet side of life.

ODYSSEUS. (*lighting a cigarette*) Maybe. But they were not Odysseus.

CIRCE. Of course not; neither are you Odysseus. Odysseus is a figment of your imagination. He is a dummy with a shirt stuffed full of impossible courage and a skull of wooden intention. He is the figurehead stuck immoveably before the ship of your life's course, and you cannot help but follow him.

At this point, Jimmy dozed off.

"I thought it had a rather *Caravaggio* touch about it," Aubrey pronounced cautiously, as they left at the end of the play. He took his playgoing as seriously as another man takes snuff.

Jimmy, who had loathed every word he heard and who recognised his brother's gambit anyway, solemnly said, "I thought that for *Greeks* they were far too Grecian."

"Yes, it certainly wasn't universalised enough," Aubrey agreed soberly. "I quite felt that myself. There is a provincialism of time as well as of space."

Alyson, who was with them, hooted with laughter and said, "Jimmy's being a Philistine and pulling your leg, Aubrey."

"Then he has no right to," Aubrey said without rancour. "He was asleep throughout the crucial second act. You Unloveable Young People are frightful cowards when it comes to a bit of culture."

At thirty-one, Aubrey Solent had been a solid citizen for too long. His work at BIL had sobered his mind, rendered him liable to haemorrhoids and caused him to wear gloves whenever possible. He still retained, however, many of the

63

loveable Solent traits, as he demonstrated after the play by taking Alyson and Jimmy to his club, the Quadrant.

"This hive of iniquity!" Jimmy exclaimed, pretending to hang back at the door. "That ill-lit bar packed with well-lit customers! Not for me!"

They went in, Jimmy conscious of an unhappiness rising in him which he did not want drink to liberate. He glared down at his Tio Pepe when it appeared, as if defying it to produce any chemical effect on him.

"Cheer up, Jim," Alyson urged. "It's so much brighter in here than you feared."

"Bright! These fluorescents are simply lurid. I'm never at my best when I'm turned beige."

"You do look rather like a fugitive from Eastman colour," she said sympathetically. "Drink up, here come some friends of Aubrey's."

To his relief, Jimmy found that the friends were no one he knew. Then and throughout dinner, and during another drink afterwards, he was able to keep slightly detached from the party. When he realised his ER was glowing mildly at Alyson, he detached himself altogether, sitting in a lavatory until the light had faded.

He returned home with the other two in a subdued fashion. Two days had to pass before he could see Rose. Long as it sounded to him, he had a suspicion that for Rose it might be merely . . . well, a couple of days.

So the day of revolution passed for Jimmy, its grand, imperative issues almost completely blurred. Sunday, however, brought them more sharply into focus. For Sunday brought the Sunday papers.

Aubrey went as usual to Communion, leaving Alyson and Jimmy to breakfast together, Alyson with a stiff and decorous white nylon gown over her nightdress. When, at the beginning of the year, Jimmy had first come to share his brother's flat, some embarrassment had been generated over the Alyson-Aubrey sleeping arrangements—at one careless remark of Jimmy's, indeed, the atmosphere had frozen to the size of a postage stamp; but he had soon accustomed himself to the idea that Alyson came for the night just whenever she pleased, although she generally pleased at weekends. It was not, perhaps, a very unusual arrangement: what made it unusual was the characters of those who entered into it.

"This is really rather fun," Jimmy said, smoothing out

the *Observer* beside his plate and carefully not eyeing the white nylon gown. "They've got a heap of what are tenderly called Eminent Contemporaries to say whether they are for or against Norman Lights."

"You saw Munnings' letter in the *Telegraph* yesterday?"

"Well, what do you expect! Listen to this, Alyson. Here are the big boys deciding on which side of the fence they are going to jump. Bertrand Russell: 'Consciousness is a faulty instrument which should be implemented by all possible means.' Jack Solomons: 'It's a heavy blow to British boxing.' Sir Miles Thomas is for the ER, with reservations. Koestler's against it. Lord Salisbury's against it. Priestley calls it a barbaric blow against our privacy. Dowding's for. Good old Dowding! Patience Strong is against. The Dean of St. Paul's says, 'The Act making the fitting of these things compulsory may well be condemned; but inasmuch as the devices themselves will be perpetual reminders to us of our consciences, they must be commended by all true Christians to all true Christians.'"

"There's a long article in the *Times* by Aldous Huxley," Alyson said, "Aubrey will like that—you know how much he has always admired Huxley."

Jimmy did indeed. Aubrey had caused a sensation in his last days at Oxford by taking an overdose of mescalin before going to see the film "Moulin Rouge," and passing out cold on the steps of the Ritz. As a consequence, he had seen neither Toulouse nor Dharma-body.

"Huxley has come over from California especially to observe how things work out," Alyson continued, scanning the paper while Jimmy watched her white nylon neckline admiringly. Huxley, with his usual admirable elasticity of mind, welcomed the new regime as the first valuable socioscientific innovation since the introduction of Arabic numerals from India. Emotional Registers should merely be regarded as another step forward in the domestication of sex which the declining influence of the Judaeo-Christian ethic had made possible. Thousands of ergs of nervous energy were expended every day in individual attempts to decide who represented whose next potential sexual encounter: in a community fully equipped with ER's, that problem resolved itself on sight, with a consequent release of psychepower which would be available for more constructive ends.

The two of them, Jimmy and Alyson, sat happily over

hot rolls and Cooper's Oxford Marmalade reading out bits of the papers to each other.

"Damon Goldgate, Texas oilman now in England, asks 'Could Utopia be just around the corner for the U.K.? I don't know, but I'm figgering to stay around here just so long as my firm'll let me. This is Big.' Many Americans with similar feelings now visiting Europe are cancelling Continental trips to stay in England and see 'what breaks.' Against the one disgruntled Californian who exclaimed, 'Why does a country have to go nuts just when I get to it? I came over here to get away from people talking on the one subject all the time,' may be set many Americans who regard the ER experiments as noble if dangerous. 'This is Britain's finest hour,' one of them told me at Gatwick Airport yesterday."

The *Observer* had a slightly less optimistic tale to tell of American reactions, from the President's firm view, "No statement," down to a Hollywood starlet's "Anything those Limeys can manage with their Lights, I can manage with *me*," The Major of Rapid Rapids, Iowa, said, "This could never happen in Rapid Rapids, Iowa." The College of Puget Sound was sending a sociologist, a pupil of Dr. Kinsey's, to England to make an independent report. Sophomores of a New York university voted Britain the silliest country they had ever heard of. The *Herald Tribune* predicted a dire collapse in the body social before the deadline date of September 1.

"European reactions are likewise mixed," Alyson said, "if not so outspoken. The usual boring phalanx of Soviet condemnation apart, nobody seems to know what to think of us."

"Did they ever?" Jimmy asked.

"Well, I suppose that just as it used to be a national boast that we were overmodest, we have been pretending for years that we did not have much love life, and now . . ." Alyson faltered and then said hurriedly, "Anyhow, the Scandinavians seem to think we've been progressive. And Canada and Australia approve."

It was exceedingly pleasant to be sitting in this cosy fashion, talking to an elegant creature in her elegant night clothes. Jimmy would have preferred Rose there, but Alyson made a charming substitute. He pushed his cup forward for more coffee; as she reached out for it, he seized her hand.

"You're going to look so sweet in your nunchaser, Alyson," he said. "Hurry up and get it fixed! I feel at such a disadvantage here with you and Aubrey without them."

She pulled her hand away.

"I've changed my mind about them," she said. "They're going to bring trouble. I don't want one. The whole idea frightens me, really. I'd . . . I'd rather be locked up and fined than wear one."

A pink emanation coloured the table and its utensils; Jimmy's genes were registering. Jimmy shook his head helplessly, then went round to Alyson, putting his hands on her shoulders. The view south was wonderful from here.

"I feel such a fool, Alyson," he said, "and that's something I never did with you. You must know what's going on just as well as I do. With this damned gadget turning pink over you I can't conceal how I feel any longer. I want to ask you . . ."

She got up, slopping coffee as she did so, but he still managed to keep his hands round her upper arms.

"Alyson, give me . . ."

"Take your hands off me, Jimmy," she said quietly. "You're getting too big to play these games. It's not very nice to your brother, is it? And it's taking advantage of me. You can be so maddening, Jimmy. I suppose you really think that because I'm his . . ." She stopped.

"I don't think any such thing," Jimmy said, warmly. "But now you can *see* how I feel.'

"I don't want to see!" Alyson said. "For heaven's sake go into your bedroom until the effect wears off. I wish nobody had ever invented those awful things. It's like tying a tin can to a dog's tail—he's suddenly conscious he's got a tail. And now every man is suddenly conscious—oh, for heaven's sake, Jimmy dear, clear off and cool off. You're just making life difficult for all three of us, if you only knew it; really you are. Go away and cool off."

He dropped his hands. He had never seen her angry and could tell she was not so now. Even as she told him to go away, she gave him a half-smile.

"This isn't just a flash in the pan," he said. "Can't you see that for yourself? Ever since I first came to live in the flat . . ."

"You were engaged to Penny then," she reminded him.

"That doesn't make any difference to what I was going to say."

"It does, and you know it does," Alyson said firmly. "*And* you know that wretched ER has made a difference to you. You haven't had it three days and you're quite changed!"

"How am I changed?"

"Don't think I haven't noticed—and I don't mean just because of my wet swimsuit. It's been so obvious I wonder Aubrey hasn't said something. What happened to you on Thursday night? I heard you come in at some unearthly hour. And you've been very strange ever since, dragging about with a dreamy look on your face. You hardly spoke at the Quadrant last evening. I'm worried about you, Jimmy; it's a woman, isn't it? And don't attempt to tell me it's none of my business—because you've just tried to make it my business."

He stood there stupidly, eyes downcast, thinking of fifty answers he could make.

"I wasn't going to say it was none of your business," he replied. "But I must say that I find this big sisterly attitude rather a bind—especially when you're in your dressing gown."

Alyson went over to the divider unit and lit herself a cigarette. Exhaling the smoke, she looked forcefully at him. Though her hair was the colour of ripe wheat, her eyes and eyebrows were dark; they commanded even when she pleaded.

"Come over here, Jimmy," she said.

He went to her.

She sighed. "You're too obedient, as I've told you before," she said, not moving away from him. "You're so suggestible. Oh God, Jimmy, how you and your brother do need looking after—especially now . . . I worry about you . . . All the experts and smart alecs in the country have been discussing these ER's for months, and I think they've all missed the obvious: with *the* problem on everyone's minds, we're going to be in for a wave of libertinage. Everybody's thinking about sex in a way they've never done before. Just get a hold of yourself and don't join in, hey? It's a line of country which doesn't really suit you."

Jimmy found as he fumbled himself a cigarette that his hands were shaking. He was furious with Alyson and baffled with himself. It suddenly seemed very important not to offend this girl in white nylon. She was, after all, his sort—more so than Rose, though that was something not to be considered.

"I'm sorry . . . ," he finally said.

"So am I," Alyson replied, and whisked into the bathroom.

For the rest of the day Jimmy was pensive. He passed most of the morning in his room, doing what is generally called "meditating on Life," by which we mean thinking about our own characters. As usual, the conclusions to be drawn were gloomy. Being, from an anthropologist's point of view, a typical member of a species of vertebrae in the placental sub-class of Mammalia, and of the order Primates within that sub-class, Jimmy knew little about his own physiology, or of the thryoid, parathyroid, thymus, pituitary and adrenal glands upon which his emotional balance depended. He knew even less of the grey and beautiful world of sub-atomic particles which, as Heisenberg's Uncertainty Relation first implied, served him with thought and direction, apparently for its own inscrutable purposes. Worse still, Jimmy was content to know nothing of these things. Such control as he possessed over himself was limited; like a popular daily newspaper, he was largely at the mercy of his circulation.

He had only a dim and partial vision of a fellow—himself—involved, to greater or less degree, with three girls. "Thou shalt have one God only; who would be at the expense of two? Thou shalt have one girl only; three a waste of cash and love would be." This modern decalogue, he told himself, was as binding as a moral law. If Alyson condemned him, he condemned himself—though at the back of his mind he was well aware that he desired Rose on rather different grounds from those on which he desired Alyson.

Poor little Penny Tanner-Smith came in a bad third. There at least he could at once ease his conscience and simplify his existence. Ever since he had broken off their engagement, Penny would have nothing of Jimmy's earnest attempts to reinstate himself. Very well. She was sweet and melancholy—he turned his mind away from that; if she wanted to go, go she should. He had loved her, yes; but she was of the old world, the old era. Our sexual antennae, after all, vibrate most rapidly in the presence of novelty. He would write to her and sever their relationship for good.

Jimmy's fourth shot at a letter to Penny seemed to him to contain the right admixture of firmness with gentleness, regret with relief. He had posted it before he remembered that it had been for Penny's sake he had gone so quickly to get his ER installed: so much had changed since then! For a moment he felt a flood of misgiving, a flood chock-a-block with the jetsam of antique religious, moral, super-stitious and sentimental notions; since he could not distinguish one from another, he put them all away from him as being relics from a buried past—but not before a line from an old play rose to mock him:

> Thou has committed—
> Fornication—but that was in another country;
> And besides, the wench is dead.

VI. An Interesting Theory

Such hair as Conrad Scryban possessed began high on his head. This gave him a good sweep of brow. His nose was sensitive and waxy, his mouth firm. His eyes were brown. His face looked well tended. He had the bland air of an actor who has played butlers not wisely but too often.

"You see, he makes a proper little picture of a Man-aging Director." Jimmy had complained to Donald once. "It's just too good to be true. Those eyes are too gentle and sincere to be anything but the eyes of a charlatan."

"Why should you worry?" Donald had said. "You should expect directors of crazy joints like the IBA to look like that."

Perhaps the librarian was right, Jimmy thought, as he stood gazing at Conrad Scryban now. This Monday morn-ing, the director wore green tweed and brogues; a shotgun would not have looked out of place under his arm; instead, he had a portfolio. Mrs. Wolf, whisking along beside him, gregarious as a city bred vulture, carried another portfolio. Jimmy carried his Haiti file. Donald Hortense made up the party of four; he had his hands in his pockets, carrying nothing.

As they headed for the Main Exhibition room, down a corridor which even the chic black and grey wallpaper could do nothing to lighten, Scryban was talking to them about a little book of Maginn's published early the previous century, "The Maxims of Sir Morgan O'Doherty."

"If you have a taste for epigram, you will relish O'Doherty, who used that rarefied form for some very worldly wisdom," Scryban was saying. "Much as we may raise eyebrows now at 'Cold pig's face is the best thing in the world for breakfast,' we can only admire the boldness of 'No cigar smoker ever committed suicide.'"

"There's something in that," Donald agreed. "Tobacco is the poor man's tobacco."

"Cease these Scribist jokes," Jimmy said.

"But my two favourite O'Doherty maxims," continued Scryban blandly, ignoring the unintelligible interruptions of the young, "are both highly moral. 'In literature and in love, we generally begin in bad taste,' is one. Excellent, I'm sure, you'll agree."

"Excellent," Veronica Wolf confirmed, with a little bitter smile to herself.

"And the other," Scryban said, as they entered the exhibition room, "is this, which looks absolutely splendid on paper: 'when a man is drunk, it is no matter upon what he has got drunk.'"

"That has quite a Johnsonian ring," said Mrs. Wolf.

"A Wagnerian Ring," supplemented Donald.

How curious, Jimmy thought, was this habit of Scryban's in indulging in literary conversation, as far as the fools about him would allow it. Perhaps he enjoyed talking about literature; perhaps he hoped to pass on something to his subordinates. Whatever the reason, for a literary man in England to talk about literature was unusual enough to be remarked on. Meanwhile, there was also that shattering remark about being drunk; Jimmy would have to remember that. It fitted.

"And now perhaps, Mrs. Wolf, you would kindly describe to us, mainly, possibly, for Jimmy's benefit, the sort of background effect we strive to create behind all our little displays here." Scryban said, edging round a massive commode which formed one of the items in the current "The English House as a Literary Theme" exhibition.

"With pleasure," said Mrs. Wolf, smiling at them as if she wanted to bite them. Fixing his eyes on those little teeth, Jimmy told himself he must listen carefully and forget that Rose would now be somewhere in London, perhaps within a mile of the IBA.

"Our basic premise is simple enough," said Mrs. Wolf. "Civilisation has now reached a plateau when literature may be taken for granted, much as we take constant hot water for granted. As a passing example, I may mention that the current U.N. slogan, 'The Opposite of peace is not war but death,' was coined by an Englishman educated under the Education Act of '44. Like immersion heaters, books can now be safely left to do their work unseen.

"This platitude might have seemed revolutionary even a couple of years ago, when the world was unsettled and the Cold War had not blown cold enough to be, as now, completely frozen over and safe enough to skate on—oh yes, the Russians can afford a war in the Middle East even less than we. The book in the last decade, in the fifties, degenerated into a mere article, a poor man's TV."

She smiled at Jimmy searchingly; he wondered if he should be taking notes: "Civiln. on platto. Hot water. Skate on. Poor m's TV."

"Now the book has graduated," Mrs. Wolf continued. "From being nothing more than a rather boring object, it has become an ideal—an aspiration, to use our founder's own word. 'Our concern,' as he told an intruding bookseller once, 'is not with sales but with souls.' The book's deplorable nadir as Cinderella of the entertainment world has been renounced; from now on, it is a cult, something to be worshipped and even talked about, but preferably not read—as I say, a symbol, not a cathode-substitute.

"The book has disappeared, dissolved. In its place is an *atmosphere*, vibrant, alive, creative, receptive. Anything can come out of it, and it is up to us at the IBA to see that it does."

She finished on a grand, declamatory note which had scarcely died before Donald said, *sotto voce*, "In other words, the long night of enlightenment has dawned."

"Our librarian is cynical this morning," Conrad Scryban said pleasantly. "I think we may presume that he has had a poem accepted." Turning to Jimmy, he said, "Well, that should give you a general line of campaign to follow for your Haiti exhibition, I think. If you want any help at all, don't hesitate to ask Mrs. Wolf or me."

"Thank you," Jimmy said. "But I'm afraid I don't quite see how you can tie down those principles to what, after all, is going to be an exhibition of books. I mean, you've got to have *books*."

"Not exactly," Scryban said, frowning slightly and glancing at his heavy wrist watch. "After all, you have this portrait from Clunes to start with. Try and work along that sort of pictorial line. Some gay.Haitian military uniforms, for instance—the V. and A. should have some if you give them a ring—would look attractive in the front bay. It should not be beyond you to hunt up some of the weapons of the period. But you must take care not to overload your display with books; you'll find it only antagonises the public. We must always remember the public."

"I see," Jimmy said boldly. "I have to soft-pedal the one thing we're here to promote, in the same way that everyone indulges in some form of sexual activity but is shocked when the subject is spoken about?"

Conrad Scryban put his hands into the pockets of his tweed jacket, cocked his head on one side to watch a faint red mount in Jimmy's cheeks, and said, "You draw rather an unfair parallel, but I suppose the answer is yes, in a general way. Nobody has any avidity for the sexual confidences of others. You must remember our job is not, thank heaven, to sell books but the Idea of the Book. And now I'm sure I'm keeping you all from your coffee. Please excuse me."

They watched him walk away. Donald linked arms with Mrs. Wolf and said, "Come on, kids, work's over for today. Let's take the hint and go and get some coffee."

"You carry on," Jimmy said. "I'll be with you. I've just got to make a phone call."

Hurrying into his little room, he winked at the Ben Nicholson, picked up his phone, and dialled the Debroy Dalmar. When a plastic, crease-resistant voice replied, Jimmy asked to be put through to Rose's room.

He heard a buzz, and then a man's voice spoke. It said, regretfully, that Miss English was not in.

"Can you tell me where I can get hold of her, or where she works?" Jimmy asked, instinctively disliking any stranger who could loll about in Rose's room when she was away.

"Perhaps I could convey a message. Would you give me your name and address?"

"As I haven't got a message for her," Jimmy said, "that will hardly be necessary. I want to see her."

"Then I suggest you give me your name and phone number, and she can ring you and make an appointment."

"Don't be bloody obscurantist, old boy. Just tell me where she works. I'll do all the rest."

"That isn't possible at present," the voice at the other end said, quite unperturbed. "But if you'll give me your phone number I'll see what I can do in the matter."

Jimmy weakened and gave the stranger his name and phone number. He was too irritated to go back and join the others for coffee. Instead, he sat drumming his fingers on the desk and gazing at the IBA pamphlets on people like Svevo. No doubt about it, Rose was rather a challenge. When the phone rang, it made him jump.

"Solent," he said, grabbing the receiver.

"Jimmy?"

"Hello, yes. Jimmy Solent here. IBA. Who's calling please?" The voice was familiar, but. . . .

"I understood you were calling me."

"My God! Rangey—is that you, Rangey?"

It was Rangey. There the simple miracle was: that wonderful woman was connected to him. By phone. The lounger in her hotel room had wasted little time in ringing through to her. Jimmy was flung into a pother.

"Oh look, Rangey, listen . . . hello, I mean, pet! I . . . you . . . I didn't expect you to call so soon." In his excitement, Jimmy babbled. "Look, listen, sweet, it's been an absolute age since Thursday. I've thought about you so much, all the time. Come out with me this evening. Come out to dinner or something; anything."

"It's sweet of you, Jimmy, but I'm terribly busy," the cheerful, self-contained voice said. "I can't make this evening; it's such short notice, isn't it?"

"I came round on Friday, but you'd gone."

"Round where? Here?"

"To the Debroy."

"Oh. I see." And then a silence. in which Jimmy's heart sank a little. She sounded so devastatingly noncommittal.

"I suppose I'd still be alive tomorrow night, said he with a note of forced gaiety," said Jimmy with a note of forced gaiety.

"Jimmy dear, I'm sorry, but I shan't be free this week,

not on any evening. It's not an excuse; I am simply terribly busy." He could not conceal from himself that no trace of regret was detectable in that level voice.

"I've got to see you, Rangey." He dropped all pretence now that this was not a matter of life and death. It ceased to matter whether the IBA switchboard operator was eavesdropping on the line. "I've got to see you, Rangey, really. My . . . my loins just ache for you. Desire, you know . . . physical desire. It's terrible; I've just never felt this way before. Do you understand? Have *lunch* with me. Anything. You've got to eat sometime. I've got to see you soon. Have lunch with me. Today. How about today?"

After a moment she said, "I can't get away for lunch, but I suppose you could come here. Could you?"

"Today? Of course. Where are you?"

Rose gave him the name "Ghearing and Flower, Ltd." and an address in Deptford; then she rang off. Jimmy sat limply, full of dread and hope. He was to meet her at twelve-thirty: it was still before eleven. "I've got to fight for this," he told himself. "This is something I want very badly. I've got a real, properly adult woman on my hands this time; if I make a fool of myself, she's going to throw me out. Oh, Rangey, my sweet, if you only *knew* . . . ! "

With satisfaction, he realised his Norman Light had turned a determined cerise at the very thought of her.

Until twelve o'clock, Jimmy made a pretence of studying Mackenzie's "Notes on Haiti," which Donald had procured for him. Then, in a burst of agitation, he rang through to Donald.

"I've just remembered," he said, "that I should have prepared the Holmes room for the two o'clock talk by Golding. It's gone clean out of my head, for some reason. You aren't doing anything, are you, Donald? Be an angel and push the chairs round and fill the carafe for Golding, will you? I'm nipping out now and may not be back in time."

"Just try and remain Lord of your Flies, that's all I've got to say," said Donald darkly.

A moment later, Jimmy was in the street and heading for Holborn. There, the tube swallowed him with the crowd as effortlessly as a whale sucking down plankton. Only when he was in the train did he begin vaguely to wonder who Ghearing and Flower were and what Rose might be doing in Deptford. It was terrible to be faced with these major issues in this heat.

Deptford was hot. Nobody knew Settle Place, where Messrs. Ghearing and Flower lived and moved and had their glorious being. At last, after walking hopefully for some distance, Jimmy found a man who said, "Yes, of course, Settle Place—I happen to live there, shuck my luck. Straight down here about 200 yards till you get to the Stag, turn left, then second right and it's on your right, past the Kia-Ora depot. You can't miss it. Ghearing's is a big white building."

It was already 12:25. Jimmy found himself running. The bare idea of being at Deptford at all was unlikely; the whole situation seemed to him like a dream. He dared not even stop at the Stag for a bracer.

For a wonder, the instructions he had been given were correct, and at 12:28 he debouched at a canter into Settle Place. Settle Place was black; Ghearing and Flower's was a white palace. Its entrance hall, from which several passages sprouted, was modern in an early fiftyish way, and needed cleaning. A stack of battleship-grey crates stood untidily by the enquiries counter. Jimmy gave his name to a receptionist and waited anxiously, rubbing his steaming face on his handkerchief and straightening his tie, certain that he looked unfit to be Rose's lover. His shirt was sticking to his chest; he prised it gingerly off and blew into it from above the second button.

"What do you *do* here?" he asked the receptionist, more abruptly than he had intended, when he saw her eye on him.

"Sit and read when nobody's about. Why?" the receptionist said. She was a prim, pale weed of a woman; Jimmy guessed that she was a widow far sunk into Methodism.

"No, I meant what does this firm do?" he persisted.

"Oh . . . Pills. Synthetics. You know . . . chemicals and stuff." She turned away as if the effort of hospitality sickened her.

A messenger appeared and led Jimmy along several corridors into a courtyard. It was an immense place, almost endearingly unattractive. He was ushered through a door marked "No Admittance" and left there. Jimmy found himself in an enclosure much like a big greenhouse, encased in glass and with flags underfoot. Instead of

76

flowers, small pens were ranged on either side of the walk; in some of these pens were animals: rabbits, monkeys, cats, hamsters, pigs, guinea-pigs, a pair of foxes. A smell of disinfectant filled the green air. At the far end of the enclosure, there was Rose, talking to a man in a white smock. He left her almost as soon as Jimmy appeared.

Clutching a board to which a sheaf of paper was clipped, Rose walked down the flagstones towards him. He felt himself dissolving into his component molecules. She wore an ice-blue linen tailored dress, absolutely plain except for two bold pockets in the skirt. It was perfection on her, lifting her at once above the planes of good and evil to that sphere where works of art belong.

She was smiling as she approached, the long face slewing its jaw to one side in an odd gesture all its own. Jimmy knew that gesture as though she had been doing it to him for centuries. Her eyes were that turbulent mixture of green and brown: like the atmosphere of Jupiter, Jimmy thought, opaque and deadly. She had a confident way of walking; the way you walk if your standards are the Debroy Dalmar standards. As she reached Jimmy, she popped the board and papers she was carrying into a holder above one of the pens; he caught the words "Salivation Rate" on the top paper. Swallowing his own saliva, he tried to pull himself together.

"I don't have to ask which you are, the Ghearing or the Flower," he said, his voice rattling like a loose tonsil in his throat. "I just don't know whether you're a—no, not a rose, that's too obvious—a spike of Russell lupin— or is that too phallic?—or a, yes, I think a cactus dahlia. They're my favourite flower."

"A hollyhock, cock," she said succinctly dismissing the subject. She just stood there looking at him; he had the uneasy feeling that she could smell he was sweating.

He touched a tiny patch of the crisp linen covering her hip, just prodding it in a timorous attempt to be familiar. "I had to come, Rangey, Rose. It's so good to see you again. I hope it's not an inconvenience." That was an error; he had not meant to let one word of diffidence escape him; it had damned well better not be an inconvenience. "I meant what I said on the phone. I'm just consumed by you. You're like itching powder in the blood."

She was watching him with interest. Her forehead possessed two definite creases; wrinkles ran joyously round her eyes. Yes, she must be at least thirty-five. She was not actually beautiful; you might even say she was not beautiful at all—except that in another sense it was a downright lie. For her face held understanding and frankness, character; it was a unique face.

"Perhaps it's just as well you've come," she said. "We'll go through to the canteen."

"I'm happy here, Rangey. Can't we stay here and talk?"

"I've got to eat."

As he followed her, Jimmy asked what the animals were for. Not that he cared one naked curse.

"We teach them to cheat and deceive like humans," she said, without any noticeable inflections in her voice.

The people who passed them in the corridor stared hard at Jimmy; one by one, they were momentarily bathed in his pink glow. Rose's Norman Light, he saw with sorrow, remained neutral. He had not even made it flicker. Yet still he hoped.

In the canteen, a forlorn place through which dance music whispered like a draught, Rose collected a spaghetti and egg and a chocolate mousse, loading them onto a tin tray. When she made for a table behind a beaverboard partition, Jimmy followed, bearing coffee; he had no stomach for food. The contrast between Rose and her surroundings was so great that he asked, "What do you *do* here, Rangey?"

"This is one of my uncle's firms," she said. "Uncle Felix whom I think you met. Don't you like it?"

"I've no idea," he said. Her question was so irrelevant; her answer had not been notably satisfactory either. He watched her as she tackled the spaghetti; she looked offensively healthy and composed. She was very clean. She had some freckles, a barely noticeable peppering.

"What did you want to tell me, Jimmy?" she asked, after a silence, when her plate was half empty.

"What I tried to tell you over the phone. That I'm just full of you, that my flesh is drugged by you. That I didn't expect or deserve what I got on Thursday night, but that it has . . . bowled me over, dazzled me, been quite beyond any previous experience. It isn't easy to say—it isn't even very dignified—but it happens to be the truth. It was all . . . a wonderful revelation."

He paused, to let her say something. She was still tucking into the spaghetti, looking down at her plate. She said, "Go on, Jimmy."

"I've made myself clear so far, haven't I?" he said tartly. She had just muffed her chance of saying how much Thursday had meant to her too.

"Yes, quite clear. You enjoyed yourself on Thursday. So did I, it was fun and it was beautiful. But it's over now. Thursday's not real any more. It was real at the time, but it's not now."

"You're wrong, Rose," he said in pain, forgetting to call her Rangey. "It wasn't real then maybe, just a glorious fantasy; but ever since, it has been real—more real than reality. I've got to . . . I want so badly to see more of you, to show you . . . oh, to show you how you suddenly opened up an entirely new world in me."

"You're like so many people, you want to live in the past," she said. She looked absolutely calm. "It doesn't work. . . ."

"The past! Four days ago!" he exploded.

"I'm sorry, Jimmy, but Thursday is as irrecoverable as 1066. Anyhow, I don't intend to get emotionally involved with you."

He choked on that. Up until that very moment, although he perceived that his reception left much to be desired (perhaps because Rose was ill-at-ease in these functional surroundings, had been the thought in his mind), Jimmy had looked on Thursday only as a golden prelude to a great drama of sensual and mystical awakening. Worse, he had, in his futile innocence, never realised that it could be regarded otherwise. His feelings—that ice-hot nimbus enveloping him—had been quite involuntary; to learn that Rose's were absolutely under control cut him clean through his soft centre.

Jimmy sat there staring at her as she chased a last worm round her plate. He fought off the frost working inwards from his extremities. As she put her knife and fork together on an empty plate, he said painfully, "You gave me so much. I'd hoped I gave you something in return. It's hard for me to say this, but you—you were so *eager* that night."

"You didn't give me a thing," she said. Of the whole conversation, they were almost her only words which remained with Jimmy afterwards. They would remain for

79

years, cruel and undeniable, as a fish thrown back into a lake must always carry the stab of the hook.

He could find nothing to say, and it was Rose who spoke next. She stopped spooning in mousse to look him in the eye and say it.

"If you are honest with yourself, you'll see that Thursday was complete in itself. It was fun and it was beautiful"—again that easy phrase—"but you spoil things by pursuing it. It was just an accident that happened. Why not be grateful and leave it at that?"

"But by itself, Thursday was sordid and stupid," Jimmy contradicted desperately. "Only by developing it can you give it beauty or meaning."

"In other words, you are persisting because you want to *justify* what we did, because you can't see it is its own justification," she said as levelly as a judge. "I'm afraid I've very little patience with that type of sentimentality."

No doubt could remain any longer in Jimmy's mind that they were two people completely, irreconcilably, at odds, that though Rose revealed no antagonism, Jimmy distinctly felt it. It flared up at once, as if it had always been there. He had made a mistake and had been snubbed for it, thoroughly. He hated most the thought that he had loved, and consequently had been prepared to lower all his defences and open himself before this woman—only to be sneered at. The contrast between her present self, ice-cold in the ice-blue, and the generous goddess he had glimpsed on Thursday, was beyond his immature powers of understanding.

Jimmy found himself talking in a low, guttural voice as if delivering a malediction. "I'll tell you why I came here and made such a fool of myself in front of you. I'd made a discovery. I thought perhaps I was the first person ever to make it—goodness knows why. You see, I discovered, when I was with you, that every woman is physically different, as well as mentally different; physically different, I mean, in their most intimate and exquisite details. Perhaps it was something I could have found in van der Veld or Marie Stopes, but instead it was something I found with you at first hand. It—I can't explain—it has altered all my ideas of love. I don't pretend I've had much experience of women, and you probably find me callow, and unsatisfactory, but you—your details,

Rose, they seemed so very beautiful in their own right, like a fruit, which was never a way I'd bargained to feel before. They are a lovely thing, this hidden fruit of yours, Rose, more finely made than other girls', just the way some peoples' features or brains are finer than others. Unique. As sweet as the inside of an orange. And what I thought was that to have something really fine like that, you'd have to be fine all through; I imagined—oh, it was silly—that I could read your character, your whole being, right through, by the senses. I imagined we'd got to know each other just by that lovemaking. Ever since Thursday, you see, I've never ceased to be intimate with you. Now you're showing me you're a stranger and I dreamed it all."

She fitted a cigarette into a holder and lit it from a cylindrical lighter Jimmy had seen her use at the Clunes' party.

"It is an interesting theory," she said.

She was being sarcastic, Jimmy thought, or perhaps she was utterly bored and trying to be polite; or perhaps—no, he could not guess. Her remark was as inscrutable and as dead for him as the Rosetta Stone. It was impossible to realise that this mature woman sitting in this dreadful canteen could possess any of the magical qualities with which he had endowed her. Even, that she was capable of feeling. She was less than a stranger: she was an enemy. Jimmy stared at her in hatred, and at that same instant still had to restrain himself from beseeching her to lie with him once more. He shook with loathing for all she or he had done or said, for every beastly mistaken thing that he had ever imagined had existed between them.

He stood up.

"I must go," he said.

Rose also stood, as a man might have done. When she looked into his eyes, Jimmy was again baffled; something of her expression, either in the translucent world of her pupils or in the set of her face, offered him courage. It was as if she silently said, "Life is hell, brother; that's a knowledge we both share," but Jimmy was too inexperienced to know that looks convey unmistakeably what language cannot.

"Did you come by car?" she asked.

Did you come by car . . . Ye Gods! The bitch was mad.

"Good-bye," he said.

PART TWO

BROWBEATEN BUT VICTORIOUS?

VII. As Natural as Navels

For Jimmy Solent, the succeeding weeks were empty of happiness; they rolled by him making as meaningless a noise as a runaway drum over cobbles. For the majority of the population of Britain, however, the time was a happy one or, if not happy, full of that exhilarating tension which makes an adequate substitute for happiness. Something was always happening or about to happen, for a new perspective had come along to alter their vision of their lives.

The weather, although uncertain at Old Trafford, stayed fine generally, and everyone got outdoors whenever possible, achieving their usual splendid massed effects along the beaches of the South Coast and in the parks of cities. This year, however, an additional zest filled the throngs, a zest born of novelty. The national hobby became NL-spotting: getting out to see who was "pinking" (as the new phrase had it) at whom. In the process, one was quite likely to pink oneself. The nine miles of illumination at Blackpool were at times eclipsed by the general rubefaction below them.

Many trades boomed. Hot dog and ice cream men alike did unprecedented business—particularly Ingolsby's, the ice cream firm which called an ordinary strawberry ice "Gene-cream" and sold it in wrappers bearing the exhortation "Cool down those overworked genes!" Outdoor candid cameramen were heavily overworked, and a representative of Kodak stated "This year colour photography has really arrived; black-and-white is as dead as sound radio." Everyone wanted a snap of "Him glowing at me," or "Me glowing at her." In the amusement arcades, Test Your Glow machines became as prevalent as Test Your Strength machines.

The only people who suffered a financial setback were the manufacturers of those hats and buttons which bear curious legends such as "I'm willing—Are you?" and

"Come and Get Me." Emotion Registers were capable of saying the same things more elegantly, more eloquently.

Yet even when the flood of complacency was at its height, an undertone of dissent was felt in both high and low places. Trouble brewed in the Welfare vat, but its symptoms as yet were illusive, affording everyone ample chance of ignoring them. An extra strike or two, an increased suicide rate, an attempted mutiny at Aldershot, a vast trade deficit—they had no integral meaning. The tide was coming in, but nobody bothered to move his deckchair.

England was full of overseas visitors, and England liked it. The visitors were not only tourists, but scientific and semi-scientific bodies or their representatives, investigating the brash new world of ER: sociologists, anthropologists, psychologists, documentary film-makers from countries as far apart as the Argentine and Japan, philosophers from India, two female sexologists from West Berlin.

One evening in the second week of August, Jimmy was sitting reading the new Raymond Chandler, when Aubrey came in. Aubrey nodded, half smiled, and walked into his bedroom without speaking. This behaviour was so unusual in his punctilious brother, that Jimmy instantly knew something had happened; having a bad conscience these days, he sat motionless by the window, feeling his stomach turn over and chanting to himself as a sort of protective measure, "Your sins will find you out! That's just the worst of sin: if they don't find you out, her husband finds you in!"

Within a few minutes, Aubrey reappeared, having changed his suit for a pair of cavalry twill trousers and a cream Tricel shirt. It was ten past seven.

"Let's have the looney's lantern on for the news," he said, making his term for TV sound like the frosty little condescension to joviality it was.

"You've a ministerial air about you," Jimmy said. "Is anything wrong?"

"I don't know, Jimmy. Nobody seems to think anything's wrong but me—and I'm the one who should think everything's right."

"Are you being a bit dramatic, Aubrey?" Jimmy asked; these bloody Organisation Men loved the chance of an emotional fling-about in their free hours. Aubrey indeed sounded and looked odd. His customary restraint had vanished; he stood in the middle of the Kosset carpet like Hamlet on the battlements at Elsinore.

"I think these Norman Lights are worth being dramatic about," he said, "but nobody else bar cranks and Bourgoynists seems to think so. They spell the end of freedom as we know it."

"Oh," Jimmy said, at once relieved and disappointed. His brother's attitude to ER's had been hardening of late, and they had already had several none too amicable discussions on the subject. Aubrey was one of the now dwindling minority who had still to get their ER's installed; as little more than a fortnight remained in which to obtain the discs before the imprisonment law came into force, tension in this undecided minority was growing.

"It's so surprising you take the attitude you do, Aubrey," Jimmy said; he put on a prim tone, in an attempt to compete with his brother's. "Opinion in the country is crystallising now. You can begin to see that the grumbles about the ER come chiefly from the cultural-academic camp, whereas *your* camp, the sort of scientific-administrative camp, is decidedly *pro* the new order."

Aubrey brushed this aside with less than his usual courtesy.

"I know that's so," he agreed; "I also read C. P. Snow's article in *The New Statesman*. Far more than you, I have been made to feel the party line. I just for once cannot conform. Partly, it's a religious objection to ER's and all they stand for. . . ."

"Even when the good old Archbishop himself declares they will eventually promote Christian frankness and chastity all round?"

"Even then. You only care what the Archbishop says when it suits you. But my deepest objection is a humane one: it is a gross indignity to be forced to wear these things, a violation of the human spirit."

"They're big words!" Jimmy said facetiously; he felt sick; he wanted to roll on the floor and possibly do handsprings into his bedroom, just to show his brother how very little he cared for these leader writer's phrases. Where the deuce did this nice, ordinary little anonym of a brother pick up these flatulent, self-inflating ideas? If others took to ER's without complaint, why couldn't Aubrey?

"You're hopeless to try and argue with," Aubrey said shortly, "although I notice you always begin the arguments. I've seldom met anyone so lacking in moral conscience." He turned away to the television set, staring down at it with hands in pockets until the news came on.

The new lady announcer, Tanky Craig, smiled winningly into the room and said, "The Swiss Government has just announced that, following the favourable report received from its research team which visited Great Britain last month, it has decided to install Emotion Registers on all the nation's adult population. British firms will handle the contract for the installation, estimated to be worth some eighteen million pounds. The first delivery of discs will probably commence in the middle of October.

"A spokesman in Basle today said 'We have reached the same conclusion as the British Government: that by giving our emotional life an, as it were, official standing, we shall shed light into many dark corners and eliminate most of the undesirable inhibitions and neuroses to which civilisation has hitherto fallen prey. You are now watching the scene outside the government buildings before the announcement was made. . . .'"

"Good Lord! Is that what you're feeling depressed about?!" Jimmy exclaimed, coming over to peer offensively into his brother's face with the intensity of a short-sighted anthropologist. "I should have thought it was the best news so far! Good for the bloody Swiss! After all, in spite of a pile of favourable but slightly dazed comment abroad, we have been dangerously near becoming the laughing-stock of the world. Now we're vindicated—or at least our madness is not unique. Crikey, the British were always faintly funny, even in the good old days of Imperialism, but nobody ever laughs at the Swiss!" He crossed to the divider unit, pulled open the cellarette flap. "Weep no more, brother. Drink, and forget your message for the world. This calls for a martini."

Aubrey accepted the drink warily. The soupily sagacious expression returned; he looked like Joshua Reynolds sitting for a portrait by Gainsborough.

"Your reception of the news is going to be typical of the way the whole country will take it, I expect," he said. "Interesting! I can't wholly blame you, but don't you see we're going to end up with the whole *world* wearing these piddling devices?"

"Prosit! What's so bad in that, Aubrey? Everyone in the world has navels, but who cares? In five years, ER's will be as natural as navels."

"That's what I'm dreading," Aubrey said.

"Well, it isn't a rational dread."

In cool silence, they drank their warm martinis. Jimmy let his eye wander back to the yellow cover of "The Rough Kind". It was a distinct relief to him when Alyson appeared, just as he was feeling as claustrophobicly embedded in time as a fossil in slate.

"Can't stop, pet," she said, kissing Aubrey; she wore a pert little hat and her brow was still innocent of the silver disc. "I'm just going to see Blanche, but I thought I'd pop in on my way and remind you about tomorrow afternoon. A date with Hampton Court, remember?"

"I was going to come round and see you later," Aubrey said, standing with his hands clasped behind his back. "I'm sorry about this, darling, but I shan't be able to make it tomorrow afternoon. There is a spot of overtime I must do; you know what the BIL is for keeping noses to grindstones. My time is going to be fully occupied for the next three weeks, I'm afraid."

She paused, looked hard at him and said frigidly, "I thought you had finished with that sort of thing now that the K. R. Shalu deal was tied up."

"That was chicken feed to this new project, Alyson," he told her. "This is really important." He explained to her about the Swiss decision to adopt the ER and added, "That Swiss contract goes to Iral and its affiliate companies— Norman Laboratories and all the others. BIL is handling all the administrative side of the affair for them, and backing them up to the hilt to get the deal through on time. It's going to mean a lot of work and organisation for everyone, as you can imagine. I heard about it from Sir Richard as soon as I arrived this morning; he got the tip from the Ministry late last night." Aubrey paused for dramatic effect, then added, "Everything's in ferment. Sir Richard is transferring me from the Asian branch to the European branch. It's a considerable step up for me—or it will be, by the time we've cleared Switzerland."

They both congratulated him warmly. Why, Jimmy wondered, had he created all that unctuous fuss? Could it have been because the unexpected promotion had suddenly made him unsure of himself? Jimmy got the martini bottle and a glass for Alyson and poured them all a tot.

"The new era!" he said, raising his glass, and like a sudden twinge of toothache came the thought "I last used that phrase beside Hurn's swimming pool at Walton!" Conquering a wave of nostalgia, Jimmy added aloud, "All the time you were giving me the old trot about Norman Lights being a bad show you had this up your sleeve! You ungrateful dog, Aubrey. I bet they'll double your salary. Now I can see why you looked so odd when you came in: you were worrying over whether I'd accept the MG when you bought a Daimler."

"More ambitious than that even," Aubrey said, a professional smoothness entering his tone. "I was even hoping I might be able to afford to get married."

Dodging the implications of that, Alyson said, "Anything, in fact, rather than take me to Hampton Court tomorrow."

She moved restlessly over to the window. As her profile glistened past him, topped by a tiny flat hat whose ribbons lay along her fair hair, Jimmy thought she looked thinner, slightly tired. With a catch at his heart, he recalled a line of Pound's from a poem he had admired in his undergraduate days: "The August has worn against her." It might, as he had glibly, gladly, claimed, be a new era; but on the permanent stage the Unlovable Young People were growing to be old actors; nobody plays juvenile leads forever.

A moment of sadness settled over all of them. Even between the well-intentioned, irreconcilable differences constantly show themselves. To break the mood, Aubrey said "A London girl and she's never been to Hampton Court!" as if he were reading the line.

"The maze would be heavenly at this time of the year," Jimmy said. "Chock full of Coca-cola bottles and ice cream wrappers. I tell you, kids, don't miss it!"

"You'll have to take Alyson instead, Jimmy," Aubrey said. "I hate to disappoint her, and you never go anywhere these days. It'll do you both good."

"I can't, Aubrey," Jimmy said, looking embarrassed. "It's nothing to do with me. I can't take her."

"Of course you can. Why not?"

"That's a stupid question, coming from BIL's brightest," Jimmy said agitatedly, lighting a cigarette. "I'm at a disadvantage here; sometimes I think you deliberately go out of your way to put other people in a difficult position. For heaven's sake, Aubrey, you aren't blind. You can see that every time Alyson comes past me I start pinking."

He would not look at them, but it was a relief to have the truth out at last.

"I understand from the handouts that that means you have a sub-threshold attraction for her," Aubrey said coldly.

"You know jolly well that's what it means. And not so sub, either."

"Very well," Aubrey said, standing rather stiffly. "Why should the knowledge affect me? Yours seems to me the only possible reaction to Alyson's presence, bless her. You still have control of yourself, haven't you? Your moral faculties still function, I trust? You can take her on the river to Hampton Court without throwing your arms round her, can't you? You're not a slave to that thing on your forehead, are you?"

"Stop talking about me as if I'm not here," Alyson said. "I refuse to listen to any more of this silly, meaningless bickering! You're two horrible, grumpy brothers, and I insist you fight a duel with loaded ice cubes."

"There's where the greatest danger of these things lies," Aubrey said, turning to her although ignoring her remark. "People are already beginning to think of ER's as 'Go' signals; they're not; they're 'Caution' signals. Not that I worry. I'm going to live abroad when I've made my pile."

"Switzerland, sweet?" Alyson asked. She said it lightly enough, but she looked annoyed with both of them.

On the river next afternoon, however, Alyson was her usual equable self. She was admirably clothed in a dramatic cotton dress with standaway skirt and buccaneer cuffs; her blouse was a mingling of the colours the fashion designers would probably speak of as sherry and anthracite, softening away to cream towards the hem of her skirt. She wore cream-rimmed sunglasses. Her tired look had gone and the moist, dewy one was back. "On trust, boy," Jimmy growled to himself, remembering Aubrey's stubborn belief in him.

"You look wonderful," Jimmy said. "Forgive me if I pink—my genes know a good thing when they see it."

"I don't trust you even if Aubrey does," Alyson smiled, "so just behave yourself."

But pinking was in fashion that bright afternoon. Everyone on the pleasure boat seemed to be at it as they sailed up the Thames. Ninety per cent of the population now wore ER's. To the middle-aged, they had proved an undisguised blessing; thousands of people beginning to be regarded as "past-it-all" by acquaintances were now able to show, effortlessly, that the fires of life still burned. For this reason, considerable numbers of people over sixty had voluntarily had Norman Lights installed, to prove that Hardy was not alone in feeling that power which constantly animates mankind.

> And shakes this fragile frame at eve
> With throbbings of noontide.

Alyson and Jimmy meandered through the famous Hampton Court maze, which was happily bottle-free, and took tea afterwards in an open-air café, where a canned orchestra played Suppé and Strauss. They were each demolishing an excellent meringue when Jimmy looked up to see Guy Leighton approaching. "*Quelle* disappointment! Every ointment owns its fly; this one's called Guy," Jimmy groaned to himself, and rose smiling manfully to make the introductions.

"This is Aubrey's fiancée, Miss Alyson Youngfield. Alyson, this is Guy Leighton, a kingpin in the BIL pin cushion."

Guy, in his turn, introduced the two people with him. One of them Jimmy had met at Sir Richard Clunes' party the previous month: Vincent Merrick, industrial psychiatrist. The woman with him, wearing heavy glasses much like his, but otherwise no more similar to him than Pavlov to Pavlova, was Mrs. Merrick.

"I'm glad to see you've had your ER installed since we met last, Guy," Jimmy observed. "I thought you were making a stand against them? Infringement of personal dignity and all that, eh?" Merrick was also equipped; Mrs. Merrick, in this respect, still presented a virgin brow.

"We're trying to keep off that subject, Solent," Guy replied, standing on tiptoes in an attempt at amiability. "Nevertheless, we've been on it most of the afternoon. Yes, I've got mine at last; the implacable pressures of society proved too much for me. To conform is comfort."

"These ER's will not bring conformity," Merrick said, seating himself next to Alyson without looking at his wife. "Everyone seems to regard them as a badge of uniformity; that is just what they are not. We are in for a wave of individuality. That's what I predict, anyhow. Inhibitory blocks we've come unjustifiably to regard as keystones in our society are being swept away. You should see some of the executives who have consulted me in this month! It would stagger you. Krafft-Ebing, thou shouldst be living at this hour. Without divulging any names or betraying any professional confidences, I can tell you I've unearthed two gerontophiles, a hermaphrodite, three wonderful autoerotics whose lights never go out, and a fellow who pinks at Drambuie for reasons I've yet to unearth—all within the last week."

"They sound rather extreme cases," Jimmy said.

"Oh, admittedly," Merrick agreed, wiping his glasses on a bright silk handkerchief. "But what I'm getting at is this. Ever since the second world war, our society has suffered increasingly from the desire to give up: in a word, defeatism. All over the world, we have been politely backing out —to submerge ourselves in the cosy, spineless gloom of the Welfare State."

"Oh, now wait a minute . . ." Guy interrupted.

"No, you can't deny it," Merrick said. "From markets and colonies we've been busily opting out. The world is too much with us, late and soon, and 'Couldn't Care Less' has become our watchword—coupled, of course, with 'Couldn't View More' from the avant garde of abdicators who hide their heads in Mummy Telly. Now why is all this? Surely if there is any one cause, it is simply that personal values have been lost. This terrible lust for anonymity is due solely to a profound distrust of individual worth. As a nation, we have been so heckled at from right, left and centre that we no longer realise that a man with faults is worth ten dummies without any attributes at all."

"But the Registers don't instil attributes," Alyson said. She had been watching the psychiatrist with the greatest interest.

"They don't instil attributes, no," he agreed, "but they manifest them. At least, they manifest the most vital attribute of all: sex. Men and women—and in many cases I assure you this has come as a revelation to them—are suddenly assured by the presence of these little discs that they are not mere cogs in a Heath Robinson machine, but live creatures with desires and impulses of their own. If those impulses seem at times beyond their control, so much the more exciting for them. It's an absolute shot in the arm all round, I can tell you. That it has flushed a brood of perverts is only—from my professional point of view—a beginning, a small beginning."

He beamed with interest at them, adding a "Let's have some ice cream," and waved commandingly to a waitress.

"And Vincent says the homosexuality laws are bound to be changed," Mrs. Merrick said, speaking almost for the first time.

"Of course they are," Merrick said. "Enlightenment's here at last, like it or not! Human nature's been hounded out into the open and the government must face the consequences. You'll have heard, I suppose, about the trouble the public schools are having? And then, looking further into the future, the marriage laws will have to be drastically revised. 'Until death do us part' is all very well in its way, but gene-instinct laughs at the idea—absolutely laughs. I tell you, by the first year of the next century the world will be unrecognisable."

"The world or just England?" Alyson asked.

"The world," Guy interposed, before Merrick could reply. "The Swiss move is out now. Everyone knows about it. Well, there's more to come. It's all hush hush, of course, but I've heard that Belgium's the next on the list. They'll buy the Registers—you mark my words. Their delegation was over here before the Swiss one, if you recall—I spoke to one of the members myself, very capable man. And that's the way the cat'll jump. No, tomorrow's an ER world, make no mistake. Everyone will follow our lead."

He rubbed his small, sallow hands, smiled gleefully, and accepted an ice cream. Jimmy wondered why his flesh suddenly felt cold; there were no clouds over the sun; the sensation must have been a reaction against the insane confidence of these two men. Before hubris, the wise shiver.

As they ate ices, and the talk changed course, Alyson speaking delightfully of her Mediterranean cruise the previous year, Jimmy tried to fathom why he disliked men like Leighton and Merrick; they were vastly dissimilar, but both possessed that same self-assurance. They seemed so sure of their own opinions and of their own place in society. "Perhaps I'm jealous because it's something I lack," Jimmy told himself. "Doubtless Merrick would love to tell me." Whatever the reason, he felt feeble before this kind of people.

"We're driving into the country to a pub I know for a drink and a snack," Merrick said. "Why don't you two come along? I can drop you home afterwards. We should all be delighted if you would join our party."

It was nothing Jimmy was keen to do. He weakened and waffled and passed the decision to Alyson, consenting when she did. She seemed genuinely delighted by Merrick's invitation.

"That'll be splendid, Jasmine, won't it?" Merrick boomed enthusiastically, turning almost for the first time to his dowdy little wife.

"Lovely," she agreed. As she spoke to Merrick, his light pinked vigorously back at her. The world, Jimmy reflected gratefully, was packed with surprises.

VIII. The Light That Failed

As the party came into a low lounge whose naked brick and beam were peppered with horse brasses and instruments of torture, Alyson squeezed Jimmy's hand. She removed the cream sunglasses, smiled at him and whispered, "This is fun! Isn't Vincent Merrick wonderful?"

"I think 'impossible' is the word you're looking for," Jimmy replied, but he was delighted to see she was enjoying herself. She sat on something like a church pew, arranging the ample russet, black and cream of her skirt, while Jimmy sat on one side of her and the Merricks ranged themselves on the other. Guy, well up on his toes, primped over to the bar to get a tomato juice and Worcester sauce (Alyson), a gin and lime (Jasmine Merrick), two bitters (Jimmy and Merrick) and a Pimm's No. 1 (himself).

"I always think this is such a nice inn, a real old country pub," Jasmine said, looking about with evident favour. "And Stipend itself is a nice little village. We used to come here a lot in the old days. The Minister of Health has his country place a mile up the road, isn't that so, Vincent?"

She had a tremulous voice which made her husband sound like a bloodhound when he spoke.

"Bunnian? Yes; his is the big Georgian house beyond the village," Merrick added, looking at Jimmy, "I've played golf with him for a number of years."

"I shouldn't have taken you for a golfing man," Jimmy said.

"I'm not, but Jasmine likes it," Merrick said, without elaboration. It might also, Jimmy considered, have been Jasmine's idea to visit Hampton Court; that hardly seemed the sort of place Merrick would frequent—or had he a professional affection for the maze? Did it remind him of the tangled topiary of the ego? Certainly he had come away from it quickly enough, gunning his car as if it had been a phallic symbol rather than a 1957 Triumph Mayflower.

"There will be little time for golf now, as far as I'm concerned," he said, addressing himself to Alyson as the drinks arrived. Guy supervising a man with a tray. "We must expect a wave of maladjustment throughout all ranks of society until the new order establishes itself. The general public, of course, are momentarily wallowing in mass exhibitionism; they may be relied upon to cure themselves; more sensitive spirits, the introvert element, need assistance. We may, indeed, find ourselves faced with an entirely new psychosis induced by a reluctance to admit that other people's fantasies are as powerful as one's own. I have, for instance, a very delightful actress of forty with a distinct dread of seeing an ER pink. Acute neophobia is only a partial answer. Very interesting. . . ."

"I read an article in *Home P-A* last week," Alyson said, "which claimed that the greatest proportion of unrest came from those sectors of the middle class which have subscribed most faithfully to the theory that no nice person *had* a sex life at all."

"That is approximately true," Merrick said, barking briefly with laughter, "merely because that particular stratum, owing to the repressiveness of the terms under which it elects to live, has always been a fertile source of rebellion. Now it's suddenly producing Bourgoynists and victims of vaginismus instead of writers, actors and explorers. One could possibly extrapolate from that and predict an end of all creative activity within five to ten years, except that by then the disquiet should be over. That's when we can expect the richest rewards—say a decade from now. We may, I think, at last look forward to a perfectly adjusted society; I, of course, shall be out of a job—and creative activity may be nipped in the bud that way: the adjusted, after all, need no catharsis, and all art is catharsis. Yet, on the other hand, the healthy *dynamic* person is always in conflict with himself—oh, I know that sounds like heresy, coming from me—but if you remove the conflict, where are you?"

"There's a spot of conflict going on outside the inn," Guy said to Jimmy. They turned and looked out of the window while Merrick continued his monologue to the two ladies.

On the opposite side of the road to the pub, a steep slope rose to a height of about fifty feet. A piggery or a ruinous farm, perched at the top of this slope, had formed a detritus of old cans, rusting corrugated iron, and motor tyres below it. Among these obstacles stood a dozen people, bearing hand-printed cardboard signs saying HANDS OFF SEX and LOVE AND SCIENCE WON'T MIX. These were evidently members of the Bourgoyne Group, or, as it now called itself officially since its amalgamation with the Suppression of Science Society, the Group for the Restoration of Emotional Privacy—GREP for short.

The dozen representatives of the Stipend branch of GREP were ill-assorted. Five of them were maiden-looking ladies of parched aspect; one was a motherly type expecting to mother again within the next few days; one looked like a traveller in gents' suitings and had brought his father with him; and the other four were yokels ranging in age from sixteen to forty.

"Very interesting, Solent," Guy said. "You notice what a madly mixed bag they are. As Bourgoyne claims, he draws his supporters from all sections of society, and what a curse it must be to all concerned! Just imagine those poor old dears, who so obviously are playing hookey from the vicar's sewing circle to come here, taking tea with yonder yobs. God, I can see it all! The sucking noises! The agonised looks! The pained discussions of what they don't want discussed. . . ."

"I've heard that the farm labourer as a class is more against ER than anyone," Jimmy said. "A pleasingly curious finding. The innate conservatism of the soil making its last stand. . . . The inability to change in all around I see."

He watched the group outside with interest. It was being jeered at by a cluster of village boys, one or two with their girl friends, who stood outside the pub. One of the GREP labourers was red in the face and shouting back at them; the women had drawn themselves up stoically and stared indifferently ahead; only the commercial traveller behaved in an unBritish fashion: he picked his nose, peeping back up the slope as if seeking a way of escape there.

"You don't still believe the government will fall by September 1, Guy, do you?" Jimmy asked. "I don't imagine this sort of motley gathering is going to impress anyone. And Bourgoyne represents about all the organised opposition there is."

"Oh, as you say, though I see that the Army is getting restive. At the same time, there are bigger straws in the wind. We hear about them at BIL when others don't. You'd better keep this tidbit under your hat *pro tem*, but you know, I suppose, how the PM stands to gain personally out of the ER *putsch*?"

"Gascadder? No, I'm afraid I don't."

"Your brother is tighter than a clam, Solent. He ought to educate you politically. . . . The inner story behind the whole ER deal is most frightfully instructive. To begin with, certain pressure was applied in the right quarters and certain shares changed hands. You realise, to diverge for a second, that the actual construction and functioning of the Lights themselves is top Top Secret? There are supposed to be only three people in the country who fully comprehend how the things work. Each ER is assembled from separate parts made by various of Iral's companies. An electrode which penetrates or touches the brain is rumoured to come from the parent laboratory, Norman's. An entirely new hypalgesic which alone makes the operation possible is produced at Ghearing and Flower's, another Iral off-shoot. Did you say something, Solent?"

"I just said I knew Ghearing's," Jimmy gulped. An ice-blue menace walked towards him again over the flags, and an ice-blue voice said "You didn't give me a thing." "Let me get our glasses filled up again, Guy," he said, staggering to his feet.

The glasses were duly refilled, and they forgot the demonstration outside. Merrick still talked with the ladies, though now in a lighter vein; at the bar, a man in a beret slapped the back of another man in a beret and said, "Well, cheery-bye, Eric old sport, I've got to be thighborn by twenty-thirty hours." And Guy was speaking again, while Jimmy listened with a sort of soggy detachment.

". . . . so the Min. of Health, our friend Warwick Bunnian—Vincent's golfing buddy!—gets his palm greased with Ghearing and Flower stock, while Gascadder is eased into Norman's. Thus armed, they tackle the BMA who, after their four years' struggle over doctors' salaries, weaken and give in, and agree to go ahead with the whole production. Next thing you know, in the name of sanity and a golden future, we—you and I, Solent, none other—are lining these altruistic ladies' pockets. That's how it's done behind the scenes, I tell you, every time. There's no question of any enlightenment being involved at any stage —just plain, ordinary self-interest. And if the knowledge gets into the wrong hands, up goes the balloon."

"I see," Jimmy said, thinking how inadequate it sounded. He wondered, appalled, if he was destined to spend all the rest of the evening imbibing Guy's noxious brand of enlightenment; cautiously, he edged himself back to the rest of the group.

Merrick was saying, ". . . . so I am meeting revolution with revolution. The course of treatment I have evolved represents a fresh beginning to the history of alienism. My new clinic is an attempt to orient patients into the mystique of each other's neuroses. I'm expecting it to induce temporary tolerance patterns. . . ."

A stone, shattering the lounge window, struck Merrick on his temple. With a roar of anguish, he jumped up, spilling his beer over the carpet. Amid shouts outside, a car hooter sounded and there was a loud crash. Scudding footsteps and shouts echoed in the road. With one accord, the occupants of the pub rushed to the windows to see what was going on.

"That's Warwick Bunnian getting out of the car!" Guy exclaimed, standing on tiptoe excitedly.

"The poor fellow's been attacked," Merrick exclaimed, allowing Jasmine to examine his temple.

The car from which the stocky minister emerged had stopped in the middle of the road directly outside the pub. The GREP (Stipend Branch) had just struck their blow for emotional privacy. Its reason for standing awkwardly on the slope now became apparent. When Bunnian approached, being driven home in his car, the group had released a ten gallon oil drum full of rainwater, and the drum, with accidentally good timing, had careened down the slope and struck Bunnian's car squarely just behind its offside front wheels. The mixed collection of labourers and ladies was now scrambling up the slope, led by the traveller

99

in gents' suiting; nobody pursued them yet. As a picturesque touch, they had left their slogans behind to face the ministerial wrath.

"Guerilla warfare! " Mrs. Merrick exclaimed. "Oh what fun! Warwick's chauffeur will be furious! "

"There'll be tumbrils down these quiet roads before we're done! " Merrick said, emitting another of his barking laughs. The stone had not even broken his skin. Dr. Bunnian was equally calm; leaving his chauffeur to cope with the damage as best he might, he pushed his way through a gathering crowd and came into the pub.

"That was a narrow shave, sir," Guy said, materialising at once at the minister's elbow. "Do please allow me to buy you a drink; the proletariat were behaving with grave thoughtlessness."

"That's very civil of you," Bunnian said, nodding over to Merrick in friendly fashion, "but perhaps you'll allow me to buy you one—and your friends, of course. How do, Vincent! Evening, Jasmine! I've just come from the PM, as it happens, and he has been informed that Belgium has placed an order with our country for eight million Emotional Registers. How do you like that? Talk about our finest hour, eh? It's something worth celebrating, eh? Landlord, drinks on the house, please, drinks absolutely on the house! "

When Bunnian's chauffeur arrived half an hour later to announce that another car was waiting outside, the bar was packed with happy customers. They exuded sweetness and light and Guinness. The minister's impromptu visit had been a roaring success; many customers were heard openly to exult that he was "just an ordinary chap" or "just like one of us," instead of finding this a cause for foreboding. Bunnian so exactly played the democratic role, even allowing a gentleman farmer to slap his back, that a group of imbibers near the door burst spontaneously into "For He's a Jolly Good Fellow" as the minister left; a more ribald group chipped in with "Land of Hope and Glory," but somebody struck up "You Catch a Train Now," on the piano, and in no time, the minister was forgotten in the hurly-burly of a sing-song.

In the general post which had taken place, Jimmy found himself next to the man in the beret who had earlier been addressed as Eric. He was a red-faced man in his forties who faced up to Jimmy pugnaciously.

"We didn't need all these damn red lights in the last

war," he said. "It's all very well for old Bunnian, but how do you think we'd have won the Battle of Britain if we'd all sat round looking at each other's foreheads, hey? Hey?"

"Presumably if the Germans had been busy doing the same thing it would have been O.K.," Jimmy suggested.

The man slopped his beer furiously over his suède shoes.

"You Unloveable Young Types think you have all the answers, don't you? There's too much security these days, that's the trouble. You don't know what it means to have it rough. Even the bally Russians have gone soft lately. And look at the Americans. . . ."

"*You* look at them," Jimmy said. "I've something else to do," and he began to elbow his way across to where Alyson was now speaking boredly to a blond young man wearing a tan cravat and tan shirt. This young man had Alyson jammed into a corner. He was the sort of blond young man one instinctively dislikes; a mere glance at him and the pink searchlight on his forehead, and Jimmy decided he had to go. Merrick, from another part of the lounge, had the same idea. He, too, was pushing through the crowd towards Alyson. He arrived before Jimmy did, said something smilingly, and at once the blond young man vanished into the crowd without a backward look.

"Nice work, Vincent," Jimmy exclaimed, warming to the man. "I was on the same mission myself. Who was the pallid Romeo, Alyson, may I ask?"

"Did I look so palpably the damsel in distress! " Alyson exclaimed, making a pert face at them. "He only wanted to take me on the back of his motor bike to see his mother in Guildford."

"What did you say to him?" Jimmy asked Merrick curiously. "He beat a pretty hasty rereat."

"I just used a spot of elementary psychology," Merrick said, removing his spectacles and polishing them vigorously; without them, his eyes looked deceptively cowlike. "I said, 'If you don't clear off at once I'll give you a thick ear,' and so he cleared off at once. Now, if we can muster Jasmine and Guy, I suggest we motor off in search of food; this place grows too crowded for my liking."

Jasmine and Guy were mustered, and within half an hour the party was enjoying a dinner which included an impeccable chicken Maryland in a roadhouse outside Esher. After coffee and liqueurs, they wandered out into a flowering courtyard over which dusk was gathering. A cool wind brought them a breath of phlox. Jimmy had a nicely cushioned expense-account moment of guilt about it all.

Guy said quietly, as Merrick, prompted by the scent of phlox, started to reminisce to Alyson and his wife, "Have you had any more dealings with Rose English?"

The question was one Jimmy had been expecting; something small and dark had warned him back at Hampton Court that Guy was waiting to launch this very subject. And until the actual moment when the question was spoken, he could not say whether he dreaded or welcomed it, whether he never wished to mention Rose again or wanted to talk of nobody else. He was whisked back to the hour he had left her at Ghearing and Flower's, when he hurried away from her through the thick streets, striving to interpret and master what had happened to him; the buildings about him seemed to have a slight topheaviness they had caught from Rose; the insanely stylised heads in a milliner's he passed—bronze things, dead and guillotined, nothing like Rose—reminded him of Rose.

"She didn't want to see me again," Jimmy said.

And Guy was suddenly so changed that Jimmy looked at him in surprise to hear him say. "She told me she was dedicated to her work. She will only have anyone once. It's just the way she is, Solent."

He needed to say nothing more—truth rolled over Jimmy like an eclipse. That Thursday night, once so resonant, so grand, was now firmly nailed in the paltry box into which Rose herself had already cast it. There had been a Thursday night for this smarmy little go-getter too! Thursday nights for Rose were like fish and chips gobbled on a cheap day trip to the sea; you had them because you were hungry, without wondering whether they came wrapped in the *Financial Times* or *Weekend Reveille*.

The sheer diabolic horridness of it—the physical shock of realising that this worm had burrowed into that hungry bed first, the distaste of realising that Guy too coddled the bleeding heart of unstaunched lust, the smart of reliving his own humiliation in that barren canteen—came down like a sack over Jimmy, making his chicken Maryland heave.

He hated himself, he hated Rose, he hated Guy. Breaking away from the latter, who stood by alertly, obviously ready to swap intimacies, Jimmy took Alyson roughly by a cool arm.

"Let's go in again," he said. "I need another drink."

"I think it's time we went in and went home," Alyson said. "I should have brought a coat, or at least worn something different, had I known we were going to be out so late."

"Then without wishing you cold, I'm glad you didn't know," Jasmine said. "Your dress is very beautiful, my dear. Isn't it, Vincent?"

"Very beautiful; I've been admiring it all evening. I'd like a Scotch before we set off. What can I get you, ladies?"

Over the drinks in the lounge, Guy found a chance to say to Jimmy, "I'll tell you what I've found out about her."

That would be, of course, the Leighton system: a probing word here, a circumspect phone call there. Jimmy did not want to hear a thing, but he listened carefully. Guy seemed under a compulsion to speak, and he to hear.

"There is some mystery about the Rose which I have yet to get to the bottom of," Guy said. "She's part of the Norman dynasty, but it's difficult to fit her into it. All of them are nearly as elusive as she is. Felix Garside you saw at the Clunes' party; he's the big noise of the family as well as the big noise in Iral. He is supposed to be Rose's uncle, but I don't quite see how. He has a sister called Gwendoline who married old Norman; when Norman died, Gwendoline took over his cash and his work and married a Russian emigré, Demyanski, though everyone still refers to her as Gwendoline Norman. This fellow Demyanski studied the brain under the Stalinist regime, when apparently he had some pretty gruesome opportunities for working on living humans. Demyanski and Gwendoline Norman between them cooked up the ER idea, but as he died suddenly three years ago, full credit for the invention goes to her. There is a TV programme due on her work soon. I'd seriously advise you to take a look at it, Solent.

"Gwendoline had a daughter by old Norman called Rachel, another recluse like her mother, by all accounts. Our dear Rose might well be a sister of Rachel's, although that is something I've yet to discover; nobody seems to know. Quite obviously, there is a security screen a mile high round them. I'll phone you if I find anything else of relevance, Solent."

"Thanks," said Jimmy. Relevant! Nothing Guy had said was relevant in any way to the suffocation Jimmy was experiencing. These were just tedious facts which somehow lulled Guy but brought Jimmy no anodyne. As they climbed into Merrick's car, Guy, full of brotherly feeling, patted Jimmy's arm; skilfully, Jimmy inserted Mrs. Merrick between them. Alyson rode in the front with Merrick.

As good as his word, Merrick drove them to Charlton Square. When their goodbyes were said, Alyson and Jimmy slipped quietly in and went upstairs. Alyson said she would sleep at the flat for the night. She switched on the electric fire, rubbed her arms and then went to peer into the bedroom.

"Aubrey's in bed and asleep," she announced, emerging, shutting the door again quietly behind her. Jimmy made no reply.

She looked restlessly about the room, tidied a newspaper, straightened a book. Her movements registered on Jimmy without meaning, as he stood stiffly watching her. The ghastly rudderlessness of his existence almost entirely absorbed him.

"I think we could perhaps manage a hot drink," Alyson said, regarding him for the first time since they had got in. "Oh God, always this flat feeling when the feast has finished and the lamps expire. . . . I liked Vincent Merrick very much; he seems such a positive person. Jimmy, come over here."

He went obediently over to her, still without thought. Only a vague and cold pleasure stirred in him as she put her hands on his shoulders to stare meditatively at him.

"Jimmy dear, you oughtn't to come as easily as that, I keep telling you about it," Alyson said, biting her lip and frowning. "Can't you see you shouldn't be so—well, so willing to please?"

"I'll always come, Alyson; it's never a chore, you know. Don't be silly—one day you may make me glad I came."

"All I was going to say was, you've been unhappy this evening, haven't you?"

It was Jimmy's turn to be restless. A cosy exchange of confidences was not what he wanted just now; his sort of confidences were nonexchangeable.

"It's indigestion, maybe," he said and suddenly realised

104

that, despite Alyson's proximity, his light had remained neutral all evening. Now she was divining the truth from that, or perhaps from having watched his expression while he was talking to Guy, just as he had divined Guy's full meaning without having it spelt out for him.

"The light that failed," he said, "Take no notice, Alyson; my genes are just crazy, mixed-up kids who don't know when they're well off. They're going through a phase. It's just one of those things. You can't eat your cake and have it. If summer comes, can autumn be far behind? Add platitudes to taste."

"I know when you talk in that silly fashion that you feel beastly inside," Alyson said, "but other people might not. Can't you see I'm only making a ham-handed attempt to be helpful?"

"The August has told against you, Alice," he said heavily, sitting down and lighting a cigarette. "It's told against me too; so for heaven's sake go and make the hot drink, and stop talking at me as if we were married."

Alyson gave him an odd look and went into the kitchen. Perhaps she was pleased to be ordered about for a change. He saw through weary eyes that the hem of her dress was splashed by the beer which Merrick had upset when the stone hit him. "Symbolic," Jimmy told himself, but could not think of what it might be symbolic.

IX. Whatever the Band Plays . . .

Next day, the waylaying of the Minister of Health at Stipend was headline news. The papers gave publicity to both Bunnian and GREP. Photographs of the little man who looked like a commercial traveller featured in several reports; falling into a pig's trough during his hasty retreat, he had been unable to extricate his leg, and so had been apprehended by the local police. His name was Roger Wellknock and he got six months.

Within twenty-four hours, four women in different parts of the country came forward and identified Wellknock as their husband. Thus the Secretary of the Stibend and Rural District Branch of GREP stood unmasked as a bigamist— quite, as Donald Hortense remarked with relish, quite a big bigamist. So the first physical blow struck by the Bourgoynists brought the group into disrepute. Wellknock had the best of reasons for not wishing to wear the truth-revealing ER; so, it transpired, had a good many other members of the group. As generally happens in such cases, the unfavourable publicity this minority received blanketed out the good intentions of the majority of the group.

Big Bill Bourgoyne himself was above suspicion; he was till the last the staunch defender of the good old status quo, and as such earned vast and vociferous (but otherwise inert) support from the gerontocracy of the rich retired. Looking back, we can only feel surprise that this fugal, murmurous chorus, containing as it did the descants and swan songs of many prominent citizens, most of them older than the century, did not more influence public events; perhaps it is that the average man who leads, if only economically, an unsheltered life, is apt to laugh at all grey-haired defenders of the status quo, for he realises, however inarticulately, that there is no such thing as a status quo. There is, instead, a continual rate of change, only noticeable as one becomes unable to change oneself.

The GREP, however, never became merely a figure of fun. This was partly due to the integrity of Bourgoyne himself and partly to the number of hooligans who rose unexpectedly, towards the end of August, to join the ranks of the maiden ladies. They were out for excitement. Oil drum rolling was a pleasure. Suddenly they turned into rebels with a cause and became Bourgoynists. Young delinquents who had had their hands on nothing else carried HANDS OFF SEX placards and flung stones at 10 Downing Street.

As the fine August days shortened towards September, a wave of unrest swept the country. Of this wave, the GREP, smashing a window here, bashing a constable there, was only a spearhead. Most of the unrest came from people who accepted the ER's without being able to adjust to the enlightenment they brought. In particular, the shy, the reserved, the defeatist, found that now they revealed their feelings involuntarily they had demolished the greatest barrier which kept them from mingling with others. A life of fulfilment was no longer beyond them. They broke with the old withdrawn ways each according to his nature, some cautiously, some violently, as pent-up desires saw opportunity for release. It was chiefly from this class of people that the outburst of licentiousness predicted by Alyson Youngfield came.

The effect of this minor disturbance was to make life generally more gay, more hectic. "Pinking parties" became the thing; the Unlovable Young made whoopee on a scale which exceeded the mad twenties, as they toasted the forthcoming September 1, "the September Revolution," when the kill-joys without headlights would be slung into clink.

Even their seniors, the middle-aged, joined in the optimism. As Mrs. Pidney, the landlady at 17 Charlton Square, remarked sagaciously, "It's something that's taken people's minds off unnatural things like films and TV." It had indeed. Beauty contests enjoyed a new vogue; their judging was infinitely simplified now that the pinking output of the judges could be recorded and measured. The 900-page novel "Nor On What Beds" by Zanadu Timms swept to bestsellerdom by virtue of its climax in a Norman-lit *wagon lit*. John Osborne's new play, "A Grave for Hodges" (with what Kenneth Tynan called "the light motive as leitmotif"), was extremely successful. The Ealing comedy film, "Forever Crimson," starring Alec Guiness, did highly funny and highly topical things in Technicolour. It was even reported that Samuel Beckett was writing a cheerful play.

This vast diversion in public life did not fail to divert Jimmy Solent. Yet he could not be called a happy man. His rejection by Rose he had borne as best he could; but Guy Leighton's chance words had been the last straw which made everything intolerable. He threw himself with sick energy into the organisation of the IBA Haiti exhibition.

In this, however, he was unable to absorb himself completely. Alyson and Aubrey began to prove an unexpected worry; as the time for them to make a final decision on wearing NL's drew near, they grew increasingly nervous. The dark patches under Alyson's eyes darkened.

On the last Tuesday of the month, when less than one week's grace remained to the people still without registers, Jimmy presented himself at Donald's house. Donald was celebrating the receipt of a cheque for a poem published two years ago in a Glasgow little review. An ally of Donald's happening to be in that centre of industry, had descended on the editor and threatened him with a black eye if the cheque was not immediately forthcoming. The cheque, for two guineas, had been immediately forthcoming, whereupon Donald had bought five guineas' worth of drink to celebrate.

"Where's your brother and his girl?" Donald asked when Jimmy arrived. "Aren't they coming?"

"Aubrey's working late as usual," Jimmy said. "The BIL is a sort of high-class sweat-shop nowadays, but they're hoping to try and drop in later. What on earth's that concoction you've got there, Donald?"

Donald was squatting by the fireplace in a room full of men, boyish-looking girls, and girlish-looking boys. Bottles of madeira and cheap red wine stood by the fender, while in an electric frying pan the IBA librarian brewed a murky mixture from which murky fumes wreathed.

"It's chilly tonight," Donald said. "End of the heat wave, probably. I thought a drop of Brontosaurus Blood would warm everyone up. We can shove the Unloveable Young corpses under the bed as they fall."

"The thunder lizards give their gizzards up to Bacchus' altar," Jimmy began rhyming to himself, as he sipped half a Woolworth's tumblerful of the brew, but was unable to think of an apt conclusion. "Gibraltar, Malta, halter? Despite our brains, would our remains make booze sweeter or salter? This is a childish habit, James; you must grow out of it, or else write it down and send it to *Punch* . . ."

The Brontosaurus' Blood proved, in fact, rather insipid. The conversation, too, was the kind one usually met with at Donald's. Donald lived with a commercial artist called Spud Witherd who worked in an advertising agency. During the day, Spud painted insanely healthy people throwing beach balls about; at night he painted ferocious, worm-like things which swam in geometrical puddles. The worm-like things were called oscillids; Spud sat on a bed now, explaining it all carefully and patiently just as Jimmy had once heard it explained to him. He wondered if Spud enjoyed saying the same piece over and over again, and had to presume he did.

"My oscillids are merely the logical, evolutionary climax to which all art has always tended," Spud explained carefully to a pair of novices. "Art, after all, is a compromise between disturbance in the artist's psyche and certain objective principles of symmetry—something, in other words, poised in the area between chaos and the straight line."

"Yes, I can see that," one of the novices said relievedly.

"Good. Now instead of leaving that compromise to chance, I *compute* it, I harness it to a mathematical

108

relationship. Oscillids are temperament curves plotted against spatial duration. They are *graphs*. They are *balances*. The canvas functions merely as a fulcrum between the inner and outer worlds. The only variable is what I might call the psychic flux, which naturally changes from hour to hour—otherwise, I should just paint the same picture over and over. Get it?"

"The funny thing *is*," a girl in slacks said at Jimmy's elbow, "that although Spud's theories are an awful lot of cock, his paintings really have something."

That was just it. The pictures of people with beach balls could not bother anybody, but these gangrenous worms could oscillate their way into bothering you quite seriously.

"That's how the world works," Jimmy said, eyeing the girl with a growing ghost of interest. "The obvious shouldn't interest anybody. If it does, it's because people have been bred silly, like chickens. I mean. . . ." But what he meant, in the noise and smoke, eluded him. It was going to be something large and grand that he recalled; it would have impressed the girl. What was that dreadful smell, Donald's brew or the varnish burning on the boards under his frying pan? "I've been haunted for weeks," he ended, "by something which sounds obvious but wasn't so to me. A girl said to me. 'You don't give me a thing,' and I couldn't understand it."

"Sounds simple enough," the girl in slacks said. She had a black sweater, long eyelashes and short pigtails; she looked vaguely like Aubrey Hepburn. She also looked vaguely like moving on at any minute.

"Oh, don't worry about it; I don't," Jimmy said hastily. Various faculties, waking as if from sleep, were prompting him that this girl was attractive.

"I wasn't worrying," she said.

"Now you're blushing."

"I'm not. It's your Norman Light. It's gone a disgusting colour. And I may as well tell you now, if you're thinking that sort of thing, you're wasting your time. I prefer female company."

The faculty curled up and went to sleep again—almost, for you never knew when a spot of physiotherapy might not convert these borderline cases. In its place, another faculty awoke and informed Jimmy that music was playing.

"Let's dance, beautiful," he said at once.

"Nobody else is dancing."

"*Here*, that's a reason for dancing."

"You're a funny fellow!" she exclaimed without animation.

"Oh, call me Jimmy," he said in boredom; what the hell did it matter anyway? To his mild surprise she came into his arms, and they jogged about among the crowd, which showed few signs of resentment. He developed a slight albedo again, and the pink light lay along her smooth cheekbones.

They jogged round the room somnambulistically, occasionally encountering among the throng another couple who had set up in opposition to them. The now unremarkable pink glow had settled over every corner of the room; only with difficulty in such cramped space could one tell who glowed at whom.

"It's all old hat," Jimmy told himself. "Already it's old hat. The shine's worn off the shiners already. Someone bring on the dancing girls."

He realised he had spoken aloud, but Jean, Andreina's girl, did not seem to notice.

He had shuffled past one corner half a dozen times before noticing it contained a TV set, which was switched on. The face of a woman of about sixty looked out of it; she talked without a sound being audible in the noisy room. She had a strong jaw and good cheekbones and was still handsome. There was, Jimmy thought vaguely, more of the teacher than the mother about her, and then he knew of whom she reminded him: Rose! This was the programme Guy Leighton had told him about, a feature on the invention of ER's.

Forgetting all about Jean, Jimmy released her and knelt down beside the set to turn the volume up. A fellow in a check shirt whose back he brushed against turned round and said curiously, "Aren't you the New Zealander who got chucked out of Zombie Sexton's the other night?"

"Yes," Jimmy said, twiddling the knob.

The volume on the set came up with a roar and the grey-haired woman bellowed across the room. "It was at that time that I first met Ivan Demyanski." A waggish member of the party applauded and called "Here, here." Spinning the knob, Jimmy got the speaker to continue, at a manageable decibel output, "Of course I was familiar with his work. Ivan was a friend of Pavlov's and, working along similar lines, had been getting similarly notable results. What I was not familiar with was Ivan's great charm. He fled from Russia to the west, arriving in England in very poor health."

"And I believe you personally nursed him back to health?" prompted an unseen interviewer.

"I did. In the process, exchanging information about our pet lines of research, Ivan and I came to the conclusion that by pooling our knowledge we might make an original contribution to science. Meanwhile, although we were getting a bit long in the tooth, we fell in love, got married in 1948, and by then the theory of Emotional Registration was well on its way."

This was Gwendoline Norman then, a close relation of Rose's, according to Guy. She not only resembled Rose; she spoke in a similarly direct fashion which came over even in a scripted talk. For Jimmy, this similarity made painful watching.

He was now spared further agony. Gwendoline Norman's face vanished, supplanted by miles of gleaming Norman laboratory, as other voices took up the tale.

Jimmy quickly lost interest. These shots of microscopes and hypodermics, these diagrams of the brain, were all standard stuff. Even as a layman, he could tell that the scientific patter gave nothing away. The Norman empire, as Guy had pointed out, had too much on the ball.

Sighing, Jimmy lay back more comfortable to listen to Gwendoline who had now reappeared on the screen.

"Our world grows increasingly complex," she was saying. "This is nothing to be feared; the way, not only of progress, but of mere survival lies in continual mechanisation. It is useless for us now to cry for the abolition of machines. To adapt a current phrase, the opposite of progress is not retrenchment but stagnation. Without machines, this island would be over-populated far beyond subsistence level; with them, we all live comfortably. What we are entitled to complain of is the threat to the individual in the increasing standardisation which mechanisation involves. All of us at times experience a desire for some key to the maze about us; we wish to see below its surface. We find our acquaintances depersonalised, and long to know what they really feel. The device Ivan Demyanski and I have developed is offered as a key to that question. I do urge those of you who have not yet had your Emotion

Register installed to get one free during the next week, and join our great and growing new society. Remember, you won't feel a thing, and . . ."

"Sales talk!" the man in the check shirt shouted. "Switch this crap off for cry's ache!"

This roused Jimmy. He had been so raptly watching the lineaments of Rose in Gwendoline's face, and so intently trying to listen through the noise in the room, that he had failed to realise how much this noise had increased in his corner. Looking up, he found he had made himself comfortable with his head on Jean's lap. She was sitting, her legs tucked under her, arguing with an older woman who spoke shrilly and wagged a nicotine-stained finger at Jimmy. The woman also had a nicotine-stained upper lip and fierce eyes; Jimmy guessed at once that this was Andreina. He sat up immediately in order to get off her property.

"What do you think you was doing?" the woman asked in a strong accent. "Just I turn my back for get a drink and this happen. How you like come to a party and be seduce, hey?"

"It all depends," Jimmy said apologetically, and was swallowed in abuse.

"Leave him alone, Andreina," said Jean sulkily. "He was only watching TV."

"Watching TV. That is a fine excuse! And what you do there—bake a cake?"

Smiling feebly at Jean, Jimmy beat a retreat.

The man in the check shirt shouted something about Zombie Sexton; Jimmy, who had never heard of this gentleman, nodded his head enthusiastically, winked, and disappeared into the crowd. He then, for about an hour, rediscovered the profound truth that, exciting as the promise of a party may be, its actuality is generally dull. He had resigned himself to the nonarrival of his brother and Alyson and was composing himself for his own departure, when a diversion occurred.

Presumably to offset the effects of the Norman broadcast, the Bourgoynists had turned out in strength. Two lorries, loaded with supporters and equipped with loudspeakers, were coming down Victoria Street from the direction of Cannon Street. A queue of private cars, trade vehicles and No. 24 buses followed them. Hecklers surrounded the lorries. The amplified voices were almost drowned by shouting and the derisive hoots of passing cars.

112

Objects were being thrown both from and at the lorries. One of the minor obstacles working against the GREP was that eggs that summer stood at only two shillings a dozen, cheaper than they had been for years. Eggs were being thrown now.

The tone of the crowd was distinctly more hostile to the GREP than it had been. Thanks particularly to the daily papers, who enjoy a little injudicious levity, the GREP had come to be regarded mainly as a crackpot organisation. If this attitude had hampered the group's serious aims, it had at least protected them so far from serious opposition, if not from police intervention. But now even the dimmest of the public realised that the whole success of the government's ER campaign lay in *everyone's* wearing a light; in the country of the three-eyed, the two-eyed man is king.

The procession had drawn opposite Donald's windows when a man, leaping from the crowd, broke two empty jam jars under the tyres of the first lorry. Amid a squeak of escaping air, the vehicle stopped. The driver flung himself from his cab in an attempt to catch the jar-thrower. A fight developed like a flash. A little man, an anti-Bourgoynist bearing a notice saying MAN CANNOT LIVE IN BED ALONE, brought his wooden board crashing down on a charging head. The more fiery male members of GREP launched themselves off the lorry into the fray, while their gentler companions stood up and cheered them on. The loudspeaker in the rear lorry barked, "We are not pacifists! We shall not hesitate to use force! We warn the government we shall not hesitate to use force! We warn you all we shall not hesitate to use force! "

Nor had Bourgoyne allowed his flock to go unarmed among the ravening multitude. As the crowd tried to storm the tailboards, the occupants of the lorries produced pick handles and walloped any skulls or fingers within reach. A man staggered away howling, clutching a dented headlight.

The partygoers had crowded to the window to watch.

"What are we waiting for?" Donald Hortense exclaimed. Uttering an obscene Scribist war cry, he charged from the room and down the stairs, a quarter of his party following him. Jimmy, Brontosaurus Blood broiling in his veins, was only a few steps behind his friend.

They issued into the crowded street just in time to see a taxi, which had nothing whatsoever to do with the GREP, heaved over onto its side by the mob. The rear door falling 'uppermost opened and a man climbed out; he was promptly punched on the nose by one of the rioters. He half turned to shield his face, and in that instant Jimmy saw it was Aubrey.

"That's my brother! Come on!" he shouted, seizing Donald's shoulder, and the Scribist party elbowed their way over to the taxi. The street was in an uproar. Someone from a nearby window was flinging buckets of water down on the crowd; glancing up, Jimmy saw it was Andreina, Jean's bosom friend. Police whistles sounded, the loud-speaker still blared angrily, but already the crowds were thinning. Blows had given way to running kicks, attack to retreats down the nearest passages. The GREP on the lorry, all boarders repelled, sang "Sons of the Sea":

But you can't beat the boys of the bulldog breed;
They made old England's name.

The driver of the overturned taxi, fists raised, back to the roof of his vehicle, offered to take on all comers; but the comers were too busy going. Skirting him, Jimmy peered into the back of the wreck. As he had expected, Alyson was there.

"Fancy meeting you!" she exclaimed somewhat breathlessly.

While Donald and some of his party took Aubrey by the arm, leading him back into the house, Jimmy helped Alyson climb out. Although pale and shaken, she had suffered nothing worse than a few bruises. She leant gratefully on Jimmy as he helped her upstairs.

There the party had come to a reluctant standstill. Andreina and her friends had, in their excitement, tipped the Brontosaurus Blood out of the window.

In the street, miraculously emptied now except for a few unhappy witnesses talking or refusing to talk to police-men, posters saying DON'T BE BROWBEATEN and HANDS OFF SEX lay covered with footprints, and the driver of the overturned taxi swore with melancholy vigour at the driver of the ambushed lorry.

Aubrey, his nose bleeding profusely, lay on the floor of Donald's bedroom with a key down his back. Alyson sat on the bed smoking a cigarette. Over the bed, reminder of Donald's Scribist sense of humour, a bit of Devonshire poker-work bearing the Ilfracombe crest said "All the

World's Queer Save Me and Thee, and even Thee's a Little Queer."

The man in the check shirt bustled in with an inch of red wine in toothglasses, medicine for the two victims.

"Just like Zombie Sexton's," he said cheerfully to Jimmy, shaking his head with evident relish. "Do you take trouble with you wherever you go?"

"It's the old Auckland heritage," Jimmy said modestly, making himself frightfully busy with Alyson.

"I'm sorry we were so late," Alyson said to Donald. Her hand trembled as she lifted the cigarette to her lips. "We got held up behind the procession. I've never heard so much propaganda in my life. And so really depraved! Love is something degrading which should be neither heard about nor seen—according to the GREP. I've lost all the sympathy I ever felt for them."

Jimmy found himself wondering once again why a reasonable girl like Alyson had not, like all the other reasonable girls, had her ER installed. Aubrey had his religious reasons, thin as they sounded, for defection; not so Alyson. Perhaps she had a loyal desire to give Aubrey what support she could; but to hear that she had undergone a change of heart was a great relief to him.

"Norman Lights'll never iron out society," the check shirt said, "because society has too many crinkles in it, but if they just succeed in revealing the homosexual laws for the nonsense they are they'll have done a worthwhile job."

"Are you one of those?" Aubrey asked from his prone position.

"So they tell me," the check shirt said lightly, but he turned to face Aubrey as if answering a challenge in the other's voice.

"I'm afraid I don't much care for your sort," Aubrey said.

Then began a painfully embarrassing scene. Aubrey, his nostrils still seeping blood, began to denounce the check shirt and all his kind. He put forward the usual and valid arguments, managing to make them sound like a personal affront. His words came out in a sudden spate, like an unexpected gusher of oil over which, once started, he had no control. The check shirt interrupted hotly once or twice, but Donald restrained him. Alyson sat silent on the bed, not looking at anyone, her cheeks hot.

When Aubrey had finished, the check shirt said angrily,

"You realise, don't you, that *we* realise there's something wrong with you to make you talk like that?"

"Why should that be so?" Aubrey asked. "You would accept objective judgements in other spheres; why not in this?"

"Never mind arguing! You've had your say," Donald told him. "I don't believe you know what you're talking about, but you've had your say. Now will you get out?" He turned to Alyson, said tartly, "I'm sorry about this," and walked from the room. After a moment in which he surveyed Aubrey with murderous contempt, the man in the check shirt said, quietly and with impressive ambiguity, "Whatever the band plays, you've always got your own music."

Then he too left the room.

"Get up and let's get home," Jimmy said savagely. "I wonder they didn't paste hell out of you, Aubrey, and I'm not sure I oughtn't to do so now. You come here, you're invited here, you accept their hospitality, and all you can do is go off your head about pansies. I told you weeks ago that Donald was queer, and if you didn't like it, you should have stayed away. If I were Donald, I'd . . ."

"Be quiet, Jimmy," Alyson said. "Can't you see Aubrey's not himself? He's been frightened. Go and get us a cab, can't you? Let's just get out of here."

Back at the flat, Aubrey staggered into a chair, buried his face in his hands, and started groaning.

"I'll draw the curtains," Alyson said. As she did so, she looked down into Charlton Square. Nobody was in sight there. Although the central grass looked brown and parched after the weeks of sunshine, a kind of freshness came up from the tree-fringed space. The mere absence of humanity was a tonic in itself; it was good to be reminded at intervals that the world was not man's, that he was nothing more than the temporarily dominant species on an enduring planet.

Nevertheless, it was quite a party he was having.

"It's a nice evening," Alyson said, bundling all her thoughts together into the tritest possible words.

"Don't be funny," Jimmy said irritably. "Cart this goon off to bed, will you? He's been drinking."

"Come here, Jimmy darling," Alyson said without fondness.

116

"I'm not in the mood," Jimmy said.

"What if I have been drinking?" Aubrey asked slowly. He pulled his face out of his cupped palms and turned it towards them; it was unrecognisable. Its circumference was white, merging to a bile yellow towards the middle, where, dead on target, a swollen proboscis hung like a mature Victoria plum.

"What if I have been drinking?" Aubrey said a second time. "Everything's in a muddle, isn't it? You're too damn busy enjoying yourself, but I've got a responsible boast—post, I mean, damn it. I mean I don't want to be immodest, but I've got a responsible post, and if we aren't careful, the whole thing's going to fall through."

"What thing are you talking about?" Jimmy asked impatiently.

"The thing, of course, the deal. The deal we're doing with Switzerland, the eighteen million pound deal to supply ER's. Now do you understand? I've got commitments. We can't let the Swiss down, but this bloody strike is going to put us all behind-hand."

Shaking his head, Jimmy looked appealingly at Alyson.

"What strike does he mean? The strike he got on his nose?"

"Why don't you read the papers?" Aubrey asked savagely. He heaved himself out of the chair, standing tensely erect. The blood was returning to his face now, making him look less like a Chinese mask at a Kung Hee Fat Choy festival.

"I'm too busy to read the papers," Jimmy said.

"Yes, too busy enjoying yourself!"

"I'm not enjoying myself!"

Crossing heavily to the dinerette, Aubrey pulled the evening paper off one of the chairs. Dramatically and offensively, he held it under Jimmy's nose. Black headlines announced that steelworkers were striking all over the country, following a lead set by Cadaver Alloys, manufacturers of the metal discs of the ER's. So much Jimmy saw before knocking the paper from his brother's grasp.

"Let's go to bed," he said.

Alas, the discrepancy between what we intend and what we do is frequently obvious even to ourselves. Once between the sheets, Jimmy realised that far from putting his brother in his place, he had merely behaved boorishly.

Aubrey was under strain and obviously needed a little consideration.

Jimmy had, in fact, read of the strike in the steel industry. It had made so little impression on him that he had failed to connect it with Aubrey, or even with the BIL. Strikes, after all, were pretty remote affairs staged in pretty remote factories, except for occasional unfortunate exceptions like the transport strike of '58. It was well known that those sort of people were out for all they could get.

Besides, the papers were full of gloom at present, if you looked hard enough. The drought. The British Ambassador kicked out of Jordan or wherever it was. The plague of caterpillars in Somerset. The recession in America making itself felt over here. The Pope's condemnation of ER's. The birth of three- and four-legged babies in Japan. Outbreaks of mutiny here and there in the British Army. And all the rest of it. One had to take it with a pinch of salt.

It was no good being pessimistic.

X. Scryban Becomes Involved

The Haiti collection was growing. A Bible belonging to the mulatto President Boyer; contemporary lithographs of the sumptuous coronation of Emperor Faustin I; the white, yellow, green and crimson uniform of the first Count of Limonade; a tattered poster from the theatre at Port Royal; a blow-up, loaned by BOAC, of the citadel on La Ferrière; the photographs of Marie-Louise's grave in Pisa; and many other enticing exhibits had already been assembled. Jimmy sat in his room in the IBA, staring rather blankly at them all.

The organising of the exhibition had become more than a job of work to Jimmy. Haiti with its tropical climate and extraordinary history had ensnared him. Above all, it was the brief reign of Henri Christophe, the king known simply to his subjects as "L'Homme," which fascinated him. That Negro, who created a fully functioning state out of chaos by persistent resolution and ingenuity (and who made all that the British government was now doing look unimaginative), seemed to Jimmy the most surprising, if not the greatest monarch, who had ever lived.

This morning, however, after the enormous *gaffe* made by his brother the previous night, Jimmy had other things than Henri on his mind. He shrank from meeting Donald, fearing that their friendship might now be frosted over; for although he resented how fashionable Donald's affliction had become generally, he was personally very fond of the librarian.

The inter-com phone rang. Jimmy jumped.

"Solent," he said.

It was Donald.

"Jimmy? Your book from the Sam Untermeyer Heights University has arrived. Would you like to come up and get it?"

"I'm on my way, Don."

As he climbed the stairs, nodding dumbly to Mrs. Charteris—there still seemed nothing to say to her—Jimmy knew Donald had not changed. His voice over the phone betrayed no hint that anything had happened. Charladies burst gossiping from lecture room to lecture room. Behind the door labelled "House Organ," Bloody Trefisick could be heard bellowing at his secretary. All was well with the world, now as ever.

Donald was still unpacking the book, loaned specially for the Haiti exhibition, when Jimmy entered his work-room behind the library. It was a small, calf-bound volume entitled "La Partie de Chasse du Roi," 1820, and was the last book ever to issue from Henri Christophe's royal press in the shadow of La Ferrière. Within a year of its printing, Henri was self-slain by a golden bullet, his son murdered, his Queen and daughters smuggled off to Europe. Just to hold the volume filled Jimmy with a stir of emotion.

"Having *books* in your exhibition!" Donald said. "What would our founder say?" He did a curtsy in the direction of the nearest photo of Clyde B. Nitkin and put on a broad transatlantic accent. " 'Material wealth is when both ends meet; intellectual poverty is when book ends meet.' Moral: don't leave your wooden elephants cheek to cheek or Nitkin will take you to tusk."

"Cease this elephantine humour," Jimmy said, adding as he caught sight of the science fiction magazine on Donald's desk, "What's Campbell on about this month?"

"Evolution and religion," Donald said. "It's quite in-

119

teresting. The theological view is that Earthmen are in a fallen state, consequently any improvements in our lot the sciences may effect are not worth a curse. From the evolutionary point of view, on the other hand, we cannot be fallen since we've hardly had time to rise: it's only some two hundred and fifty generations since the Bronze Age. The climb we've got to make is worth making for its own sake, whatever may be at its destination."

"It is if we think it is."

"Do you think it is?" Donald asked.

"Frequently. Just as I don't believe in Heaven but am fully cognizant of hell, I don't believe in progress but fear stagnation."

"My dear fellow, how very contemporary of you!" Donald said. "Your intellectual flowering is wasted in this backwater—it's positively gilding the lily!"

"How do you feel about it then?" Jimmy asked, unsure, as he often was, whether Donald was indulging in sarcasm or self-defence.

"I have no right to any feelings about progress or evolution," Donald said. "Your brother made it quite clear last night that people on the right side of the fence regard my kind as anti-evolutionary. And of course from that point of view he's perfectly right. This horrible, blind daft, thing called evolution has no interest in feelings; its only concern is propagation of the next generation. But to return to science fiction, these boys are really happy about the Norman Lights, you know. It's something right out of their stable. They haven't been more cock-a-hoop since the Earth satellites went up."

Grateful for this change of topic, Jimmy said, "Did I ever tell you Scryban caught me reading a collection of science fiction stories when I was first here? He picked it up, examined it, and then quoted Shakespeare: 'This is an art, which does mend nature, change it rather; but the art itself is nature.'"

"Hm. He did the same thing on me. Same quotation."

"How disappointing of him! A neat little tag for every situation. I regret to say I always suspected it of him."

"Well, you know what they say, Jimmy. Doesn't matter how bloody daft you act, provided you talk sense."

Jimmy slunk back to his room, clutching the precious copy of "La Partie de Chasse du Roi." He threw it onto his desk and sat down with a sigh, Donald's words echoing in his mind, "Doesn't matter how bloody daft you act. . . ."

"If anyone has ever acted bloody daft, I have," Jimmy told himself. "Getting mixed up with Rose was the work of an idiot. Getting mixed up about her is the work of twenty idiots. God, but it's like poison in the blood; I can't get rid of it. It's like a fatal illness. The mere brute fact that I shall never see her again—that I hate and detest her—makes no difference. I still want her. I had carnal knowledge of her, and now I'm in a state I can only describe as carnal ignorance. It's like a smell under your nose; it may be a beautiful smell, but you don't want it with every lungful of air you take. If only I could shake it off, pull myself together."

He was still sitting there picking his past over when Mrs. Wolf came in. It had become a habit with her to drop in and chat for a few minutes, generally before coffee; though they could hardly be said to have much in common, they passed the day pleasantly enough. This morning, though, Mrs. Wolf had more than gossip on her mind.

"Jimmy, my dear, have you spoken to Conrad Scryban this morning?" she asked, her mascara'd eyes wide. When Jimmy said he had not, she continued, "Without wishing to say anything at all behind his back—you know how I feel about good personal relationships—I really fear the poor dear man has gone crackers."

"You intrigue me. What makes you think that?"

Mrs. Wolf said: "Conrad has joined the Bourgoynists."

Thoughtfully, Jimmy took his fountain pen off the desk and sucked the end of it.

"Yes, it is odd; I mean, I know people are still signing on with the GREP, but old Scryban's hardly the type. . . ."

"It's more than odd," Mrs. Wolf said impatiently. "It's frightening. I can't think what's coming over people."

She broke off, looking round in surprise as the door burst open. Martin Trefisick, the Devon-born Cornishman, came in, his face a deep crimson enlivened by touches of aquamarine.

"Veronica," he shouted at Mrs. Wolf—it was the first time he had spoken to her for weeks—"Veronica, has Scryban had you in his room this morning, maundering out his bloody rubbish?"

"Yes," she said. "Though I would hardly call it *rubbish.*

I was in there with him about ten minutes ago, and he had Miss Redfern in before me—"

"He's having the whole bloody staff in there one at a time," Trefisick shouted. He stamped round the room in fury, breathing like a pair of bellows.

"What is all this?" Jimmy asked. "What did Scryban say?"

"Say? What did he say? What do you think he said? He had the confounded cheek to ask me—*me!*—to join the Bourgoynists."

"That's what he wanted me to do," Mrs. Wolf said, adding coolly. "But I should have thought he was on more promising ground with you, Martin. After all, you have stubbornly refused to have your ER installed."

"So I should think! A pity there aren't more individuals like me about! But just because I refuse to be regimented, is that any reason why I should be expected to associate with that crackpot of a fellow Bourgoyne and his rabble? Do use a bit of sense, Veronica! Bloody sauce, I call it, interfering with our private opinions—not that I've ever attempted to keep my opinions private. I hate the mere thought of wearing a silly tin medal in my skull."

In the heady glow of fulmination, Trefisick knocked heedlessly into the bookcase, sending a pile of IBA pamphlets slithering to the floor. Jimmy grew very tired of this display; the man was plainly enjoying this excuse to wallow in his anger like a sausage in batter.

"If you feel so badly about Norman Lights, I should have thought your obvious course was to join the GREP," he remarked, cutting off Trefisick in full spate. "As you say, they take all sorts."

Thrusting out his jaw, Trefisick turned on Jimmy.

"It's all a question of principle, Solent. I wouldn't expect you to understand. Your generation is all the same; you don't know how to vote or think or act. You're stumped from the word 'go', a poor wishy-washy lot. So just keep your mouth shut, will you?"

"I like that!" Jimmy exclaimed, jumping up. "You barge in here and lout about round my room like a prison warder with all Dartmoor to himself, and then you expect me to say nothing while you air your ruddy prejudices. You can—"

"Solent!" Trefisick roared. "Solent! I'll have you flung out of here on your neck! If you think I'm going—"

The house phone rang.

"Please both of you stop shouting and answer that phone," Mrs. Wolf said. "There is really no need to argue."

"That's the whole trouble with England today!" the Cornishman said, changing his tack. "Nobody can see any need to argue. 'Never mind discussing anything, let's join a group; then we needn't think.' Do you wonder the whole bloody system's falling to bits? Veronica, you surprise—"

"Yes, Solent here, Mr. Scryban," Jimmy said with emphasis into the mouthpiece of the phone, smiling cynically when Trefisick instantly fell silent. "Yes, I'll come up at once."

He put the phone down again.

"Your turn," Mrs. Wolf said, with detectable complacency. "Now don't you let him talk you into anything."

Going out through the exhibition room, Jimmy nodded wordlessly to Mrs. Charteris and took the lift up to Scryban.

Scryban sat at his desk with his hands clasped on it, rolling a little tub of harlequin matches to and fro. His pipe with the amber mouthpiece was clasped between his teeth, unlit. He looked at once grave, flustered, and a little pleased with himself. A slight red line on the jaw of his well-tended countenance showed that this morning Scryban had cut himself shaving.

Nodding to Jimmy and indicating a chair, he said, in a brisker manner than he usually employed, "From the roaring I heard over your phone, I take it that Martin Trefisick was with you; in which case I have no doubt that you arrive with some notion of what I am about to say."

He glanced sharply at Jimmy, continuing without waiting for his assent.

"It is Thursday today. On Saturday evening the ER Installation Centres will be closing down all over the country. On Monday, September 2, fines and imprisonment will be the lot of all those who have declined to visit the centres. It will be called prosecution; it will be persecution.

"Perhaps you will realise that my views of politics have tended to incline, in the past, towards the frivolous. I admit it—and it is a common error, Solent. For though politics is a weighty matter, who can take politicians seriously?

123

If you remember your 'New Grub Street'—an underestimated work by an underestimated man—you will recall Reardon's riddle, 'Why is a London lodging-house like a human body?' and its answer, 'Because the brains are always at the top.' In the body politic, this does not apply. The talkers are on top, the thinkers underneath; the dissemination of Demosthenes, that smooth-tongued lawyer, by our public schools and universities, has combined with methods of televisual publicity to corrupt our governmental system from the top; Or perhaps it is as the Persian proverb has it, that a rotten fish stinks from the head. It is difficult to diagnose certainly when one is oneself part of the malady. However,—"

It occurred to Scryban that he was wandering from the subject. He frowned at the lapse, at the same time stroking his tonsure with some complacency.

"To reserve judgement is an English habit," he continued, "and that is what many of us have done since ER's were first introduced. We hoped indeed that the governmental view of these devices as simplifiers of life might prove correct; in the event, I think it has proved incorrect. The end has failed to justify the always doubtful means."

"I can't quite agree with that," Jimmy said, his voice husky with disuse.

"I am talking not of particular cases, but of the country generally. Trouble is universal, violence endemic, licentiousness rampant. There is mutiny in the army, idleness in the factories and, so I hear, unrest even at the Foreign Office. All this is attributable to the introduction of Norman Lights. They are, you see, installed under a terrible misconception, which should have been recognised as such months ago, before the whole lunatic scheme was put into effect. The misconception is, of course, that sex plays a dominant part in people's lives."

"You mean you think it doesn't?" Jimmy asked in surprise. With the plastic venetian blinds down against the sun, it was quiet in Scryban's room. The traffic in the Tottenham Court Road snored distantly.

Allowing himself a sickly sarcastic smile, Scryban said, "Sex is as much the preoccupation of this century as reason was of the eighteenth. Unfortunately, we have the mechanical means of raising our preoccupation to godhood. We shall be enslaved by that which we should conquer. That is why there is a twofold reason for rejecting the ER. In a not unimportant sense, we become slaves of our government when we permit these things on our forehead; in a much deeper sense, we also become slaves of ourselves. Our baser selves."

Although he delivered this speech with earnestness and what, for him, was simplicity, Conrad Scryban spoilt the effect by leaning back at the end of it to survey Jimmy with a kind of proprietorial interest. The mere look of him turned Jimmy into an Unloveable Young Person.

"I can see you are naturally worried about what will happen to you next Monday," he said, "but what can *I* do about it? I've got my ER, I'm content with it, and on the whole I think they're a good thing. All right, there's a spot of bother in the country just now, but it'll sort itself out once the new system's working properly. Any new invention seems like the end of the world when it first appears, especially to the older generation."

Scryban jumped up and walked about behind the desk, ineffectually trying to light his pipe with a succession of harlequin matches.

'You won't think for yourself," he said. "As I tell you, I originally reserved judgement. But all I can see is that conditions are growing worse."

"That seems to me more a question of temperament than judgement," Jimmy observed.

"It's no good getting irritable," said Scryban irritably. "I've had a circularised letter from Bourgoyne this morning; that's why I'm speaking to you all personally. He points out that the country will be ruined, economically and financially, by the end of the year if present trends continue. The government must be forced from office and the compulsory ER laws rescinded."

"What does Bourgoyne expect you to do about it?" Jimmy enquired curiously.

"You've heard about the Protest March on Sunday?"

Jimmy did not like to admit his ignorance: he sat tight, letting it be presumed he took the question for a rhetorical one.

"So you haven't heard?" Scryban said, to let him know the gambit had failed. "Well, this is Bourgoyne's last attempt to stir up public feeling in the country. To my mind, he has chosen a ripe moment; when people know the government will be forced to act drastically next week.

He is personally leading a Protest March from Wembley Stadium to Chequers, where Gascadder will be in residence. The marchers leave the stadium, after an oration and a blessing from the Bishop of Coventry, at nine o'clock sharp on Sunday morning and reach Chequers by tea time. I have decided to join the march, and I was hoping that you would care to come with me, as a sign that your personal and social conscience is not dead."

Something rather helpless in his look of appeal almost won Jimmy over. He would have liked, for Scryban's sake, to march with Scryban. Then he imagined the other people he would have to march with, pictured the rash of Aertex shirts; the damp patches underarms; the hideous frocks of the women; the yelps of unwearying urchins; the accompanying impedimenta of bags of buns and bottles of pop; the silly banners; the aroma of sweat when the march was on and the bathetic milling around when it was over; and above all the spurious camaraderie engendered by the whole self-conscious affair, expressing itself in the shared vacuum flask, the would-be witty joke, the slap on the back.

"Sorry. It's not my cup of tea at all," he muttered and stood up to end the interview.

"It's so much easier not to get involved in anything, isn't it, Solent?" Scryban remarked without sympathy as he watched Jimmy walking out. After another abortive attempt at lighting his pipe, he turned glumly to the phone and summoned Donald Hortense.

No sooner had Jimmy emerged into the corridor than he was seized by Mrs. Wolf. She almost dragged him into her room, digging her sharp and brightly painted nails into his wrist. She shut the door behind them with a little gasp.

"I had to get you in here or that terrible man Trefisick would have cornered us again!" she exclaimed, staring avidly up at him. "Oh Jimmy, I've only just got away from him—he'd talk the hind legs off a donkey. He's outside now. Well, what did Conrad have to say to you?"

Jimmy offered the she-wolf a cigarette and took one himself. He was not sure how comfortable he felt about being closeted in here.

"Quoted Gissing, said the country was going to pot, wanted me to hike out and talk to the Prime Minister about it—me and some others," he summarised briefly.

"Poor dear Conrad," Mrs. Wolf said unexpectedly. "I

do so sympathise with him! I have always thought of him as the martyr type, one who would one day impale himself on a lost cause. He's out of his wits, and yet . . . He may be wrong, but he's admirably wrong."

"Oh, I don't know, you know," Jimmy said; it was his blundering attempt to suggest that Conrad Scryban might be right and the idea of a protest march wrong; but that in neither case was he sure; and that he rather distrusted the certainty with which other people seemed to weigh up a given situation.

"He's a Cambridge man," he added, thinking vaguely that to know all was to excuse all.

Anxious not to argue, Mrs. Wolf brightened and seized his arm. "Never mind, Jimmy," she said. "I've an idea; why don't you come and spend the week-end with my husband and me; we get on splendidly now, so there will be no embarrassment; and my mother will be there—you'll like her. I can drive you down with me on Saturday afternoon. The protest marchers will be bound to pass through Surrogate on their way to Chequers. We can watch them from the house; we should get a splendid view from the upper rooms. It will be rather fun to see Conrad Scryban at the head of them, striding along with a banner; perhaps we can offer him refreshment as he goes by. You will come, won't you?"

"That is exceedingly kind of you," Jimmy said.

"Not at all, not at all; I should have asked you before, had things been easier between Kenelm and me." She had the authority and the colour of good luggage as she whisked back into the corridor, still talking brightly—eager, scaly, metropolitan.

At the head of the stairs, by an unseeing bust of Nitkin, Bloody Trefisick was waylaying Donald Hortense, exhorting him not to go in and listen to Scryban's nonsense. Donald, who evidently knew what was in the wind, wore an ominous look of patience like a mask on his face.

"All I'm trying to say," Trefisick emphasised, banging his fist on the newel, "is that Scryban is overstepping his authority by speaking to us at all on this subject. *Books* are his line, not politics—or sex, for that matter, ha! You'd be well-advised to ignore his summons, Donald, believe me. The man shouldn't be encouraged. It's none of his bloody business."

Donald presented the appearance of one locking himself inside a tomb of self-control.

"Mr. Trefisick, Scryban is a diffident man. In his contacts with us, he shores up this diffidence behind a little dyke of learning and quotation. You can imagine then— or you could if you had any imagination—the great effort of will-power it must take for him to speak to us on this matter; it shows how strongly he must feel about it. The least we can do is humour the man and listen to him and let him get it off his chest."

"But he's got nothing *on* his chest except a lot of hot air about some bloody silly parade! "

"I'd prefer, if you'll let me by, to listen to that rather than your blood-and-bluster."

So saying, Donald pushed past the would-be Cornishman.

Trefisick's neck turned plum colour.

"You're all the same, you Unloveable Young People— think you've seen through everything, and you can't see the nose on your own face! "

Without answering or looking around, Donald knocked on Scryban's door and entered.

"God Almighty," Jimmy remarked to himself as he went down to the cafeteria and collected his morning's coffee. "Here you have a simple thing, Scryban's wish to discuss something important. And you have four of us, the she-wolf, Bloody Trefisick, Donald, and me, all more or less of the same chunk of society. Yet we all four react differently. Amazing how even between people with much in common, irreconcilable divergences can exist—Rose English and me, for a painful example.

"Everyone's muddled up, even those who pretend to know. I was wrong myself, of course, in the first place. I'm always dashed well doing the wrong thing; I wonder just how noticeable it is? I thought that getting an ER was simply a personal decision. It's not. It's not that, and it's not an open and shut case either.

"Oh God, it's politics, of course. The fate of the country depends on it, and the destiny of Western man. It's the way out of the intellectual traffic-jam of the sixties. (Funny how directly you get onto a political level, the clichés flitter up like humming birds, cutting you off from reality.) But Europe never thought of ER's; it's too sunk in pessimism. How many people over here really care about what's happening, really care enough to be pessimistic?

I know I don't. I *try* to care. But I don't. I'm a materialist bastard; I don't really want it, but I've swallowed the materialist bribe, swallowed it whole. New clothes, a smart woman, a car, wine—God, I've fallen for the lot and I never really meant to. It's funny. . . . Once upon a time, I intended to be the cultural type. You don't think about it for months at a stretch, then you suddenly realise where you've got to.

"But after all, where the hell else is there to go? Certainly not on this ostentatious hiking lark with Scryban."

Finishing his coffee, Jimmy headed back for the peace of his room, but was stopped in the foyer by a cry from Mrs. Charteris.

His conscience still sore, Jimmy imagined she was at last about to burst into a tirade and confront him with never finding anything to say to her; instead, to his relief, she announced that a call had just come through for him.

"I'm going to my room. I'll take it from there."

"Thank you, Mr. Solent. It's from a Mr. Guy Leighton."

The conscience ceased to worry as the heart began to nag. Jimmy knew this was going to be something about Rose; his heart whirled up and down inside his chest like a maniac's yo-yo.

XI. "A Bit of a Let Down"

Guy Leighton was coy; Guy Leighton was forceful; Guy Leighton was, as usual, knowing. Guy, in fact, had found out "all about Rose," as he put it. But Guy Leighton refused to divulge his latest knowledge over the phone, and accordingly Jimmy arranged—reluctantly, with misgivings, but nevertheless arranged—to meet him at a public house a good deal nearer the BIL than the IBA.

Jimmy arrived first. Before he got there, a fight had broken out in the saloon bar; the loser had been carted off by his friend, but the winner, a sturdy young fellow without an ER, was still there celebrating. Although he took no interest in the affair, Jimmy gathered from snatches of overheard conversation that the quarrel had been about the wearing of Norman Lights. The loser had called the winner "a sexless so-and-so"; the winner had called the loser a "dirty little conformist"; and so blood and beer had been spilt. The atmosphere was still extraordinarily tense with the sort of itching-trigger-finger sensibility more usually associated with the bars in Hollywood Westerns.

Jimmy could not care less. A newspaper soaking on the bar by his elbow announced an unofficial strike at Smithfield Market; porters there were refusing to load lorries driven by men belonging to a union whose secretary had spoken sympathetically of the GREP movement. Life was indeed complicated, but so were Jimmy's feelings. He downed a dry sherry, following it desperately with a drambuie as he wondered why he had agreed to come here at all.

When Leighton came padding in on the balls of his feet, with the awful air of a ballet dancer turned cabinet minister, Jimmy tackled him straightaway.

"Look, Guy, old lad, I'm sorry about this, but I'm really here under false pretences. I may have given you the impression over the phone, in a moment of weakness, that I still retained some sort of interest in this woman Rose. It isn't so. She's right out of my system now, and it would bore me stiff to hear about her. So let's talk about the weather, eh?, or the unofficial strike at Smithfield. And how do you feel now about the plague of caterpillars in Somerset?"

Without bothering to look as if he had heard a word, Guy seized Jimmy's arm and led him into a corner. Scowling, he looked over his shoulder at the nearest drinkers.

"For heaven's sake, stop being so ruddy impressive," Jimmy said loudly.

"Ssh, not so loud, Solent. You're not yourself this morning. Listen to me: this woman is one of the Normans, *the* Normans."

He paused to let this register, then continued.

"What is more, she's the crucial Norman. She's *Rachel* Norman, ma Gwendoline Norman's daughter by her first husband. Do you realise she's the king-pin of this whole business? She's the king-pin, Solent, hiding under the alias of Rose English. Now do you wonder we bit off more than we could chew?"

Jimmy shook his head.

"I'll get us a drink," he said.

He returned, slopping two beers, to find Guy sitting in the corner and staring blankly into space.

"Are you *sure* about this, Guy? What did she go and change her name for?"

"It's an alias," Guy said stupidly. "She's that kind of woman. You know, you expect a woman to be just a woman—not a woman, absolutely a woman, with the qualities of a man. Honestly, Solent, I'll tell you frankly, it's still like a knife in me to think of her, and I've not seen her since the night she picked you up at Sir Richard's party. And it was a couple of months before that that I . . . oh, that she picked me up."

He lapsed into glum silence. Jimmy knew what Guy was looking at: that same terrible image that he was, an image of a determined body powered by an equally determined mind, an irresistible whole that had its own flavour like poison. Jimmy faced it now, after dodging it with fair success for several weeks. It was at once obscene and comforting to have Leighton here suffering in the same way.

It churned all over in his mind again, the apocalyptic evening by the swimming pool, the inseparable, no less revealing, conversation in the canteen. He was detached enough from it to judge it now. The moralists were perfectly, boringly, undeniably, right about promiscuity. He had not known what he was letting himself in for, and he had been harmed. But Rose—Rachel—she was not promiscuous; it was not a word one applied to her; she only lived her life.

His life was a mere caper through a sherry jungle. On the way he had met a man-eater.

"For God's sake, Guy," he said, "why did she change her name?"

"I tell you, she invented the NL," Guy said. He took a gulp at the beer, pulling himself together, and something of his BIL manner returned. It was like an oyster closing its shell. "At least, she almost invented it. She is Gwendoline's daughter by her first marriage. As you know Gwendoline Norman—or actually Gwendoline Demyanski—remarried in 1948, after the second world war. She and Ivan put in the neurological theory behind the Emotion Register project, but Rachel contributed just about all the technical side, which represents the really big advance."

He shrugged rather wearily.

"She's a dedicated woman, Solent. That's the whole truth of her. A dedicated woman. Nothing stands in the way of her work. Hence the assumed name: it enables her to carry on incognito, without publicity or fuss or other interruptions. But, by golly, they're a tight lot. Iral's an establishment within the Establishment. I told you I was investigating. Well, even at Ghearing and Flower, where Rachel works *pro tem*, they don't know who she really is. Still I sorted it out. There are ways if you ask the right questions in the right places."

In a little flush of complacency he drank again.

"Probably only half a dozen people in the world know what she does," he said. "And probably only half a dozen people know who she is. I don't think Sir Richard knows. I hope you're impressed, Solent."

Solent was unable to raise the fished-for compliment.

"It took me all my cunning, Solent, believe me. Do you know, she has a permanent suite at the Debroy Dalmar—under her assumed name—with a sort of personal bodyguard in attendance."

"What good does this information do now you've got it?" Jimmy enquired bluntly.

Leighton's eyelids half-closed; perhaps he was inwardly crossing himself.

"The truth, Solent, shall set you free. I hoped to show you the impossibility of hope and the futility of desire where Miss Rose English and you were concerned."

"That's a bit of a *tu quoquo*," Jimmy answered grumpily. He suspected altruism formed no part of Guy Leighton's character. That he had told Jimmy at all probably signified only that he was burning to divulge his surprising news somewhere and had divulged it where he knew it would hurt most.

They began to speak perfunctorily of the awful state of the country. But there too Guy had inside information that the worst was yet to come; feeling extravagantly tired of him, Jimmy stood up and announced he must get back to work.

"The tragedy is," Guy said, rising also and abandoning all pretence of interest in any subject but Rachel Norman, "that she seemed to have the ideal attitude to—well, to anything; she appeared the ideal woman. They're frightfully hard to come by; the more you see, the more choosy you get."

"She was a bitch," Jimmy said vindictively. He kept seeing her, sitting back detachedly, saying, "You didn't give me a thing." Of course he had given her nothing; his comprehension of the erotic impulse was entirely amateur.

As he and Guy got to the door, preparing to part, Guy said, "This is all top secret, Solent; perhaps I was foolish to have spoken. I must put you on oath not to tell a soul what I have told you."

Already he was regretting his indiscretion.

"My lips are sealed," Jimmy said.

"If I'd had more cash in the bank, I might have had better—longer, success with her," Guy said bleakly as he turned away. Moving off in the other direction, Jimmy reflected how much of himself Guy inadvertently revealed in that remark. He would recall the remark again—and with dismay—before the week was up.

He did no work that afternoon. He sat at his desk in a brown study, the sound of traffic coming to him like Matthew Arnold's melancholy, long, withdrawing roar. Nor was anyone else in the IBA building much more active. Nor was the IBA alone in this. Bourgoyne's circular making a last appeal for support had gone out in its hundreds of thousands, sowing dissension everywhere. A week earlier, it might have been screwed up and forgotten; but the timing was good. On Monday—everyone felt it—the world would be changed. It would be a new, an ER world.

Even the great majority who had scrambled to be first to wear the new toy, even those who genuinely saw in the Norman Light a new, better, way of life, paused and wondered. An epoch was ending; nostalgia blossomed for it overnight, and the universal fondness for the safe, unalterable past burst baying like a hound onto the scene.

It found eloquent expression the next morning, Friday, in a procession of stage and cinema actors and actresses who made a three mile march round central London. Some of the best-known names in show business were there; although the press raised a delighted, high-pitched shout about it, the procession itself observed the utmost decorum. Indeed, everyone was dressed in black and carried black umbrellas, though the sun shone bright. They mourned the death of the drama.

At Hyde Park Corner, a mock funeral was performed, and over the corpse of past glory the First Lady of the Stage pronounced these words: "We come not to praise drama but to bury it. Its death is our death. How can we any longer face the footlights when from Monday on all of us will wear headlights? Equipped with a flashing disc, would King Lear have the power to make us weep? Would Oedipus's plight seem anything less than ridiculous? Would Eliza Dolittle make sense? No, my friends, we are cut off from our past by the Emotion Register. To act in any play written before this year is to falsify it and ridicule ourselves. The modern world has finally eclipsed all that was good or valuable. Therefore we weep today, and on this ancient and honoured body I do not throw rosemary—that's for remembrance."

The actors mourned for artistic reasons. The strikers struck for financial reasons. Following closely in the steps of Switzerland and Belgium, Japan announced that it too would adopt the Emotional Register. This caused more consternation and excitement than the two previous announcements; Japan turned the whole business into a competition. In no time other countries would join the scramble. It was felt that they hung back only to see whether or not the British constitution had saddled itself with something it could not support.

Faced with this inrush of orders and the prospect of more, the country's industry trembled. A breath of inflation stirred the leaves of paybooks everywhere. To the discontents of those who were forced to work overtime were added the discontents of those unable to work overtime. It only needed the dismissal of an arrogant shop steward at Cadaver Alloys and machines idled everywhere as what the workers regarded as a fight for fairer conditions developed into another round of the teratogenic struggle between trade union and government.

The members of the armed forces who mutinied did so at first for very simple reasons. They were ordered to polish their ER's.

To soldiers whose nerves were already tried to the utmost by the rigours of peace, this order came as the last affront to their personal pride, the last straw in a haystackful of disciplinary needles. Almost overnight, the British Army became as active a group of freethinkers as the French Army in 1916.

In yet another group, that amorphous mass vaguely castigated by Mr. Noël Coward as "This Happy Breed," discontent was also rife. The Happy Breed—happy even at

134

the worst of times because of their amiable ability to find perpetual consolation in small things—had an uneasy feeling that something was awry. Mrs. Pidney put her finger deftly on the matter when Jimmy came home that Thursday evening.

"You look a bit brassed off, Mr Solent," she said, emerging from the kitchen as he let himself in.

"I was just going to say the same about you," he remarked.

"Go on! How did you guess? I been out this afternoon and bought myself a new dress just to try and cheer myself up, but somehow it didn't work." She shook her head sadly, making her veritable gazebo of hair tremble with regret.

"What's the trouble then?"

"Well, I suppose it's silly of me at my age, but you know it's these here ER's we've all got to wear. I was quite excited at first, I must say. I suppose I was expecting too much from mine. I mean, we all have our disappointments in life, of course, but these things come along and somehow I reckoned—well, it was just a feeling, if you get my meaning—that I'd get another chance, like. In the lists of love. You know, the beginning of a new era, see what I mean?"

"I do indeed," Jimmy said, leaning sadly over the banisters. Hilda Pidney was but echoing what he himself had said when dancing like a fool round the Hurns' swimming pool.

"The trouble was, they cracked these ER's up too much to start with," Mrs. Pidney said. "The Government at fault as usual. Here, I've got some tarts in my oven—I must go. But you see what I mean. We were all sort of excited at first. But now—well, nothing's much different from what it was before, see. I mean the baker pinks at me, but so what? We don't neither of us *do* anything about it. It was rather a lark at first, but we don't take no more notice of it now. It's all a bit of a let down, really."

She retreated sadly to deal with her tarts.

Wearily, Jimmy went upstairs. He lay on his bed reading until nine o'clock, when he took a bath and retired to sleep, resolving not to dream of Rose-Rachel. He had started with her on a Thursday, he wanted to finish with her on a Thursday—this Thursday.

On Friday a spurious peace reigned over the land. The nation, or such of it as was not on strike, unemployed, in mental homes or similarly disqualified, went to work as usual. Friday, even in time of crisis, is one of the more attractive days on which to be incarcerated in shop, office or factory since it both precedes the week-end and is commonly pay day.

At the IBA the business of diluting culture for the common good went on with almost its normal speed. Trefisick remained in a pet; Scryban remained in his room. Only in the evening was Jimmy Solent jolted out of that sunny complacency which never deserted him for long.

He was alone in the Charlton Square flat finishing his late tea when Alyson Youngfield came in. Aubrey still had not appeared; he usually worked on at the BIL until after eight o'clock these evenings. This explained—and Jimmy regretted that it was so—why Alyson appeared so little at the flat of late.

He stood up as she came in. He had forgotten how tall she was but not how delightful. She looked at him as if looking was not something just everyone did, smiling with that deceptive friendliness beautiful women achieve so easily.

"Hello stranger! Long time no see. Wur you bin all my life, honey? How the hell do you think your poor old uncle James survives without you, eh?" Jimmy asked, hoping desperately she could see through this asinine way of talking.

She could.

"I haven't exactly liked staying away, Jimmy," she said, coming over to him. She dropped her small handbag onto a chair and eyed him speculatively. Then she smiled, patting his arm.

"Er—Aubrey's not back yet."

"I know," she said. "I've been to see Vincent Merrick this afternoon. You know I was immediately taken with him when I met him."

"He's powerful, isn't he?" Jimmy agreed, instantly cast down by this news. "You don't mean—I mean, you aren't actually attracted to him, are you?"

"If you mean physically, of course I am not," Alyson said briskly, emitting a tiny laugh. "That's something you will be able to determine for yourself quite easily, when I get my disc. I went to ask Vincent's advice. By the way, the new Merrick-Kind clinic—Kind is his Canadian partner—opened this week. He has invited me along on Monday afternoon and asked me to bring you as well. It should be interesting, don't you think? Apparently he has some sensational new method of treatment. Societal therapy, he calls it."

"Wait a minute! " Jimmy exclaimed. "Do you say you are going to get your ER at last?"

Alyson dropped her gaze and then turned away in a sort of embarrassment Jimmy could not understand.

"I think I really must," she said. "That was one of the things that I went to ask Vincent Merrick about."

"Oh, why ask him?! Why not ask me?! " Jimmy exclaimed. "I've been saying so for months. And all this week I've been worrying, Alyson—really I have. The thought of your having to go to prison—I should have gone mad or something. You mean so very much to me."

He had never understood why she had hesitated. In his delight at her capitulation he took her bare arms and swung her round. She had to smile at his overjoyed face. Pink light seemed to swirl round them like candy floss. Thoughtlessly he kissed her.

Throughout his system, corpuscles, chemistries, and compounds leapt into action, like firemen on a practice alarm. Her lips stirred a powerful confusion in him; his arms went round her in dizziness and love, making the confusion worse. The firemen, unsure of their proper posts, ran hither and thither, madly.

"Darling," Jimmy said, drawing breath, "darling, oh Alyson. . . ."

Over her shoulder, through the gold strands of her hair, he saw the door open and Aubrey enter, neat, precise and self-contained.

Immediately the firemen retired to their bunks. The fire had gone out. Alyson, Aubrey and Jimmy just stood there, looking and not looking at each other.

"You've got your Norman Light! " Jimmy exclaimed, at last taking in his brother properly.

The welter of guilty annoyance at being caught kissing Aubrey's mistress momentarily vanished under the crowning astonishment of seeing, in the middle of his brother's forehead, that blank silver disc.

His exclamation gave Alyson all the chance she needed to recover herself.

"I'm so glad you've got it, Aubrey," she said; and then, to Jimmy, "I rang him up from Vincent's to tell him that Vincent advised his getting it."

Still Aubrey said nothing.

Alyson spoke again.

"I had just come round to ask Jimmy to escort me down to the Installation trailer, to give me a little moral support while I had mine installed."

"*Moral* support!" Aubrey echoed ironically.

"I knew I should capitulate in the end. I couldn't hold out any longer. Unfortunately I'm not the stuff of which martyrs are made." She seemed not to be addressing either of them in particular; it was even doubtful whether the capitulation she mentioned referred to wearing an ER or to Jimmy's charms.

By accepting the former alternative, modesty and prudence dictated to Jimmy a way of escape from this trying tableau.

"I'll come down with you at once," he volunteered.

As he and Alyson moved tentatively to the door, Aubrey said, "I'd rather you stayed and spoke to me, Jimmy. Alyson will be all right; you don't feel a thing. She can come back here afterwards if she cares to."

"How hospitable of you," Alyson said coldly. Seeing Jimmy halt, she gave him a meaning look he was unable to interpret and left the flat. The brothers listened until they heard the flat door close behind her before either of them stirred.

Moving in an abstracted way, Aubrey went over to feel the teapot Jimmy had recently been using, nodded to himself, and fetched a cup from the kitchen. Having poured himself some of the lukewarm brew, he raised the cup as if toasting Jimmy.

"The old panacea!" he said, unsmiling.

"Aubrey, this is an extremely beastly situation," Jimmy began, but Aubrey interrupted him at once.

"I should like to explain to you exactly why I have gone against my better judgement and equipped myself with an Emotion Register," he said. "First of all, perhaps I had better tell you that I have ascertained just what will happen on Monday to anyone without a disc. The police are empowered to arrest them on sight. By mid-week summonses will be issued on all those whose names are not down on the Installation Centre rolls as having undergone the operation. They will be told to present themselves at the local court within twenty-four hours. So you can understand that by the end of next week all believers in the freedom of the individual will be under lock and key.

"As I have tried to explain before, I believe these discs are evil; they encroach on territory always regarded as sacred—a man's right to his private feelings. A few years ago brainwashing was universally condemned. How the ER, something infinitely more immoral, has come to be accepted, is beyond my comprehension."

Moodily, Jimmy looked out of the window, only half listening. He had heard Aubrey's sermons through before, believing it his duty as younger brother to listen, or appear to listen. He knew, moreover, that all this talk—however Aubrey himself regarded it—was merely a smoke screen behind which an attack on the Solent-Youngfield position was developing; and he resented the indirectness of the manoeuvre.

Looking down, Jimmy saw the grey trailer standing deserted in the middle of the parched space. The inhabitants of the square had ceased to notice it, although after tomorrow, when it was gone, they would doubtless miss it. In the doorway a man appeared in white overalls. He smoked a cigarette and looked across the cracked earth where grass had grown. Somewhere inside, behind him, Alyson would be lying back in a surgical chair while the little drill whatever it was bored a neat hole through her forehead bone.

As his mind veered queasily away from that thought, Jimmy became aware again of what his brother was saying.

".... only my difficult position at the BIL has persuaded me to overcome my moral objections. I cannot afford to be absent over the next fortnight serving a prison sentence. Our organisational problems increase daily; so much Iral sub-contracting has had to be switched to other plants at an hour's notice owing to impending strike action. If I were to let down Sir Richard now—well, I could hardly hope for consideration in the future. So I shall swallow my principles and submit to the operation.

"But I want you to understand how much anxious thought has gone into my—"

"Oh, I understand well enough," Jimmy said. "You

can't afford to be locked up or you'd lose your precious chance of promotion. It's as plain as black and white. Now let's talk about Alyson instead."

"Very well," Aubrey said, lighting a cigarette from his case with hands that shook slightly. "You realise for a start, don't you, that after what has occurred you will have to leave the flat. You have broken faith, haven't you? I won't pretend I'm not pretty disgusted."

"Ah, for heaven's sake, stop turning everything into moral riddles. Where does it get you? Why don't you face the facts?"

"All facts happen to have moral connotations. I've no wish to lecture you, but the sooner you realise there are certain definite rules of conduct the easier you'll find life."

"Let's go back to Alyson! I didn't mean to kiss her. It's something I've wanted to do for a long time, but all the same I didn't plan it that way. But do you think I'd have done it if I hadn't felt that, in theory at least, she also wanted me to do it? You can tell, Aubrey, you can always tell, unless you've blinded yourself with theories."

Aubrey was very pale now.

"And what if you can tell?" he asked. "Does that make it in any way right?"

"Does it make it in any way wrong? I know you've got a good old Christian theory that any natural instinct is wrong, but I've got a good old pagan idea that what a man wants is ultimately the best thing he can have. Where's the use in arguing with you about it though? We're just opposed. I think all the evidence proves my view is right, but that doesn't stop you clinging to your bigoted, outworn—"

He stopped.

From the corner of his eye, he saw movement in the square. Two people were moving by the trailer. The man in the white overall had tossed aside his cigarette and was leading Alyson down the ramp. She thanked him, coming on slowly alone. She was heading towards the flat. In the middle of her forehead, looking flat and dead in the waning light, was an Emotion Register.

"She's coming back here! " Jimmy said. "And she's got it on."

His hands felt decidedly clammy. He wanted Alyson; it had been a hypothetical need before she had actually been pressed against him. Now it was something for which he would fight Aubrey to the death. In a few minutes, however, Alyson herself would involuntarily show her own preference; that was something she was no longer able to conceal.

Jimmy looked furtively at his brother. Aubrey was adjusting his tie, smoothing his hair, lighting up another cigarette. Jimmy cleared his throat unhappily; smoothing his hair and adjusting his tie, he said, "Give me a cigarette, Aubrey, will you?"

As Aubrey held out his case, they heard Alyson coming slowly up the stairs.

XII. The Invaders Have Nice Manners

"The car's round the corner in Gower Street," Mrs. Wolf said, as she and Jimmy emerged into the sunshine from the cool interior of the IBA. She was in excellent form, her creased face matt-surfaced and thrust well forward. She took Jimmy's arm in a manner of half predatory, half motherly.

It was the Saturday lunch hour, and the streets ran with determined, rapid people. The week-end was upon them, the desire to leave London had them by the tail; already their inner eyes were upon some dusty picnic spot in Epping Forest, some flashy rendezvous in Surrey, some creaking deck chair at Brighton. And over the animated scene, cyclamen-coloured flashes played an erotic semaphore which no one heeded—or very few. Londoners had settled down to rubbing shoulders with sex in the same spirit that their seventeenth century counterparts had mingled with the plague.

"I'll get a paper," Jimmy said, jostling his way over to a news vendor.

"I must stop as we go through Chalfont," the she-wolf said. "I want to get some face tissues."

"It'll be wonderful to be away from London. The last few days have been pretty exhausting as far as I'm concerned."

"Me too. But Jimmy, you know we're the only two at the IBA who really believe ER's are a benefit to society."

They had been shouting at each other over intervening heads. Now, as Jimmy stuffed the newspaper into his pocket, they rejoined; again Mrs. Wolf ardently took his arm. It started a certain trail of thought. His Norman Light stuttered at her.

"I'm terribly sorry," he said, confused.

"Jimmy, you absolutely don't need to be. The car's down here. Soon this kind of thing will be accepted; nobody will take any notice of it, and we shall all be the freer for it. By nature I am no optimist; my life has been full of disappointments, but here I really see great hope for a more balanced future."

Their arrival at the car saved Jimmy from delivering a reply more cautious than might have chimed with Mrs. Wolf's mood.

In a few minutes they were edging into the rapacious summer streams of traffic in Southampton Row. Nothing is more pleasant on a pleasant day than to drive through the streets of London. On the one hand, the stop-and-go method of proceeding gives one a heady sense of competition with the vehicles packed tight on either side, on the other hand, the congestion promotes companionship, one passes and is in turn passed by drivers whose faces soon grow remarkably familiar; while on the third hand, the heat and petrol fumes rising in the narrow thoroughfares gradually induce a gentle euphoria in the voyagers. Jimmy slumped back in his seat relaxedly, fished his paper from his pocket and opened it.

His heart sank like shares in a Wall Street recession.

GREP COUP
NORMAN INVENTOR AND HEIRESS SEIZED
Bourgoyne Warms P.M.—"Take My Terms"

Beneath this barricade of headlines was a staggering tale of the kidnapping of Rachel Norman, daughter of Gwendoline Norman. Her name came up and hit Jimmy hard between the eyes. His Rose by any other name. . . !
She had been abducted from her London flat at breakfast time. Half an hour later a message had been received at 10 Downing Street from Big Bill Bourgoyne. He stated that Rachel Norman was in his hands and would be surrendered only upon a published governmental assurance

that no proceedings would be taken against the minority of the population who had refused to adopt ERs.

That, in effect, was all the news. But of speculation there was plenty. Would the government yield to this blackmail? And if they did not, what would become of this rich and beautiful girl who had so unselfishly, so inventively, served her country? Either alternative raised forbidding issues. If P.M. Gascadder and his government weakened, it was intolerable to think of the few people without Norman Lights remaining without for good, thus creating another privileged minority in a land already so overstocked with privileged minorities. But if Gascadder remained unmoved—well, nobody liked to think of that fantastic Bourgoyne posting that poor little girl to Number 10 in little parcels just like wedding cake!

This last desperate act of Bourgoyne's placed him, of course, outside the law. There was a reward on his head; police and military units were already combing the country for him. But Bourgoyne had gone to earth; no trace of him or his captive had been found.

"What's the news?" Mrs. Wolf asked, glancing round momentarily from her driving.

Jimmy told her, naturally omitting any mention of the way his and Rachel's paths had crossed.

"Don't sound so upset," Mrs. Wolf said. "They'll catch the blighter. He has made his last and biggest mistake, that's all."

A soggy mixture of lust and guilt settled on Jimmy. He loved Alyson; for her he would spend his years in toil and respectability, given the chance. But with Rachel it had been precisely the lack of the necessity for such prosaic ingredients in their love that had made it a thing unique. The best fed of us can remember an ice cream stolen in childhood all our lives.

"'Cheer up! '" said Mrs. Wolf, smiling flashily as she drove busily on.

And Jimmy did cheer up.

Chez Wolf was a comfortable house standing in about four acres of land on the outskirts of Surrogate. Surrogate itself was inconsiderable. The hill at its northern end formed an eminence from which Grey Cotes—for such was the name of the house—surveyed an acceptable amount of the surrounding countryside.

Mr. Kenelm Wolf was roughly twice the size of his wife and half as bright. He had a big, beefy face with a good nose and shiny complexion. His manner was invariably genial, though in repose his expression was glum; although he talked a great deal, chiefly about the glories of the insurance business, this hardly mattered to Jimmy since Mr. Wolf spent most of the week-end in a potting shed converted into a dark room. Microscopic photography was his hobby. A twice-decorated colonel in the Korean War, Kenelm had since worked his way up to one of the loftier pinnacles in the insurance world.

It would hardly be necessary to give even this brief précis of the life and works of Kenelm Wolf were it not that such facts, and many others, were the common stuff of almost every conversation Jimmy was submitted to in Grey Cotes. Mrs. Wolf and her mother, the aged Mrs. Crinbolt, spoke of practically nothing but Kenelm. It became evident that the installation of an ER upon a man hitherto regarded by those nearest and dearest to him as sexless had greatly increased his attraction. From a failure he had turned overnight into a mystery. Mrs. Wolf, with an avidity only the sex-starved can show, had seized upon every implication of the affair.

"You see Kenelm is different," she told Jimmy as they strolled down the drive after lunch on Sunday. "As he explained to me, there are many kinds of love. The ER's register only sexual love, don't they? But many other varieties of bond exist between couples. Spiritual bonds, and that sort of thing—I did tell you Kenelm studied Buddhism when he was in Korea, didn't I?"

With wonder, Jimmy reflected on the way Mrs. Wolf was made: perceptive one hour, self-deluded the next. It gave them, he felt, plenty in common.

On impulse he began telling her of the entanglements which existed between Alyson, Aubrey and himself. They reached the end of the drive as he began to speak.

The country lay brown and heavy and still all around them. Thick cloud piled up overhead, seeming to increase the heat. A jeep rattled surprisingly down the road with an officer driving and two other officers sitting alertly in the back, headed for Surrogate.

". . . . So Aubrey and I had what was for us a pretty bad row," Jimmy said, "and then Alyson came back to the flat with her Norman Light installed."

144

"It must have been a nasty moment!" Mrs. Wolf murmured.

"It was. I thought Aubrey was going to be sick. And you see until Alyson came in and saw which way her Light pinked, I really believe she wasn't sure how she felt about us herself. Your mind can be confused, but the Lights by-pass your mind. So she had to confront us with the truth."

"And which of you ...," prompted Mrs. Wolf.

It began to rain, the slightest, lightest patter in the beech trees, the first rain the Home Counties had experienced for weeks.

"She pinked at me." Jimmy said. "She couldn't help it, but she pinked at me. Just as I've been doing at her for months."

Mrs. Wolf squeezed his arm in congratulatory fashion.

"I hope we'll get married; I don't want to mess about as my brother has done," Jimmy continued dreamily. "But Alyson and I have had no chance to talk it over yet. I shall have to look out for a small flat of my own tomorrow after this row with poor old Aubrey. There's such a lot to do. . . . She's such a wonderful person. She seems to understand life; I mean, she's capable of judgement without judging all the time. Do you think we'll be suited?"

This unpretentious murmur was hardly intended as a question, but Mrs. Wolf answered it by saying, "How can I tell until I see her? You must bring her here one week-end."

They moved under the shelter of a beech tree, idly watching the rain scamper across the faded green countryside.

"But even if you saw her, how could you tell if we were ideally matched?" Jimmy asked in a sudden agony. Appearances never told you who was suited to whom. He had a memory of the formidable Vincent Merrick, for whom Alyson showed such respect, pinking at his dowdy little wife, Jasmine. There was a happy couple; it was a weird thought. The question arose, why were they happy? *How* were they happy?

Could it be because Merrick, as a psychiatrist, was intellectually capable of choosing the ideal partner to match his own inward nature? Or had he for this occasion put intellect behind him and trusted to his emotions, his intuition?

Would a time ever come when Jimmy might be able to formulate these questions in words to Merrick? No. That was certainly out. English society had so developed that the important questions might never be asked.

Mrs. Wolf did not reply to Jimmy's outburst. Instead, she said with forced brightness, "This must be the first rain for weeks. It will damp the ardour of the GREP protest Marchers. Poor Conrad! We had better get back to the house before we become too moist."

The rain fell very gently. Under the beech trees the drive remained parched and dry. As they walked back up it, a helicopter flew by, low over their heads. Since it seemed to be descending towards Surrogate, Jimmy turned to look at it. They had gone far enough up the drive for a section of the road on the other side of the village, hitherto eclipsed by nearby hedges, to rise into view.

Exclaiming aloud, Jimmy stopped and pointed at it. No more than a mile away, the stretch of road was clearly visible through the light curtains of rain, which had yet to reach it. A mass of people filled it from side to side, with vehicles and banners interspersed among the mêlée. The Protest March was on its way through Surrogate to Chequers.

"Grey Cotes stands in a very strategic position; let's go and watch from the house," Mrs. Wolf said. "They'll pass by the bottom of the drive. I only hope they are orderly and don't break down the rhododendron hedge."

As they climbed the front steps and entered the hall, with its genuine Brangwyn and reproduction Russell Flint, Mrs. Wolf called to her mother. Mrs. Crinbolt appeared almost at once, coming down the corridor and beckoning anxiously. Although nearly seventy-five, she was still a large, solid woman who bore herself well. Her white hair was fashionably but simply arranged. Through her thick, horn-rimmed glasses, she bestowed on the world the same vigilant and penetrating stare her daughter did.

"Veronica!" she said now. "I'm so relieved that you have come back. A man has just walked across the paddock—I saw him from the sun room window. I'm sure he has gone into the orchard to steal apples."

"Then you should fetch Kenelm, mother," said Mrs. Wolf. "Where is he?"

"He's in the potting shed."

146

"Then the man will have to help himself to apples. I have no inclination to go and confront him. There's nothing but maggotty windfalls this year, anyway, with the drought. Come up into the attic with us, mother, and watch the people going to Chequers; they'll be past the gates soon."

"How very wet the poor things will get. And perhaps the rain will drive the man out of the orchard. I shouldn't mind betting that it's one of the Spinks brothers; they're a real bad lot."

So saying, she followed slowly up the stairs after Jimmy and Mrs. Wolf, pausing on each landing for rest.

In the attic they arranged themselves in ancient, dusty chairs and looked out. The view was indeed magnificent, although its full extent was concealed by the rain, which still hesitated and withheld itself like a coy lover. The village of Surrogate lay in plain sight at the bottom of the hill, a genuine sample of rural England. It consisted of a corrugated iron cinema; a Strict Baptist chapel; a filthy garage; several dilapidated chicken farms; a seedy general store selling sweets, socks and jazz LP's; the Farmer's Boy Inn; a gigantic station like an aerodrome, labelled *Grass Research Establishment*; two military rows of council houses; three nondescript cottages; one nondescript bungalow; one wooden café, permanently closed; one power sub-station; a Low Baptist chapel; and several piles of gravel by the roadside.

The column of protest marchers had reached the village. Its head halted opposite the filthy garage while the rest of it was dispersing with curious alacrity into the ditches, back yards and fields on either side of the road. Of the cars also taking part in the procession many turned suddenly to left or right and bumped over the adjoining fields; none attempted to drive on through Surrogate for that way was closed to them by a tank parked sideways across the road. Its gun pointed menacingly down the road, its turret was open; from the turret an officer in a beret was haranguing the marchers through a megaphone.

"They've been stopped!" Jimmy exclaimed. "Good God, they're being turned back."

"But they aren't turning back," Mrs. Wolf said. "They're simply flowing round the obstruction."

"Oh, this must be the result of the special announcement on the wireless," Mrs. Crinbolt said. "I was going to tell you about it—it sounded so serious—and then seeing that fellow going into the orchard quite drove it out of my head."

"*What* special announcement?" Mrs. Wolf asked sharply.

Mrs. Crinbolt looked flustered.

Listening closely to what was being said, Jimmy was still looking out of the window watching the tiny figures down in the village. The rear part of the GREP procession was still moving up as the front dispersed. Meanwhile more soldiers had appeared, strung out thinly in lines on either side of Surrogate; they carried light machine guns aimed at the civilians and plainly meant to let nobody pass. This new move had caused many of the more determined marchers to seek a way past the obstruction through the gardens of the council houses. At this the owners had acted. Several fights were in progress. Jimmy saw a row of bean poles, heavily loaded with foliage, heel over as two men fell against it. Khaki figures ran up the road to squash the trouble.

It was all as remote and unreal as something happening on a military sand table; yet its very remoteness and smallness lent it an unnerving air, like something dreamed.

The officer with the beret, perched in the tank, suddenly doubled up and fell out of the turret. With the tank obscuring his view Jimmy could only see one leg kicking as the man rolled in the road. The GREP had fired its first shot in anger. Many of them now surged past the tank, which looked helpless with its slowly swivelling gun. A soldier jumped up in the turret and hurled something at the crowds.

As the smoke cleared over the road, boy figures could be seen clasping their eyes and blundering about.

Mrs. Crinbolt's clear voice was saying. "The announcer said a state of emergency has been proclaimed throughout the country. There had been rioting at Coventry and Bristol and somewhere else—Edinburgh, perhaps it was. Somewhere North, I know. A lot of people were hurt. The Prime Minister has forbidden demonstration of any sort, and the police and military have special powers—oh, and there's a curfew, Veronica. I was so appalled, I'm afraid I didn't get all the details. They are going to be repeated again at half past three."

"It's nearly that now," Jimmy said. "We'd better go down and hear what's happening. By the look of things a battle's about to begin in the village. The government are certainly doing their best to break up the protest march."

He ran down the stairs ahead of them, full of a strange excitement, far from unpleasant, rather as though he was going to see the second act in good drama. As he took the last flight a plane roared over the house. He ran full tilt into the drawing room where the radio and television were. An army captain was just entering the french doors from the terrace. Jimmy stopped abruptly.

"What do you want?" he asked.

The captain drew a revolver, pointing it at Jimmy. He was a rugged man of about forty-five, with a big rectangular face and an unmistakably pugnacious expression. A large square of sticking plaster covered his ER. As if to confirm that this was the man Mrs. Crinbolt had seen going into the orchard, an apple leaf adhered to the grizzled hair protruding from his beret. Wrapped round the gun butt, his right hand was large and red and hairy. He gave Jimmy a fighter's grin.

"How many others in the house, Jack?" he asked Jimmy, ignoring the other's question.

"What are you doing here?" Jimmy asked, staring fascinated at that raw beefy hand. "I suppose you realise this is a private house?"

The joyless interchange of questions was broken by Mrs. Wolf's entrance, her mother following closely behind. With grim authority the captain made them sit together on a sofa near the fireplace. Standing in front of them he surveyed them. He kept the revolver in his hand and looked very much in command.

"No harm'll come if you sit still," he said. "It just so happens that this dump is in a nice handy spot for us. We'll be using it for a couple of hours, and then you can have it back. *If* you behave. If you *don't* behave, I shall be forced to use this on you." He patted the gun.

"You have no right to speak to us like that in our own home," Mrs. Crinbolt said. "Don't think you'll be allowed to get away with it."

"I'm not going to argue the toss," the captain said, looking very ill-tempered. "Just bloody well keep quiet, that's all. Sit still and shut your traps and we'll all be okay."

Jimmy risked a side glance at Mrs. Crinbolt; her appearance suggested that she had never been sworn at before. The captain turned his back on them, walking over to the far side of the room, where a phone stood in an alcove. Perching himself on the flimsy phone table, he picked up the receiver, dialled "O" with the muzzle of the revolver and waited.

"Hello," he said at length. "Who's that? Put me through to Major Hobbes. This is Captain Biggs here. Put me through to Major Hobbes and buck up about it . . . Major Hobbes? Ken Biggs here. Yep, I'm in the house. No trouble at all. No, in the bag. How's it going with you? Good-o! Okay, yes, I'll stand by, Roger, good-bye."

"They must have captured the telephone exchange," Mrs. Wolf whispered agitatedly to Jimmy. "That's at Amersham. There is a barracks there."

As he hung the phone up, a clock struck three-thirty. The rain redoubled its strength.

"Excuse me, do you mind if I close the french doors?" Mrs. Crinbolt said. "The carpet is getting wet."

"It won't hurt. Leave it," Captain Biggs said. Going over to the wireless, he switched it on.

A state of emergency existed, said the tinned voice, gathering strength. Strikers at protest meetings throughout the country had been causing damage in several main centres of population. Some Army units had mutinied en masse and were causing trouble, chiefly by disrupting lines of communication. Agitators had stirred up violence, and there had been much damage to shops and government property, especially at Coventry, Bristol and Glasgow. Hand-to-hand fighting in the streets was still going on in parts of Liverpool and London. Everyone was advised to stay indoors. It was hoped that all unruly elements would be crushed before dark; in the meantime, a curfew—

"They'll be bloody lucky," the captain exclaimed. "They've got a civil war on their hands, did they but know it." He switched the set off with unnecessary violence.

Nobody said a word. The captain grew restless and walked up and down, thrusting his jaw out.

He turned with obvious relief when another khaki figure emerged from the pouring rain to stand at the french windows.

"May I come in?" the newcomer asked.

150

"Of course you can come in, Mainfleet," Biggs said. "You don't have to ask. Where are your blokes? You've taken ruddy long enough."

"On the contrary, we are ahead of schedule," the man addressed as Mainfleet said. He entered, closing the glass doors carefully behind him. Like Biggs, his ER was covered with sticking plaster. Also a captain, he was some years younger than Biggs, presenting a contrast to that gentleman in almost every way. The first difference that hit the eye was that where Biggs was dry, Mainfleet ran with water. He brushed wet hair from his forehead and nodded with a certain embarrassment at the three on the sofa.

"Meet the owners," Biggs said jeeringly.

"Sorry about this," Mainfleet said, and Jimmy took heart. He saw in the other's pleasant, rather soft face, a type he liked and recognised: his own.

"There's a towel in the kitchen," he said. "You look as if you need one."

"Just keep quiet, please," Mainfleet said and turned to talk in low tones with Biggs.

My mistake, thought Jimmy.

After a minute's discussion Mainfleet hurried through to the front door. He flung it open and blew a whistle. A vehicle had evidently been waiting with its engine running at the drive gates. It roared up to the foot of the front steps. A tailboard crashed down. Three soldiers appeared smartly in the hall, two of them carrying piled boxes of ammunition, the other with a machine gun over his shoulder. Under Mainfleet's direction they all proceeded upstairs.

"What are you doing with my house?" Mrs. Wolf groaned.

The scent of action had done wonders with Biggs' temper. Though he still cuddled the revolver, he smiled.

"Your house will be okay, lady. It's the blokes outside who have to worry. We're bringing off this *coo*, see, and one of your top rooms happens to be an ideal spot for a temporary machine gun post."

"Good God, you really mean you're prepared to kill people over this business?" If anything, Jimmy's sense of unreality had deepened.

"That's right, chum. That lot in Surrogate'll be wiped out by now. They're the enemy as far as we're concerned.

We've got a fleet of captured lorries waiting to take all Bourgoyne's marchers on to Chequers, those still fit to fight. Chequers is already under siege. No mucking, I tell you! All the government will be dead by morning."

"What's the machine gun going to do upstairs?" Jimmy asked stupidly as they heard the sound of breaking glass somewhere above them.

"Pick off any intruders coming either way, of course. There's going to be a lot more blood shed here before we're through, believe you me. But you lot sit tight and you'll be okay."

"We can't sit here for ever."

Biggs' affability vanished instantly.

"You sit there till I tell you to get up," he said, "and not before. Get that quite straight in your thick noggin, chum."

Rising, he went over to the phone. For five minutes he was busy talking, dialling, talking, dialling, talking. While he was sitting at the instrument, Mainfleet came downstairs again to report the gun in position. Nodding, Biggs passed this information on to his superior. Mainfleet brought out a cigarette case and offered it to Biggs; Biggs picked a cigarette out and produced a lighter.

"*Could* I have one?" Mrs. Wolf asked.

"Why not?" Mainfleet agreed. He came over and presented his case. Since Biggs made no move with the lighter, he produced his own and held it out to her.

"Thank you," Mrs. Wolf said, inhaling smoke gratefully. "Now why don't you let me make us all tea, revolution or no revolution?"

"Splendid idea," Mainfleet said, smiling engagingly.

"No! " Biggs said. They all looked at him. He dropped the freshly lit cigarette and ground it savagely into the carpet. "For God's sake, don't let's turn this into a picnic. Go thirsty for once in a good cause. Let's keep on our bloody toes."

Rather helplessly, rather sulkily, Mainfleet went over to the window. In the rain-filled silence they heard a distant explosion.

"I keep worrying and wondering how Conrad Scryban is faring," Mrs. Wolf whispered to Jimmy after a while. "It's so terrible to think of him out there in all that fighting and rain."

Jimmy nodded dumbly. He felt that their own position

152

might very well be worse than Scryban's. The phone rang. Everyone jumped.

"Biggs," Biggs said, grabbing the receiver.

He listened intently, his face growing set.

"Black sedan. Heading for London. Right. Well get it, sir. Ring you back."

Slamming the phone down, he called to Mainfleet, "The C.O.'s escaped. Heading this way. Hang on here," and ran upstairs to the gun position. The three on the sofa listened to his footsteps ascending and turned their eyes to Mainfleet, who had now drawn his revolver.

"Can you please tell us what is happening? I find it very unnerving not to know," Mrs. Crinbolt said.

"The situation is quite simple," Mainfleet told her. "A growing section of the community, including a proportion of the army, believe the present government, and the measures imposed by the present government, to be corrupt. We intend to overthrow the government. To that end we are cutting communications to London and seizing the Prime Minister."

"You're only a handful!" Jimmy exclaimed. "Once they get organised you'll be wiped out."

"We intend not to be. With the Prime Minister in our hands we shall be in a position to negotiate a strong peace. The attachment to which I belong is mopping up the forces opposing the GREP marchers. We then load the GREP into lorries from our Amersham base and proceed north to take Chequers. Captain Biggs and I will probably remain here to provide cover from the rear."

A rich and deep-piled silence fell over the room.

"You mean you are going to kidnap the Prime Minister . . . ," exclaimed Mrs. Crinbolt at last. "I never thought I'd live to hear such wickedness."

Mainfleet ignored her.

"If you don't mind, I'm going to switch on the electric fire," he said. "I am rather damp."

As he bent to do so, the machine gun in the attic opened fire. Jimmy had already detected, through the rain, the sound of a car travelling fast along the road. Now the house echoed with noise. Mrs. Wolf jumped to her feet; Mainfleet's gun was instantly levelled at her. Clenching her fists, she sat down again.

From the road came a squawk of tyres on wet tarmac

and then the prolonged racket of a car battering itself to pieces among trees.

"Oh my dear, oh my goodness, what ever shall we do?" Mrs. Crinbolt gasped. Mainfleet went to the inner door where he could see through the hall window and down the drive. Biggs and one of the machine gunners came thundering down the stairs; they ran out into the rain to investigate their target.

A minute later a solitary shot sounded. Two minutes later Biggs and the private returned, looking grim and beating the rain from their uniforms. Biggs returned to the phone.

"Major Hobbes? . . . Major Hobbes. Biggs here. We got the bugger . . . Yep, Roger."

Unexpectedly Mrs. Wolf burst into tears. Mainfleet turned to the private, who stood on the threshold of the room, gazing in with a sort of gormless awe.

"Robinson, go and see if you can rustle up a cup of tea for all of us," he said.

The private departed.

Mrs. Crinbolt looked up from the task of patting her daughter. "Well, I'm glad to see you still have some manners," she observed.

Despairingly Jimmy tried to analyse why he thought this remark one of the most ghastly he had ever heard. He had already decided that if he tried to make a dash for the door, it would be Mainfleet who would shoot him first. Mainfleet believed in the cause. Biggs was only doing his duty. Biggs was rough and ignorant and probably covering his envy of anyone who owned a nice house in the country with a display of aggressiveness. Mainfleet, on the other hand, was an educated man who disliked having to incommode anyone of his own social class. He would shoot first and answer questions afterwards. It was precisely this mixture of the genteel with the murderous that so appalled Jimmy.

He became increasingly aware that Kenelm Wolf would soon be emerging from the potting shed in search of tea, like a mole blundering topside after insects.

With some surprise Jimmy saw there was indeed someone coming to the French doors. With more surprise he saw it was not Kenelm Wolf but Guy Leighton.

XIII. Hot Pursuits, Cold Shoulders

"This is a scandal, an absolute scandal, and considering that I am completely in sympathy with your cause, I think you're both behaving abominably," Guy Leighton said, a few minutes later, wiping his wet face on a cushion as he addressed the two captains.

"Just keep quiet," Biggs said abstractedly, going back to the phone and busying himself there.

Little more relish for the newcomer was shown by Jimmy, Mrs. Wolf and Mrs. Crinbolt. Room on the sofa was limited and Guy was very wet.

Irritably he explained what had happened to him. Driving towards Grey Cotes, he had almost reached Surrogate when a mortar shell exploded in the road a few yards in front of him, shattering the spurious Sunday calm. Flying fragments struck his car as he swerved violently into a ditch. Although Guy was unhurt, the car was wrecked.

Climbing out, he saw three armed men, one in civilian dress, running towards him. They shouted at him. Taking fright, Guy plunged through the nearest hedge. A bullet pinged over his head. He hid in a deserted chicken run. The armed men made a cursory search, lost heart in the rain, and retired.

After some meditation and one cigarette, Guy decided to make for Grey Cotes on foot. This he managed to do by avoiding the main road and keeping to the cover of hedgerows. Happening, by luck, to strike the grounds by the kitchen garden, he had approached the house behind a brick wall, thus avoiding notice by the machine gun post in the attic.

While he was telling his tale, and as Jimmy explained what he knew of the Surrogate coup, they heard lorries rumbling along the road towards Amersham. Several aircraft droned by overhead without making any attack on the rebel forces.

The private brought in tea and disappeared upstairs.

"What I don't understand, Guy, is why you were coming here in the first place."

Guy, whose usual savoir faire had deserted him, snorted.

"I hope you are not being deliberately obtuse, Solent," he said. "I called for you at the IBA yesterday morning but just missed you. Someone there—a facetious sort of individual called Hortense—gave me this address. Unfortunately, owing to pressure of important business, I was unable to get away from town yesterday. But doubtless you can guess what I wish to talk to you about."

"If it's about Rose—Rachel—again, I don't want to hear it."

"Not so loud!" Guy hissed. His own voice had already dropped to a mutter. "It's not about Rachel—or only indirectly."

He looked round hopelessly, as one embedded in a sea of fools. Biggs was having a long, glum talk on the phone.

"Have you got a plan for escape?" Jimmy whispered, huddling into a corner against a bowl of dahlias.

"Now, Solent, you and I are in rather a precious awkward spot. Things have turned nasty, as I long ago predicted they would. This bit of nonsense, for instance, is going to hit the nation where it'll feel it most—in the pocket. However, you know my views on that. The point is this. Rachel Norman has been kidnapped by Bourgoyne; you know that much, I suppose?"

"For heaven's sake, Guy—"

"This is what I'm trying to tell you, Solent. On Thursday, you will recall, I managed to establish the true identity of this woman we so unhappily became entangled with. I passed that knowledge on to you with the genial feelings one has towards a fellow sufferer. You and I, in other words, are the only unofficial holders of this important secret."

Guy's was not a volatile face; it registered as a general rule only two expressions, the imperious and the impervious. Nevertheless, searching it now, Jimmy found something else there, something he instantly connected with all he knew of Guy, and in particular with his casual parting remark on Thursday: "If I'd had more cash in the bank. . . ." In that moment he saw the cogs that drove Guy on.

"Leighton!" he exclaimed. "You *sold* that information! My God, you sold it to Bourgoyne!"

"Not so loud!" Guy exclaimed, looking round. Mainfleet was watching them suspiciously. "All information has a cash value. *We* couldn't use it."

"You're mad, Guy. Why—then it's through you Rachel was kidnapped!"

"Do we owe her any love?"

It was an unfortunate way of phrasing it. Jimmy did not feel about love that way; he did not feel about anything in Guy's way. A flood of resentment at everything in his present position rose up in his throat; it obscured his senses. He glared through a fog, like a drunk peering through beer-smeared spectacles. Swinging forward, he hit Guy Leighton on the jaw.

The bowl of dahlias and the table on which it stood went flying as Guy sprawled and sat heavily on the floor. Mainfleet was there in an instant. Grasping Jimmy's arm, he swung him half across the room. Caught off balance, Jimmy fell backwards into an armchair. It skidded backwards, crashing into a glass-fronted cabinet. The room swam with breaking glass and shouting. Both Biggs and Mainfleet looked as if they would shoot everyone at a moment's notice.

"Are you all right, Jimmy dear?" Mrs. Wolf cried, running over to him.

One of the privates came charging downstairs to see what was happening. Pulling a shattered Guy to his feet. Mainfleet pushed him back onto the sofa. The phone rang urgently. The rain stopped of a sudden, leaving a restless silence behind.

"The next one to cause any trouble will be shot out of hand," Mainfleet said savagely.

"Biggs," Biggs declared, grabbing the phone, still pointing his gun at the party. He listened for a while, answering in low, angry tones. Jimmy, still straggling over the armchair and therefore nearest the phone, caught the words, "but if that's so, we can't wait for him. . . ." An argument ensued, which Biggs evidently lost. Looking at his watch he announced grudgingly, "We'll give him till 1700 hours then," and slammed the phone down.

"What was all that about?" Mainfleet demanded.

"Looks as if Amersham has had it," Biggs said. His face was red and sullen. He did not even bother to keep his voice down, so the others heard all he said. "Bloody Hobbes tells me the tanks have been called in and the RAF are strafing the barracks. Our lads and the GREP lorries are cut off just up the road. The whole blasted operation's come unstuck. An armoured column's moving up from the south, and if we don't get the hell out pretty smartish, we're going to get it in the seat of the pants. They'd lob a six inch shell into this house soon as look at it."

He ran out to the foot of the stairs and bawled up to Robinson. "All you lot come on down with the hardware. Move to it pronto and get it mounted in the back of the truck. We'll be with you in a minute."

"We'd better get cracking," Mainfleet said. He had gone very pale.

"Hang on till five o'clock," Biggs said. "It's only ten minutes. We've got to act as escort to a V.I.P. across country—our luck. He'll stop his car in the side lane, and we get round and join him there. Where's the side lane, you?"

He directed this last question at Mrs. Wolf by sticking a finger at her.

"If you originally entered by the paddock, you must have come from the lane," she said.

"You lot'll have to be locked in an upstairs room," Biggs said. "We can't have you running about yelling your heads off. You'll have to take a chance on being shelled."

"Please, we'll be no trouble—" Mrs. Wolf began, but he cut her off. Someone was coming round the side of the house from the back, their footsteps audible on the terrace. With one accord Mainfleet and Biggs dived for shelter, revolvers aimed towards the french doors. Everyone tensed Jimmy with a horrid certainty that Kenelm was about to appear.

Instead, a tall, bearded man with a powerful presence stepped into the room.

Mainfleet and Biggs rose sheepishly.

"Are you my escort?" the newcomer enquired. "Are you ready to move?"

There was no mistaking the owner of that resonant voice. It was Big Bill Bourgoyne himself. In a plain grey raincoat he looked entirely in control of the situation.

"We'll just get this lot locked up, sir," Mainfleet said respectfully. "We had word you were due to arrive." He motioned to Mrs. Wolf and her mother to get up.

"We have no time to waste," Bourgoyne said briskly. "The enemy are moving up on this position rapidly. We will evacuate as soon as you are ready."

As if to reinforce his statement a low-flying squadron zoomed overhead.

"They'll have seen your truck outside and be back to investigate it."

"Please don't leave us here to be bombed!" Mrs. Crinbolt cried.

"Get 'em out of here," Biggs said savagely, hoisting Guy to his feet. "Get 'em upstairs and lock 'em in somewhere."

Guy broke away from him and ran in front of Bourgoyne.

"Don't leave me here," he said. "I'm one of your men; these officers have no understanding of the real situation. We've not met, but I spoke to your secretary over the phone. I've done a lot for you. My name's Guy Leighton; you'll know it, of course."

"You'd better come with us," Bourgoyne said, hardly pausing to consider the matter.

In a sudden zest of relief Guy bounded over to the window. As he went he indicated Jimmy without actually looking at him.

"My friend here also knows all about Miss Norman," he said.

Jimmy was so surprised at this he hardly realised that Bourgoyne was calling peremptorily to him to follow Guy.

"I'll stay here, thanks," he said, "and take my chance with the ladies."

Bourgoyne, striding over, seized his arm.

"You'll come with me, young man. If you know so much of my business, I don't want you about loose at a time like this."

At this remark Guy's face clouded considerably, as he perceived he might be less rescued than doubly captured. But no time was allowed for further argument. Biggs had ushered the two protesting ladies upstairs, locking them in a bathroom. He ran out of the front door, driving off with the gunners to keep the rendezvous in the lane with Bourgoyne's car. Meanwhile Mainfleet stayed with the rest of the party as they made off through the French doors towards the paddock.

Outside the potting shed a soggy figure lay on its face in a puddle, its old raincoat rucked up about its knees. Jimmy stared at it with horror and remorse as they passed it; he knew now why Kenelm Wolf had never made his expected entrance. He must have emerged from his hideout just as Biggs was prowling through the grounds wary for trouble. Ever since then he had sprawled in the pouring rain with his skull broken in.

The two vehicles headed westwards for the best part of an hour, Bourgoyne himself driving the lead car, Biggs tailing grimly at the wheel of the Army truck. In the early stages of their journey they passed several tokens of the unrest sweeping the country: a smashed car, a wayside inn with hastily dug trench in its front garden, a line of light armoured vehicles with their drivers smoking peaceably on the grass verge, a bullet-riddled caravan, and a still smouldering cottage with the village fire brigade in attendance. Very few people were about.

These melancholy evening reminders of the morning's ambitions prompted Captain Mainfleet to ask Bourgoyne if Herbert Gascadder, the Prime Minister, had been captured.

"The whole grand plan has failed, my friend," Bourgoyne said, not without a certain gloomy relish. "The English have less fight left in them than I had hoped. They're a great disappointment to me. From now on we can only count ourselves as a decadent nation. The struggles we would once have staged on the battlefield are now to be confined to the bed."

Still recalling Kenelm Wolf sprawling on the terrace, Jimmy said, "I should think that shows an advance in civilisation."

"Naturally you would," Bourgoyne remarked tartly.

The somewhat fruity silence which now fell was broken by Guy, who began to speak in low tones to Jimmy.

"I'm still trying to forgive you for that loutish incident back at the house, Solent," he said. "Though I must admit I find it uncommonly hard to do so. When you attacked me, I had not even made plain the purpose of my visit—my ill-timed visit. Are you listening?"

"Continue."

"Solent, this is a delicate matter. I am trying to make you a little present. After all, I can afford to; it would give me pleasure to. Between you and me, Bourgoyne paid very generously for that information. I feel it would be a nice gesture on my part to . . . more or less split the proceeds—that is, if you will promise me never to reveal to a soul the nature of this deal. You see, I may have acted

160

rather on impulse; and if the truth ever came out, well it might be rather difficult to explain."

"Damned difficult, I'd say."

"Well then, how about fifty-fifty?"

"Go and jump in a lake, Leighton!" Jimmy growled, and the fruity silence fell again.

After a prolonged tour of narrow byways, during which the following truck lagged further and further behind, they came on the closed double gates of a big estate. A notice fixed to the wrought iron announced that the property was for sale. Fifty yards further on the wall which bounded the road had collapsed. Swinging the wheel over, Bourgoyne drove the car across the rubble and so into the grounds. They bumped through a small plantation.

The house, when they came up to it, stood in sinister decay. It was not old but neglected, not large but cumbrous. Nobody could love it now. It had been constructed (perhaps about the time that Galsworthy was painfully building Robin Hill) of the yellow brick sometimes referred to, quite adequately, as "lavatory brick." Evidently it had been deserted for some while; the windows were grey and uncurtained.

Approaching from the rear, they drew up in a rough courtyard formed by a number of outbuildings, a garage, a stable, an anonymous outhouse, a greenhouse with smashed glass, a corrugated iron bicycle shed. Grass grew between cobbles. Ivy crawled in at a downstairs window. Nettles flourished obscenely in the shattered greenhouse. A masterly touch of dereliction was lent by a wooden farm cart loaded with hay, which had evidently stood by the house for many summers; on top of the hay grew a splendid crown of cow parsley, burdock and dandelion.

Three spinsters with sporting rifles ran up to challenge the car, their pugnacious front melting in cries of delight as they recognised Bourgoyne.

He was very brisk with them.

From the questions and answers which followed, Jimmy gathered that Bourgoyne had been in hiding here for a couple of days, together with a number of loyal supporters —most of whom had forsaken him in the last hour or two, after learning of the afternoon's reverses from the B.B.C.

"We must all be out of here within half an hour and the whole place cleared," Bourgoyne said. "Captain Mainfleet, please take these two young men upstairs and lock them in separate rooms. The nursery rooms with bars at the window will do best. We shall move the quicker without being encumbered with them."

He moved smartly into the house, followed rather forlornly by the three women.

"Come on!" Mainfleet said, waving his revolver at Jimmy and Guy. "You heard; up the stairs smartly, please."

"I should have thought you could see by now you've picked the wrong side," Jimmy said to him. "Bourgoyne's a spent force! Why don't we all get back into the car and move away as fast as possible in the direction of the nearest policeman? Guy and I would then say you had rescued us from Bourgoyne, and you'd probably get a pretty light sentence."

"On your way," Mainfleet said, but he looked as if he might be privately considering Jimmy's proposition. Whatever his personal feelings, he did as Bourgoyne bid him. Jimmy and Guy were pushed upstairs into separate rooms and left.

By now Jimmy was far from his usual sunny self. An unexpected dislike of being ordered about rose in him. Looking round the room, with its frieze of mildewed teddy bears, he determined to escape at once. Mainfleet had locked the door; the window was firmly barred. No sort of weapon lay anywhere about the room: window, grate and door formed the only breaks in its box-like aspect. As he roved round looking for something, his heel went through a patch of dry rot in the floor.

Jimmy was down on his knees at once, peeling away huge wafers of floor board. This done, he could get a grip on a sound board and lever it up. Wedging this board under the door handle so that nobody could get in to bother him, he returned to his hole and had soon enlarged it sufficiently to climb into. He imagined that with any luck he might be able to crawl between floors until he reached an unlocked room.

The ceiling below seemed capable of bearing his weight. Testing cautiously, Jimmy lowered himself slowly into his hole. He let go of the cross beams, putting his full weight on the lath and plaster. It was as rash as letting go of morals and trusting to conventions; the ceiling caved in.

With a squawk Jimmy fell, and the whole ceiling fell with him. It came down like an avalanche about him, dust and lath and plaster, until he felt he was being pelted with wedding cake. Vaguely through the choking white mist Jimmy discerned the outlines of an empty room with a broken window at one end. Groaning, he picked himself up, found with astonishment that he was unhurt but for a twisted ankle, and hobbled over to the window. Pushing it open, he fell through it before anyone could come to investigate the noise.

He lay breathing hard, covered from head to foot in chalky dust.

He had tumbled out behind the garage; it cut him off from the rear courtyard with the haycart, while the house cut him off from the front. In effect, he was in a little isolated square, the other sides being formed by ragged elder bushes. A small helicopter stood untended in the middle of the square.

But it was not the helicopter which held Jimmy's attention. Even as he fell through the window he had heard a vehicle roar up to the front of the house, and now someone was bellowing through a megaphone.

By standing up and peering through the room he had just left, where the dust was now settling, Jimmy could look through an open doorway and a further corridor window. There, drawn up facing the building, was an Army truck. Over its raised tailboard the snout of a machine gun turned to and fro, as if seeking a target.

From the concealment of the truck the megaphone bawled its message again.

"Bourgoyne! Big Bill Bourgoyne! We know you're here. Come on out with your hands raised. Don't try to mess about, or you'll be shot down like a dog. Anyone else in there, you better come out quick with your hands raised before the shooting starts. Come on, everyone out! You've got two minutes."

Distorted though it was by the megaphone, Jimmy recognised that voice. Captain Biggs, for all his lack of education, had been more intelligent than his colleague, Captain Mainfleet; he had recognised the winning side when he saw it and hastened to join. What was more, he looked like hitting the jackpot.

Jimmy could now make himself useful by sabotaging the helicopter. As he turned to do so two shots rang out from the building, answered at once by a burst from Biggs' machine gun. The noise, Jimmy reflected, was fairly intimidating. He had not yet come to the age where the idea of dying is a familiar prospect and was still inclined to regard it as a rat-trap to be avoided at all costs.

As he hesitated he saw that he was being watched from one of the ground floor windows in the wing. A woman stood there, looking out. It was Rose—Rachel Norman.

Immediately Jimmy fell prey to the old sickly mixture of ambivalent feelings. The sight, touch, smell of her, her unbearable outspokenness ("You didn't give me a thing"), the passion to which—one night long ago! —she had so admirably given free rein—all were vividly before him again. He loved Alyson, yes, but this was the woman who had given him the glimpse of another world, wild and trackless.

Of course it was logical to find her here—Bourgoyne's captive at Bourgoyne's headquarters! —but Jimmy hardly thought about that. From the main part of the building behind him shots were being fired. Bourgoyne, Mainfleet, the three women, and anyone else who might be around were sniping at Biggs' truck. With a roar and an answering burst of fire it backed into a more sheltered position. Ignoring the racket, Jimmy sprinted across to Rachel's window.

Her wrists were tied against her body with a wealth of bandaging. She wore a tweed skirt and a green cotton blouse streaked with dirt. Her hair was untidy, but her long, rough-hewn face looked out composedly at Jimmy. His immediate feeling was one of awe to find this impressive woman, so strong, so vital, standing quietly helpless; this changed to sorrow as he saw that she did not recognise him in his present literally plastered state. Once more she was giving him the cold shoulder.

Rachel's window had rough bars across it on the inside. Waving and pointing, Jimmy signalled to the captive that he would go round the other way to let her out. She nodded, giving him a faint smile. As she did so the door of her room burst open behind her; she turned to confront a tall, thin man with a face like a baby's coffin.

Jimmy ducked down out of sight below the sill. Like everyone else, the thin man was armed. The outlook for Rachel was obviously threatening. Sighing, Jimmy saw he would have to do something about her. "I'm sure that being mixed up in all this violence is not good for me," he muttered.

Running round by the garage, he found a good, solid two-by-four about a yard long lying in a patch of couch grass. It would serve as a useful weapon if he could get behind the thin man. Peering out from the other side of the garage. Jimmy surveyed the desolate rear square, with its clutter of decaying outhouses and haycarts. Someone was moving behind the bicycle shed.

The thin man emerged from the building, holding Rachel by the arm. Her wrists were still tied; she walked briskly, even eagerly, her assured, top-heavy walk. They were coming towards Jimmy. He shrank back, but they went down the other side of the garage.

At the same time the man by the bicycle shed half rose, hurling a spherical object towards the house. It struck the wall and rolled over, hissing. Jimmy flung himself down on the ground. Sheepishly, he stood up again. A cloud of mist spread from the bomb towards the house: tear gas. And in the bushes beyond the bicycle shed a line of figures was advancing. Rescue or arrest was at hand for all and sundry!

Running back behind the garage, Jimmy saw that Rachel and the thin man had climbed into the helicopter. As he ran into the open the engine burst into life, the blades beginning to rotate. Looking up from the controls, the man reached for his gun and took a pot-shot at Jimmy. Jimmy flung his two-by-four and swerved. Dodging round to the other side of the machine, he seized the handgrip and bellowed to Rachel above the noise.

"Get out! Get out! The rescue party's here! They're just coming!"

He thought she said, "I'm going with this man."

"He must be one of Bourgoyne's chaps! Get out, for God's sake! Rescue's here! Rachel!"

The din increased. A gale raged round Jimmy.

Jimmy put his foot on the step as the helicopter shifted. Next minute it was lifting. Rachel made no attempt to move. The thin man was shouting. Jimmy was shouting. Someone—a dizzy glimpse revealed him—was shouting and waving from the roof. Bullets were flying. The motor roared. Of all the noises Jimmy's yells were loudest.

Staggering under its unbalanced load, the helicopter climbed with a reluctant crabwise motion over the garage, barely missing its roof. Jimmy hung on frantically, shouting. He saw the thin man, his dark, narrow face wizened in anger, lean across Rachel and strike out with the clubbed gun. The butt came down on Jimmy's knuckles.

He let go. He was falling, the helicopter seeming to lurch away from him. Next second he hit the ancient hay-cart, landing bottom first on the pile of antique hay, sprawling among cow parsley and nettles. Under his sudden weight the rotten axles of the cart broke, the wheels crumpled outwards, the body crashed to the ground. An immediate exodus of rats was partially screened by a vast outward-bound cloud of hay particles which obliterated everything from view.

XIV. Camera Obscura

Mrs. Pidney placed the baked custard reverently on the table in the dinerette, adjusting the frill round the dish as she spoke, much as a mourner will adjust his tie at the graveside even when the coffin is being lowered into the earth.

"It ought never to have happened to him," she said. "Such a nice, inoffensive young man. But there you are—as always, there was a woman at the bottom of it. Shairch-ay la femme as Mr. Pidney would say."

"She must have been a horrible creature," agreed Alyson.

"Horrible," emphasised Mrs. Pidney. Shaking her head, she looked towards Jimmy's bedroom door. "And there poor young James Solent lies. . . . I've had such a job keeping the reporters off; they got no respect at all."

"He's only tired," Alyson said. From Mrs. Pidney's tone one might have assumed that Jimmy was dead on a slab rather than asleep on his bed. "The police questioned him for hours."

"Having his picture in the papers and all," Mrs. Pidney said, shaking her mop of hair in anguish. "And to think none of us knew a *thing* what was going on, us living in the house with him. He always seemed to get on so nicely with you, dear. I wonder he didn't tell you."

"He's been keeping rather to himself lately," Alyson said uncomfortably.

"Well, what I always say, everyone ought to have someone they can talk about sex to, no matter who. It's a sort of outlet, like. That's why I bless these nunchasers, as the

166

boys call them; they sort of give people more of a chance to come out with things."

"They've brought Jimmy a lot of trouble, Mrs. Pidney."

"Maybe. But when everyone's settled down with them they'll be a blessing in disguise, you'll see. I'm ever so glad you got yours in time, dear—it does suit you, you know, suits your complexion. And I saw you pinking at him when the police brought him back home."

The look of discomfort on Alyson's face deepened.

"I'm in rather an awkward position at present," she said. "I'm afraid I have obligations towards both the Solent brothers."

Mrs. Pidney waited, expecting elucidation. When it was obviously not forthcoming she said, "If ever you feel like telling me about it, you're welcome. I'm very broadminded. You either can tell some people or you can't, that's what I find, and no one knows what decides who you tell and who you don't. Like I say, most people have got someone they can talk about such details to; the funny thing is, it isn't always the people they marry, not by a long chalk, and don't I know it."

When she had gone, Alyson still stood silently in the middle of the room. She was struggling with a great desire to cry. It was Monday afternoon, and she had not bothered to go to work.

A sound made her turn. Jimmy was standing on the threshold of his room in pyjamas. He yawned, stretched, and smiled at her. Both of their ER's began to glow.

"What's the time, Alyson?" he asked. "My watch has stopped."

"It's half past three and high time you woke. How are you, my dear? How are the bruises? Are you hungry?"

"Yes. Yes, now you mention it I'm ravenous. And just a bit stiff; my behind's slightly black and blue."

"Mrs. Pidney has just brought you up a baked custard. She's been terribly concerned about you."

"How nice of her. What's in the larder?"

"An apple pie I made yesterday."

"With six cloves?"

"With six cloves as usual."

"You're wonderful, Alyson. I'd rather eat that than the baked custard. Come and sit down and talk to me as I eat."

"I'm sorry, Jimmy, I oughtn't to stop. I'm about to go out."

"I see. You sound rather formal, Alyson. Is anything the matter?—I mean, apart from the fool I've been making of myself over the Norman woman?"

"Apart from that, no."

Still not entirely satisfied, Jimmy fetched the splendid pie and commenced to eat. Watching Alyson from the corner of his eye, Jimmy saw that instead of making ready to go she was delaying her departure. He put his fork down.

"You don't have to pretend with me, Alyson," he said. "What is bothering you?"

"Nothing," she said. "It's just that I've got an attack of nerves. I'm about to go round to the Merrick-Kind clinic. You know I promised Vincent I would."

"Vincent Merrick's experimental clinic?" Jimmy said. "Good Lord, I'd forgotten all about that in the excitement —he asked us both round, didn't he?"

"In the circumstances, he'll be sure to forgive you for not turning up."

Jimmy looked hard at Alyson, aware for the first time how anxious she seemed. Always there was something fresh to be puzzled out, he thought tiredly. "Throughout the syzygies our visages wear a satiety of anxiety; lack of care has become as rare as natural piety."

"Would you like me to come with you? A dose of other people's troubles would be like a tonic to me now!"

Jimmy much liked the way her eyes lit up.

"I'll wait for you, if you're sure you feel up to it," she said.

"This is probably the last meal I shall eat here," Jimmy said, as Alyson seated herself opposite him. "There's a spare room in the house where Donald Hortense digs, and I'm going over there this evening; I can stay there until I find something more exciting."

He refrained from mentioning Aubrey. Alyson did the same. An awkward silence fell between them. Jimmy began to tell her such details of his eventful weekend as he had not related the night before. He broke off suddenly.

"But here I sit chattering . . . tell me, Alyson, what the hell's going on in the big world? Why aren't you at work? Is the country plunged into bloody revolution?"

"England? Of course not! I stayed away from work just to be about here in case I was needed. No, Jimmy, the collapse of your haycart was pretty well synchronised with the collapse of all organised opposition to the Emotion

Registers. Bourgoyne's house was surrounded by loyal troops, Captain Biggs will receive a citation and promotion, your little dark friend Guy was rescued, everyone else there was arrested—except Bourgoyne. He managed to escape by car but was caught down at Deal this morning. Quite exciting, really."

"And the helicopter? What happened to the helicopter?' Alyson smiled an acid smile.

"It was found deserted in a field less than a mile away. The occupants are still missing."

Helping himself to more pie, Jimmy tactfully asked about the country generally.

"Oh, now the big attempt at a rising over the week-end has failed, I don't think anything else spectacular will happen. After all, the trouble-makers in the army are now either shot or arrested. Over two hundred people were killed yesterday. The Amersham business was a storm in a teacup compared with the pitched battle at Glasgow; you must read about it in the papers when we come back from Vincent's."

Her nail varnish was chipped, her shirt crumpled. He saw that although she spoke carelessly enough, she was still tense. A longing to go round the table and hug her, to throw everything over in loving and comforting her, assailed him, but he was not sure enough of how they stood to do it.

Finishing the pie, he stood up.

"I must phone Mrs. Wolf before we go," he said.

"She's phoned you twice this morning, once after lunch."

"My God, what did she say, Alyson? Was she O.K.?"

"To tell you the truth, Jimmy, I didn't much care for the sound of her. She seemed to be taking the death of her husband very lightly."

"Nobody loves that woman but me," Jimmy said, heading for the phone. Seeing the look this remark summoned onto Alyson's face, he added hastily, "And don't forget she's twenty years older than I am."

He dialled the IBA. Mrs. Charteris put him through to Mrs. Wolf. An incessant shower of talk poured from the receiver. Mrs. Wolf was apologising for Jimmy's harrowing week-end. She was saying that she should probably sell the house; that her mother, Mrs. Crinbolt, had been sent home; that some nice RAF Regiment men had rescued them from their bathroom prison; that she had to come to work to get away from the dreadful atmosphere; that she hoped Jimmy was all right; that even Bloody Trefisick had been kind to her; that there had been shooting outside the IBA that morning; that she had Jimmy's suitcase safe in her office; that dear Conrad had at the last moment never gone on the GREP march to Chequers at all owing to a slight cold; that he had shown himself personally interested in her future; that he had said he hoped she would not forget he would be thinking of her while he was in prison; and that had he an ER it would undoubtedly be registering at the member of his team he valued most.

Out of breath himself, Jimmy put the phone down.

"She's going to marry Scryban, our managing director; so that lets me out," he said.

"What, today?!" Alyson exclaimed.

"No, silly, after the funeral."

He went and shaved and dressed, presenting himself to her within twenty minutes, ready to go to the clinic. Jimmy wanted to take her arm but did not.

Alyson talked fairly cheerfully as he walked to the bus stop, but he sensed that she was still quietly disturbed, and that the cause of the disturbance did not lie in him. Becoming aware of this momentary perceptiveness in himself, a perceptiveness based on no acknowledged powers of reason, Jimmy asked himself how many other such abilities had died out since man began to cultivate his intellect, and whether, especially, the increasingly intense study of man as a psychosomatic unity had not—like the sunbeam which puts out a fire in a grate—damped down those same delicate effects it had set out to investigate. Perhaps in Jimmy Solent then there was a vision, however vague, of the future as we are now living it, when ER's are as universal as foreheads; for under the intense scrutiny which Emotional Output has enjoyed since ER's came in, sexual activity has slumped to an unprecedented minimum, and birth rates everywhere have dropped to a small percentage of their previous levels. One happy result of this decline is that the world famine so frequently and zestfully predicted throughout the forties and fifties of this century has been, like Utopia, indefinitely postponed.

This year the tourist season was lasting longer than usual. The London pavements were still crowded with an ambling multitude from Toronto or Trieste. A spiv selling dummy NL's which were secured round the head with an elastic band was doing good business with overseas visitors. As they passed a news theatre, Jimmy peered eagerly at the placard outside it; under the enigmatic BROWN: SECOND OVAL CENTURY was the headline GREP COUP FLOPS. Jimmy thought sadly, I ought to go and see that; the one time I enter history I also flop.

Merrick's clinic, though established in a fashionable part of town, looked disarmingly ordinary from the outside. If hell is a city much like London, it follows that purgatory may resemble an address in Mayfair. Even the dazzlingly new plate on the portal saying The Vincent Merrick-C. B. Kind Societal Therapy Clinic did little to warn them of what they were about to find. Alyson and Jimmy entered and were ushered into a waiting room.

Alyson's nervousness visibly increased. She stood looking out of the single window at a white-washed wall three feet away, drumming her fingers on the sill.

"We don't have to be here if this place gives you the whim-whams," Jimmy said, going over to her.

She turned and rested her hands in his.

"I've got to stay, Jimmy," she said. "You see, I persuaded Aubrey to come here. He should be here already."

"Oh, yes, that does make it rather difficult. What did you ask him for? He doesn't know Merrick. We shall only quarrel; you know he's at my throat since he found that you and I—"

"Aubrey's coming here for treatment," Alyson said.

There was not time to say more. The door opened and Merrick came in with his confident tread, the thick lenses of his spectacles gleaming. Something very heartening in his presence made itself felt. He held Alyson's hand warmly before turning to Jimmy.

"I must congratulate you on the brave part you played in one of yesterday's unfortunate episodes," he said. "I'm delighted that you feel fit enough to come here today."

"Just a few bruises here and there. May I ask how you heard about my insignificant part in things?"

"I was told privately by somebody who is actually on the premises at the moment," Merrick said mysteriously. "I do hope you will both come out with Jasmine and me one evening soon, when I can spare the time, and tell us all about it."

Jimmy was uncertain whether this was something he wanted to do.

171

"Is the national situation settled enough for us to be able to plan ahead?" he asked.

Merrick laughed gently, a pleasant laugh full of assurance, as he produced a cigarette case and offered it round.

"Absolutely," he said. "Absolutely. I think the whole pattern of the next few years may be predicted with some confidence. Whatever is new is questioned; that is both inevitable and reasonable. One saw the same thing a few years ago—you would both be at school then—with the introduction of TV. All kinds of unexpected side-effects, arising from permanent factors in society such as unequal distribution of income, awareness of class difference, bondage to family shibboleths, make themselves felt. But their very expression—and we must regard the troubles of the past weekend as such an expression—dissipates them and becomes, in fact, the first stage towards the acceptance of the casual innovation. No, ER's are a fait accompli; all we have to watch for now are the minor irritations inseparable from a time of adjustment. And this clinic, I fancy, will be able to deal with most of them."

Merrick was about to add something more when Alyson, looking strained, broke in with an enquiry about Aubrey.

"My dear Miss Youngfield, you have nothing to worry about," Merrick assured her. "Your fiancé is here, has been examined, and is already undergoing societal therapy. My colleague, Mr. Kind, and I have both talked with him, and we are in complete agreement that his condition is one which will yield easily to curative measures."

"It did not seem to yield to my curative measures," Alyson said diffidently. She bent her fair head to avoid the enquiring glances Jimmy was directing at her.

"Aubrey Solent's is a fairly uncommon kind of impotence," Merrick said. "As I told you before, the essential point for you to remember is that it is in no way a reflection on your own—delightful qualities."

"Impotent! Aubrey impotent!" Jimmy exclaimed. "I don't believe it! I don't believe a word of it!"

"You were perhaps less advantageously placed to discover the truth than Miss Youngfield," Merrick said blandly. "The condition, in any case, is only intermittent. And now, if you will come with me, I will introduce you to my co-partner in this new venture, Mr. Kind."

Mr. Kind, Mr. Croolter B. Kind, was an unfrocked Cana-

172

dian alienist with advanced ideas and a slight stammer. He wore, unexpectedly, a Harlequin sweater with a giant letter K sewn on the back and a pair of black pin-stripe trousers. He greeted Jimmy and Alyson amiably, although some of his cordiality vanished on finding they had not come for consultation.

"Sorry," he said, laughing ruefully and scratching his crew-cut. "I thought you were obscures rather than what we c-c-all c-c-c-clears. Well, any friends of Vince's are friends of mine. We've got q-q-quite a set-up here, and if you have a loved one here undergoing treatment—what we c-c-call c-c-c-clearance—you'd better come along and look in on the session that's just started. How do you say, Vince?"

Vince Merrick nodded his head.

"Yes," he said. "I think you would be interested. As intelligent young people you ought to be. You may find it all rather startling at first, of course; societal therapy is rather revolutionary."

"Ah, we'll shoot them full of dope and they'll take anything without turning a hair," Kind said, opening a swing door into a surgery. "Just c-c-come into here, boys and girls, and we'll set you up."

Entering the surgery, he selected a hypodermic syringe from a bowl and commenced to fill it from a small phial. Seeing the indecision of Alyson's and Jimmy's faces, Merrick put a hand on their elbows and led them gently into the room. Unction flowed from him.

"This is not going to hurt at all," he said. "We have here a drug we have recently synthesised called Peyocalan. Originally it was derived from the cactus peyotl. It is a harmless euphoric which will induce in you a feeling of withdrawness from and indifference to your surroundings. A small injection would be advisable; at first glance our treatment is, as I say, apt to be startling unless one has some prior fortification."

Feeling that old helpless sensation which always oppressed him in the presence of anyone who knew more about his interior than he did himself, Jimmy enquired, with an attempt at humour, "Do we bare arms or buttocks?"

"Hell, you choose," Kind said. "It's all the same to us."

He brought the syringe over to them, squirting out a little peyocalan for practice. Alyson and Jimmy took the needle in the arm; Kind swabbed their punctures with cotton wool and said "O-k-k-kay, let's go. This way for the freak show. Have your tickets ready, please."

Merrick led them up a corridor to a sound-proof door. They went through this and found themselves in a small cinema. "The programme has only just started," Merrick said, peering towards the screen. The differences between this and a normal cinema were several. They had come directly onto the balcony, which was divided by thick plate glass from the rest of the auditorium and contained only six comfortable seats. Down in the stalls, some thirty seats, only half of which were at present occupied, accommodated the "obscures," those mental sufferers who were undergoing the Merrick-Kind societal therapy.

The obscures all wore dominoes over their eyes and sweaters on which large numbers were sewn, so that Jimmy was reminded of a Harvard football team preparing for a masked ball. The pit in which these people sat was draped with black in contrast to the ginger and orange stucco which serves many cinemas for internal decoration. But the most radical point of departure from tradition here was the four screens set one beside each other.

Different films were being projected onto each of the screens. The thirty seats in the pit revolved, each on its own axis, so that their occupants might view each film with equal ease. They rotated slowly and ceaselessly.

Now a curious effect, like the aftermath of making love, began to steal over Jimmy: an effect compounded of lethargy and lightness. The peyocalan was at work. He found himself, from eyes as blank as the ports of a bathysphere, gazing out at the eerie ocean depths, nonchalantly watching the screens on which men and women, as much under pressure as any denizen of the Pacific deeps, underwent a thousand postures and humiliations. Sometimes in pairs, sometimes in solitude, occasionally in solemn groups, the human race filled four screens with its gyrations in search of fulfilment. With the same sort of baffled earnestness, Jimmy muttered to himself, "Yes, yes, yes. . . . This is terribly important."

"This balcony is soundproof, so I can tell you something of what is going on," Merrick said. His voice came to them from a point many light years away and lingered uncannily in Jimmy's ear. "Basically, of course, all mental healing is concerned with adjusting an individual to himself. Many individuals have to be helped to find a balance;

174

Croolter and I offer such help. But we offer much more—and here, as I think you will appreciate, revolutionary ideas creep in. All over the world, mental sufferers are being sent back into the world labelled 'cured' by their psychiatrists. They *are* cured, in the sense that they are adjusted to themselves, but they are not adjusted to the other personalities around them; they find that the world is a mill. The random impingement of these other personalities knocks them off balance, and in no time they are back at the ward door begging for readmission.

"We have changed that; at this point societal therapy steps in. Here, in this theatre, we show our obscures (so termed because their view of the right external object is obscured) that the world teems with idiosyncrasies—perversions may be the word you are more familiar with—many of which are more grotesque than their own. That is what they must understand of the mill of the world. Once they have faced and accepted it as an irrefutable fact and faced it in the presence of other obscures, they are suitably prepared to adjust to and to accept themselves. By the end of this course they will be different beings. Now just look at this variation coming up on the second screen and see if you don't think it one of the most fascinating . . ."

The respectable little man in pince-nez was creeping through hotel rooms, disarranging beds, selecting pillows by their smell, he removed the pillow cases, carrying them furtively with him until he had collected six of them. His nose twitched uncontrolledly. He then bound various parts of his body tightly with five of the cases, fell on to his hands and knees, and crawled into the sixth case.

On adjacent screens a cunning attachment to a mangle was giving a woman the beating of her life, a strange creature danced in white nightdress and gumboots, a boy of fifteen stroked an Alsatian dog and smiled angelically.

Waves of sex flowed out overpoweringly above the audience, drowning them like a breeze from an Indian village, splashes from an octopus-breeding tank, accelerando passages from a fly-blown Grand Romantic symphony. It was hard to believe that out of this unsavoury chaos would emerge a balanced world.

"What you have to grasp," Merrick said, glancing at the fish-like, hypnotised countenances of Alyson and Jimmy, "is that these scenes have a very definite connection with what you regard as the ordinary world. They are merely, one might say, a slight parody of it. Man has free will, but he is also under compulsion. Some compulsions are acceptable to our present society, many are not; what I hope to see—what ER's may bring about—is a disintegration of the present society. But it must be a slow disintegration, not the crude GREP attempt to shatter it, which would inevitably have brought economic chaos in its wake.

"I firmly believe we shall see an *evolutionary* disintegration. Society will rearrange itself on lines more in alliance with reality; it's inevitable—when everyone daily gets an insight into the workings of sex through the ER. It is ignorance which creates taboos, not morality."

"Mmm. . . . Terribly important," Jimmy murmured. He had hardly grasped a word in his efforts to concentrate on the antics of a gigantic negress and a bald man in suspenders.

"Terribly important, but I don't like it," Alyson sighed.

From the fuggy dark behind their seats the fuggy genial face of Merrick's partner loomed. He nodded his crew cut at the quadruple screens.

"These extremely interesting movies are only available to members of the medical profession," Croolter B. Kind explained. "No doubt you have heard of a very excellent association c-c-c-called AA, Alcoholics Anonymous, which aids anyone afflicted with alcoholism. These films are shot by an equally courageous outfit calling itself PP, Perverts Pseudonymous. Their obscures act out their idiosyncrasies for the c-c-c-cameras."

Before the posturing images the clinic's fifteen obscures revolved in their seats like chickens turning on spits, as if commanded by some modern Dante. All of them bar two wore ER's, which fluttered and blinked, gleamed and dimmed, as their wearers reacted to the varying stimuli of the screens; they resembled agitated, rose-tinted searchlights seeking out enemy bombers. To add to the frenzy of the scene some of the obscures were twitching or pointing at shots which particularly roused their errant genes. Uninvited, two lines from Meredith's "Modern Love" crept to Jimmy's sluggish mind:

You burly lovers on the village green
Yours is a lower, and a happier star!

176

Now the village greens were deserted or had blocks of flats built on them, and the burly lovers lost weight and came creeping in for Merrick's therapy. With an effort Jimmy turned to look at Alyson; her face was momentarily illuminated by the light reflected off giant thighs; she was crying. The sight did a good deal to clear Jimmy's head. He had forgotten that his own brother was turning on a spit down in that thigh-blown purgatory. Perhaps Aubrey was No. 5, or perhaps No. 12, curled up there quietly in his sex dodgem-car.

Heaving himself forward, Jimmy raised his hand and touched Alyson, numbly attempting to comfort her.

"That's right, you kids, go ahead and neck," Croolter said encouragingly. "These movies do have that effect on some people. I might inform you that on the black market they fetch quite a whale of a price."

"I ought to tell you that some of the obscures in our audience below," said Merrick, resuming his commentary, "occupy trusted positions in industry and in society. One holds an important post in the Treasury, one is a key woman in ultrasonics, one, indeed, is a Minister. Croolter and I can tell which each is by the number on his sweater, but all obscures are anonymous to each other."

"I don't want to hear anything more; I think it's all terrible—ghastly—inhuman!" Alyson said.

"Terrible and ghastly maybe," Croolter replied, "but all too human." He chuckled appreciatively.

"Well, I want to get out into the clean daylight again," Alyson said, rising shakily. "And I want to take Aubrey with me; I'm sure all this can do him nothing but harm."

Pulling himself together, Jimmy got up and went over to her. When he took her arm, he could feel how much she was trembling.

"Please calm yourself, Miss Youngfield," Merrick said. "Do leave, by all means, if you feel you must—though I should be sorry to see you go—but you must believe me when I say you would be ill-advised to remove your fiancé; he needs this opportunity to come to terms with his life. You should leave him here unless—" He paused abruptly.

"Unless what, Mr. Merrick?"

"Forgive me. What was that noise outside?"

"I heard it too," Croolter said. "Sounded like firing to me. Some guy downstairs told me there was more unrest in London today, after the news that Bourgoyne had been put in the c-c-c-cooler, than ever he managed to stir up here when he was loose; I'll never understand you British if I live to be a hundred."

"That's nonsense," declared Merrick. "Naturally there is some unrest after the climactic week-end."

"What were you going to say about Aubrey, Mr. Merrick?" Alyson persisted. But Merrick was saved from answering by a minion who entered the gallery to announce that a truck-load of men armed with rifles were firing on the police in the street outside.

Merrick tut-tutted as if he, too, sometimes had his doubts about the British.

"You'd better haul the Minister out of the pit in case there's any trouble," he told the minion, peering down into the aptly named pit where his seekers of the right external object still rosily revolved. "He's No. 8 and we can't afford to lose him. Drag him out and give him the phenobarbitone routine, then bring him up here."

"Yessir." The minion showed a dirty pair of heels.

A solitary shot sounded outside, followed by the spanging howl of ricochet. Jimmy, who had had his fill of guns for a while, said uneasily, "What good do they think hooliganism will do?"

"It's a valuable outlet for the hooligans," Croolter said without taking his eyes off the changing pictures.

"Bourgoyne had a good case," Alyson said unexpectedly. "These fools outside just spoil it; everyone spoilt it, he spoilt it himself. I can't comprehend why he never got more enlightened backing than he did. It seems amazing to us now that less than ten years ago nations were cheerfully exploding H-bombs without any effective protest being raised over the danger of their after-effects. Yet future generations will be equally amazed that we did not make more ado over this tampering with the life of the individual. I suppose we're all too absorbed in the personal aspects of the problem to heed the general ones."

"Ah, you're just being archaic," Croolter said. "It was high time someone did something like this. It's a real advance, honey, take it from me."

"I don't much like the tone you take to Miss Youngfield," Jimmy said. He did not quite agree with Alyson, but he took a dislike to anyone else who disagreed, particularly when they wore sweaters and pin-stripe trousers with crew cuts.

"Permit me to repeat: archaic," Croolter said flatly. "She talks about tampering with the life of the individual! Jesus, man, ever since homo sap formed itself into groups and societies, the life of the individual has been tampered with—that is, made to c-c-c-conform. C-C-C-Conformity is c-c-c-comfort. That's all we aim to do here in this c-clinic, make folks c-c-c-comfortable. Why, they'd be quite happy with their little k-k-k-kinks if it weren't for the element of nonconformity in those said k-k-k-kinks."

"Never mind all that, Alyson," Jimmy said. He had been looking anxiously at her face and could read the tension mounting there. "Let's get out of here if you don't like it."

"You are welcome to leave by all means," Merrick said. "The shooting seems to have stopped."

"Yes, I want to go," Alyson told him, "but first I want to know what you were going to say about my fiancé. I had an idea it might be important."

"Sit down again, my dear," Merrick said patiently. "Perhaps it is important. You see, affliction from which Aubrey Solent suffers is a mental condition—impotence caused by a physical defect is extremely rare. The sense of inferiority which produced the condition is naturally reflected in the other facets of his make-up. He is reserved, conservative, never talks much about his work and conforms by going to successful plays, reading currently popular books, visiting church every Sunday—in short, by adopting a usual upper-middle-class conformity pattern; and sometimes he gives himself away—for instance, in his recent outburst against a nonconformist homosexual group of which you told me or in adjuring Jimmy to behave towards you as if sexual attraction were non-existent."

"But all that just happens to be part of Aubrey's nature," Jimmy protested. "There must be hundreds of people like Aubrey in London alone."

"I agree with both of your points," Merrick said urbanely. "And these latent stresses were brought to the surface when Aubrey met Miss Youngfield."

Jimmy turned away in disgust—these people had you over a barrel which ever way you jumped; arguing with them was like trying to do Euclidean geometry on a perpetually expanding or contracting rubber sheet. As he turned he was in time to see two minions in the pit reach the chair of Obscure No. 8; by their actions he realised for the first time the audience was wisely strapped into its chairs. No.

8 was now undone and half carried through the salacious pink *pointilliste* gloom to a guarded exit. Still slightly dizzy from the drug, Jimmy found himself peering to see if the minions carried pitchforks.

Leaning towards Alyson, Merrick, inevitably, was talking again, using an allegro comodo, professional tone of voice.

"Now you, Miss Youngfield, are an exceedingly attractive young lady, if I may say so. Aubrey certainly recognised that when he first met you; but with his rising desire for you came a dread that he might be proved inadequate. It is a tragic situation; in the old phrase, he is his own worst enemy. He could see that you were sympathetic and perhaps even inclined to mother him. No—don't protest! Every woman is a latent mother. Aubrey was intelligent; he hit on a scheme which appealed to all levels of his being. He *told* you—did he not?—of his disability and he sought your help to try and cure it; in effect, it was a way of flaunting his weakness and his strength at the same time. You fell in with the scheme."

"I was fond of him," Alyson protested. "And I was—sorry for him; I sympathised with him. I thought I could help."

"Exactly. As I say, you fell in with his scheme," Merrick agreed imperturbably.

Now Jimmy was listening with great attention. Nothing engages us more closely than unpleasant revelations about members of our family. He flinched slightly as the psychoanalyst, still talking, turned towards him.

"At this juncture James Solent came up to London and began to share his brother's flat."

"This is where it gets good," Croolter gloated from behind them.

"Aubrey's powers of love-making had been, thanks to Miss Youngfield's tact and patience—to say nothing of her pulchritude—fairly satisfactory until then," Merrick continued. "But he sensed—quite rightly—a rival in his younger brother. He was unsure of his powers; he said to himself, in effect, 'Alyson cannot love me, for I am not worthy of her; she stays with me only through pity, therefore she must have something to pity me for.' And from then on his trouble grew rapidly worse. That's so, Miss Youngfield, isn't it?"

Alyson nodded her head, not speaking.

"If you could persuade yourself," Merrick said, "to

abandon Aubrey, we could then treat him successfully by showing him his basic fears are groundless. By aligning yourself with Jimmy you have become for Aubrey a symbol of his failure that we should remove as far as possible from his life. Incidentally, he has already admitted to me that his main reason for not getting an ER, however he has rationalised it, rests on a fear of not being able to make it pink. It was this fear alone that turned him for several weeks into a nonconformist in the BIL camp."

"That at least—" Jimmy began to say, when there was a loud explosion and the building trembled under their feet. The plate glass cutting off the balcony from the rest of the auditorium cracked horizontally without smashing. At the same time a section of the wall in the pit above the left-hand screen puffed and wrinkled and fell slowly outwards. The building shook again as bricks and mortar hit the street. The collapse made a ten-foot square hole in the cinema wall. Through this gap the watchers saw an immense curtain of dust and plaster rise; as it cleared, the outer world was revealed—or if not exactly the outer world, a large poster on the opposite side of the street, on which, above and beneath a delineation of a young woman in her bed, stood the proud boast, THERE'S NINE HOURS BEAUTY SLEEP IN EVERY CUP OF VIGA-COFF. It contrasted oddly, Jimmy thought, with the lower part of a hypogastric region which undulated in close-up in juxtaposition to it on the next screen.

For in spite of the explosion the films ground inflexibly on, and the obscures perforce remained in their rotating seats. But the light filtering through the cavity into the cinema dimmed the moving images to a faded brown; they now wore in consequence a quaintly old-fashioned air; the post-Kinsey researches of PP were turned into pornographic postcards imported from Marseilles after the first World War and long treasured in some fusty bureau drawer. The earnest and ungainly antics had acquired a period charm.

Recovering from his shock, Croolter B. Kind jumped to his feet. He waved his arms with the curious retrograde movements of a lady driver learning to signal.

"We're being attacked," he shouted. "Leave everything to me and don't panic. Just k-k-k-keep c-c-c-c-c-cool! Make for the emergency orifices!"

He plunged out of the door and his footsteps padded along the outside corridor. As they died away, Merrick's minion entered clutching Obscure No. 8, a stocky figure still garbed in mask and sweater; he was panting.

"It's nothing to be alarmed about, sir," the minion told Merrick, referring to the explosion. "Just a few malcontents and Bourgoynists having a last fling, that's all. The police chased them up onto the roof and cornered them there—but not before some young fool let off a hand grenade. Apparently he was trying to blow up the fire escape and he blew down the wall instead. We can claim off insurance, sir, can't we?"

"I suppose we can," Merrick said. "I find myself nonplussed. A stone flung at me at Stipend, my livelihood damaged in Mayfair; what traumatic times we live in! Perhaps, if it is safe, we should go outside and view the damage. By so doing I feel I might perhaps recover my nerve. Would you kindly phone my wife and tell her how my life has been spared?"

As the vassal hurried off to obey, Merrick gently took the masked minister's arm and, turning to his other guests, invited them to escort him. Before leaving the balcony Jimmy looked for the last time into the pit. Dante Alighieri and Krafft Ebing had faded before Salvador Dali and Kiddicraft. Filtering daylight had banished the inferno; in its place was only a child's toy, the mechanical, twentieth century ideal of a toy, which the child must not touch for fear of hopelessly damaging the works. The chairs whirled round, the pink lights flickered enchantingly on and off, the brown figures on the walls rehearsed their meaningless postures; and over it all, one eye eclipsed by her swelling pillow, the giantess peered down in Vigacoff-induced benevolence.

Jimmy turned and caught hold of Alyson's arm as she followed Merrick and Obscure No. 8 from the balcony. Drawing her closer to him, he surveyed her anxiously.

"Listen, Alyson," he said. "I know it's hard to check either way on these psychology blokes, but is the Great Panjandrum right in all this patter about Aubrey?"

"I believe so," she said, sighing. "At least Vincent seems to have unravelled a part of Aubrey's troubles, and believe me, he has more knots than string—I just hope you aren't going to be such a handful. . . . But to think he's got worse because of me, when all the while I had tried to *help*. I can understand it in a way, but I can't understand *why*; really, thinking about people is more bewildering than thinking about God. Oh, it's so confusing—I wish I'd never come here."

He brushed back her fair hair as if trying to brush her remarks aside. Vincent Merrick and the masked obscure were disappearing down the corridor. A schwärmerei of pink light surrounded Alyson and Jimmy as he said, "It's confusing all the time, but we can blunder on quite happily. Just don't worry! I worried for so long about your not getting an ER, but I think I can see now why you hung on."

Alyson struggled in his arms, wrinkling her face in a sort of irritated-amused expression.

"You're so diffident, or you'd have seen long ago. Oh, Jimmy dear, you heard what Merrick said. I was attracted to Aubrey and then hooked by—oh, by pity, I suppose, though I hate to say it. Then you turned up. I knew if I had a disc it would pink at you. I didn't think it would pink at Aubrey at all and could guess how that would hurt him. Once I knew I couldn't control my genes, I knew I couldn't risk getting a Norman Light. Not with you about. It was only at the last moment I knew I could not bear to go to prison for Aubrey's sake."

A gay, lilting waltz was being performed by all the parts of Jimmy which normally functioned at a solid plod. He felt extraordinarily dizzy. Letting go of Alyson, he backed away, unaware of how blank his expression had become.

"Yes," he said. "I see."

Alyson burst into slightly ragged laughter.

"Don't just say 'Yes, I see,' you unloveable man!" she said. "Do something about it. We can't look after Aubrey any more. Vincent Merrick said that himself—and besides, the strain's too much; I've aged years these last few weeks. From now on it's out of our hands."

"Yes," Jimmy repeated blankly, overcome to think of the dilemma in which Alyson had been trapped. "What a bit of luck, eh?"

"Come here, Jimmy," she said, very softly, making it an invitation rather than an order. As he approached he watched with interest the way her face grew pinker. She was not blushing. Taking his face in her hands, she kissed him tenderly with parted lips.

"Hm . . . Are you two coming down to the street with us?" Merrick's voice arrived from a long way away, as if he were speaking down the wrong end of a telescope. He and No. 8 had come back along the corridor to find them.

183

"Sorry," Jimmy mumbled, breaking from Alyson's embrace. "There was something we had to get straight."

"That is rather a Freudian remark," Merrick said, "in the circumstances."

XV. Affairs of State

Turning to follow Vincent Merrick and the quaint figure of No. 8, Jimmy clutched Alyson's arm tightly. The gesture was only partly one of affection; he felt a little intoxicated and needed steadying. Optimism crawled aphrodisiac-wise through his arteries, surprising him by its presence. Rachel had not turned him into the little withered thing he had feared. He lived; he was reborn!

"How wonderful to be out of that ghastly cinema!" Alyson exclaimed, taking a deep breath and smiling at him.

"It was like a railway junction," Jimmy said. "Every human clattering along on different tracks, no contact."

"No contact, no hope," Alyson said. "Yet I suppose everyone's like that. We're lucky to be on main lines, but the poor creatures in there were out on branch lines."

As they went along the corridor the masked No. 8 tapped Jimmy's arm and said, "Forgive me, but Vincent has just told me who you are. You've been having an exciting time lately, eh? As we have met once before perhaps I may remove my domino."

He slipped the black velvet from his eyes, and obscure No. 8 was revealed as Health Minister Dr. Warwick Bunnian.

"Surprised to find me in Vincent's beastly clutches? I'm undergoing treatment for a mild touch of gerontophilism, nothing serious," the Minister of Health said, smiling genially. "Comes and goes like catarrh, you know."

"You stood us a drink at Stipend," Jimmy said, mastering his astonishment. "Perhaps you will come and have a drink with us now? I certainly feel in need of it."

"I expect you do," Bunnian agreed. "But you must allow *me* to get the liquor, old laddie; *I* can get it on prescription. Ministerial privilege and all that, you know." Uttering a laugh, he clapped Jimmy on the back and winked salaciously at Alyson; it was obvious that a spot of societal therapy had worked wonders on him. "I say, I've been informed that you were involved in the raid on old Willy Bourgoyne's hideout. Weren't you the chappie who nearly rescued Rachel Norman out of the helicopter?"

Jimmy felt himself beginning to blush, whereupon the process accelerated.

"I didn't get there soon enough, sir," he said.

"Just as well you didn't, by jove!" Bunnian exclaimed cryptically.

The four of them emerged into the upper class sunlight of Mayfair. Growing crowds trampled over pavement and roadway, necks curved like bows as they stared up at the rooftops and the damage that had been wrought by the grenade. Some police were already throwing a rope barrier round the masonry which had collapsed in the road, while others escorted four dejected rioters into a waiting Black Maria. Of all this Jimmy absorbed little, so busy was he mulling over the Minister of Health's last remark.

"I'm afraid I don't see what you mean. Is Rachel Norman safe?" he asked.

"Safe enough for our purpose," the Minister said, placing a plump little hand on Jimmy's arm. "I may as well tell you this, Jimmy, now the show's all over, but you see, that fellow who took her off in the helicopter was a Russian agent. I happen to know that by now Miss Norman is well on her way to Moscow. . . . Don't look so worried! You see, we *wanted* her to leave England. The crux of the matter was that she is a young woman of considerable drive and power."

"I found that out," Jimmy said.

"Did you? Not only did she practically invent the ER's but she sold this enormous dream of fitting everyone in the country with them to the Prime Minister and me. Which of these two feats is the greater I leave it to you to decide. The point is, once she had done all that, Miss Norman was in a more powerful position than ever. Then she revealed to us the terrible truth that the installation of ER's was only half of her scheme; the best was yet to come. The PM and I, being rather committed—we had, er, accepted some gifts of shares in Norman Laboratories and other Iral holdings—could not back out. It became imperative to get rid of Miss Norman for the country's good as well as our own. And at that juncture, as good fortune would have it, MI5 informed us that Russian agents had contacted her. I say, we can't talk out here! I don't mind giving away State secrets, but I'm not properly dressed. Where's the nearest pub, Vincent?"

The nearest pub was fortunately just across the road. They crossed the road. Bunnian resumed his domino and they settled themselves in the lounge bar behind an assortment of glasses.

"If you want him to talk, make him talk now while he's still partially under drugs," Merrick said in an aside to Jimmy. "I've got more government tips out of him that way. . . ."

"Do go on, sir," Jimmy said, clutching Alyson's hand under the table. "This is all most instructive."

"Bottoms up, old boy! —Or perhaps with Vincent here I shouldn't say that," Bunnian exclaimed merrily, sipping his double whisky. "Anyhow, as I was saying, the Russians contacted the Norman woman and offered her any resources she cared to name if she went over there to work for them, much to our delight. She liked the idea, remembering how free her step-father, Demyanski, had been to experiment. She was about to do a Burgess when this damned idiot Bourgoyne somehow got wind of who she really was and pinched her himself. However, all's well that ends well. Some of our Secret Service chaps—unknown to the Russians naturally—saw that she and the agent got safe passage to a submarine which was waiting for 'em off the South Coast in the early hours of this morning."

Bunnian looked with evident glee at the amazed expressions of those around him.

"Rachel was quite a handful, I can tell you. I don't suppose you'd have met her socially . . . Ah, well, that's another tale; I'll leave that one for my memoirs." A gentle smile hovered on his face for a moment, until he continued in a different tone, "Herby—the PM—and I had the wind up, I can tell you, when it looked as if she might miss the boat. You see Rachel really was a key figure in Norman Lights. Her step-father, Ivan Demyanski, originally located what we know now as Demyanski's Bundle in the hypothalamus of the brain, where the biological engages with what he would have termed the infra-spiritual. So the ER, like all good inventions, is Russian in origin. But it was Rachel who did all the delicate circuit work of connecting the Bundle to an external output register, the disc. There aren't half a dozen people in the world with that girl's knowledge. So you can see why she was too hot to handle. She had to be out of our way quickly—before the next general election."

He drained his glass. He smacked his lips. "Have another drink, Jimmy, dear boy. And you, Miss Younghusband. And you, Vince; do you good."

"Is that really the way policies of state are settled, Dr. Bunnian?" Alyson asked curiously as the second round of drinks arrived.

"It is in this case," Bunnian said. He winked at her through his domino, which he had reassumed on entering the public house. "Of course, Herby and I were personally interested, naturally."

"Naturally," Alyson echoed.

Jimmy said nothing. He sat back and relished the sensation of a weight lifting from his shoulders. Never mind how, never mind why; she had gone, Rachel had gone, and he would never see or think of her again. She hadn't taken a thing. The profound gratitude he felt had to be lavished on someone; he turned to Dr. Bunnian.

"How can I thank you," he said, "for all your kindness? I must admit in the past that I've sometimes run with the mob and regarded politicians as cynics, hypocrites and self-seekers. Well, I know better now. Dr. Bunnian, sir, thank you a thousand times for your honesty and your outspokeness. You just can't think what a weight it has taken from my mind. I do hope you will come to the wedding— Alyson's and my wedding, I mean."

Smiling widely, Bunnian nodded his head a dozen times in acknowledgement, swallowed his second double whisky, and called for a third.

"We do the best we can, laddie," he said. "I know we're not a popular breed. You must remember how opposed my job is to Vince's here. Vince's job is to encourage the badness out of people; the politician's job is to keep it in them. You have in the NL's an ideal compromise—they keep the badness flowing back and forth all the while. Ah, humanity's a damn bad lot, and I can't see there'll ever be any real changing us."

His sudden plunge into pessimism was most noticeable and affecting.

"Cheer up!" Alyson said kindly, watching with awe as he tucked the new whisky away. "The country's going well now. At least Vincent will tell you that we have a time of progress to look forward to. Everyone is starting again with a new outlook on life."

Bunnian pouted dismissively.

"Oh I know what you mean. GREP destroyed, opposition routed, business climbing again in the City, exports up. But the strikes are still spreading—ruddy dockers now. It'll be the railways next, mark my words. And as for the moral outlook. . . . Oh well, it doesn't do to be gloomy; no good ever came of worrying. I'm having dinner with Herby tonight, and you daren't breathe a word of pessimism to him. He bites your head off if you suggest that things aren't all they should be."

With sudden heartiness the Minister laughed and all was well again.

"By the way," Jimmy said, "I've not heard what happened to Guy Leighton yesterday."

Bunnian's smile became even wider.

"He was in the thick of it all. Aided this Captain Buggs—Briggs?—Biggs tremendously; knocked out another rebel captain involved with a well-aimed brick. Yes, Leighton came up trumps; I always fancied he would. Fellow's always on his toes, you know. We owe a lot to young chaps like him—and you, of course. I shouldn't mind having him over at the Ministry of Health. No, the country hasn't much to worry about while his sort are still in circulation. What do you say, Vincent?"

"I agree absolutely; Guy Leighton should go far and do well," Merrick said with the air of one accustomed to judging character.

Jimmy said nothing.

Bunnian laughed again, removing his domino in order to mop his perspiring face.

"Yes, it's a funny old world! " he exclaimed, looking round for approval of his bromide.

Irritation sparkled in Alyson's eye. Without wishing to spoil the well-oiled accord of their meeting, she felt bound to say. "It does rather surprise me to find you so light-hearted, Dr. Bunnian. Your government wished the Norman Lights onto the country, so that you must hold yourself responsible for all the strikes and other unrest which they have caused. Surely you must feel a good deal of apprehension about the next few months?"

Merrick looked detachedly interested, Jimmy frowned warningly, Bunnian merely laughed.

"I can be as serious and pontifical as the rest when occasion demands," he said, wagging a finger at Alyson. "You should hear some of my speeches. But after all, why worry? Look at the revolutions this country's seen! Remember the Tory rout in the 1945 elections? Didn't make a ha'porth of difference in the end. England takes a lot of shaking, young lady, a lot of shaking. And I don't mind telling *you*, it'll take more than a rash of little discs to upset the good old status quo. Don't bother about politics; they're an old man's game. You keep your eye on Jimmy—you'll find him harder to manage than a country! "

They finished off their drinks in a glow of self-congratulatory good humour, and Merrick stood up.

"I must be moving," he said, polishing his spectacles on the end of his tie. "I must see how Croolter is getting on over the road. Are you coming back to change, Warwick?"

"Just call me No. 8," the Minister of Health said expansively. "Yes, I suppose we'd better be moving. I've got a speech to prepare on the problems of old age for the Bournemouth conference tomorrow. Well, Solent, it's been interesting to run into you again; I hope you don't feel too much like a pawn in the affairs of state. . . . Thanks! "

This last remark was addressed to Merrick who, seeing the difficulty the Minister was experiencing in rising from his chair, had caught him under the armpit and hooked him to his feet. He began to walk uncertainly to the door, Merrick still clutching him.

"Just a minute, Dr. Bunnian," Alyson said. "You haven't told me what the end of the Norman Light scheme was that Rachel had in mind or why it was something that required so drastic a remedy as getting her out of the country."

"Not just out of the country! " Bunnian protested. "Not just out of this country but *into Russia*; that was essential. If she had carried her ER scheme through—as undoubtedly she would have done had she remained here—it would have meant the ruin of Great Britain and all it stands for. Democracy would have met its downfall."

He put on his House of Commons voice to say this, and Alyson and Jimmy were duly impressed. He drew himself up, beckoning to them both, seized their arms and led them into a corner where, resembling an old rugger coach in his sweater, he bent down and whispered in their ears. Merrick by the door was completely ignored; in a fit of cold anger

189

he strode over to the bar and bought twenty Benson and Hedges.

"La Norman will go over to Russia, where they do nothing by halves," Bunnian was saying confidentially in his corner. "In a year all their teeming millions will be provided with ER's and no ifs nor buts about it. Then Rachel will put over the second part of her scheme, which we jibbed at. Within a second year all the Russians will be wearing *two* discs on their foreheads.

"Now I don't want to go all technical on you young people, but these ER's, clever little things that they are, plug into a part of the brain, as I told you, called Demyanski's Bundle, through which pass other impulses than just erotic ones. By running an extension, with a suitable filter, from the first disc, you can get a different reaction on the second; and this, our Miss Norman plans, will light up with a *green* light.

"Once you've sold a population *one* disc, you see, the second is no trouble at all, particularly when you promise them that this second disc, the green light, is going to make life even simpler than the first one did."

Merrick had caught the minister by his sweater and was dragging him slowly to the door. Alyson felt a strange sympathy towards this move of Merrick's; after all, she told herself, if Bunnian really thought the NL's had in any way mitigated the complications of life he was obviously due for some more treatment.

"So in a couple of years all Russians will wear two discs, one flashing pink, one green on occasions?" Jimmy asked meditatively, following the slow shamble towards the exit. "We know what the pink one's for; what terrible thing is the green one for?"

"Perhaps you know," Bunnian said, tottering towards the threshold, "that Rachel Norman had her own ruthless moral code; it was twisted, perhaps, by our standards, but by hers it was crystal clear. She would admit of no compromise, ever; that was what made her so formidable."

"Certainly she was always painfully frank," Jimmy agreed, a faint, fading, echo of "You never gave me a thing" still in his ears.

"Exactly. She had an obsession with truth," Bunnian said. "The green lights will light up when anyone tells a lie."

"But surely . . ." Alyson said, puzzledly. "Surely that

might be a very good thing. Surely you haven't allowed such a splendid invention deliberately to fall into Russian hands."

"Absolutely!" Jimmy exclaimed, drawing back in horror. "Think how it would simplify English life if everyone in the country had such a device on his forehead."

Merrick's last vicious tug sent the Minister of Health reeling out of the pub door.

"It would have meant a death blow to British diplomacy," Bunnian said in his most ministerial tones.

Arm in arm Alyson and Jimmy emerged after him into the London air, evening-calm, gasoline-sweet.